ASSIGNMENT: BOSNIA

Map of the Central Balkans

HUNGARY
SLOVENIA
Zagreb
CROATIA
Vojvodina
RO
Prijedor
Omarska
Banja Luka
Brcko
Novi Sad
Zrenjanin
Bosnia
and
Herzegovina
Tuzla
Ruma
Fenčevo
Belgrade
Smederevo
Valjevo
Serbia
Srebrenica
Kragujevac
Sarajevo
Pale
Užice
Kraljevo
Mostar
Priboj
Novi Pazar
Kosovska
Mitrovica
Adriatic Sea
Montenegro
Nikšić
Kosovo
CROATIA
Podgorica
Balkan States

ASSIGNMENT: BOSNIA

Barry Friedman

Writers Club Press

San Jose New York Lincoln Shanghai

Assignment: Bosnia

Published by Writers Club Press
an imprint of iUniverse.com, Inc.

For information address:
iUniverse.com, Inc.
620 North 48th Street
Suite 201
Lincoln, NE 68504-3467
www.iuniverse.com

ISBN: 0-595-09648-4

Printed in the United States of America

DEDICATION

To Sue who lovingly dedicates her life to helping me get through mine.

To Carol, Steve and Roger whose talents soar far beyond those of their Dad.

To the sixteen thousand Balkan peoples of all nationalities who are still missing after the devastating war of the nineteen-nineties.

Also by Barry Friedman

Dead End

Acknowledgements

This effort would not be possible without the help of a number of people.

The following gave me valuable technical advice: John Van Egmond, radar engineer; Lt.Gen. E.J. Godfrey, USMC (ret) and Lt.Col. J.D. Howell, USMC, on assault tactics; and Ian Godwin, metallurgist.

Sofia Shafquat meticulously edited the manuscript. Marilyn Singer's recommendations have improved the work.

Of the many articles I consulted for background, Michael Kelly's excellent report, *Where Are The Dead*, appearing in the February 16, 1998 issue of *The New Yorker* deserves special mention.

A group of talented writers helped me nurse this book from its infancy. They are: Shirley Allen, Judith Hand, Phyllis Humphrey, Pete Johnson and Suzanne Middleton.

☠ PROLOGUE

April, 1994

Eighty-seven men sit or lie hip to hip on the concrete floor of their prison, a converted barn. The stinking odor of sweat and urine is mixed with that of the horse manure left by the previous occupants of these stalls. Hacking coughs and moans echo through the barn. Curled up on the few wisps of straw that litter the floor, some are able to escape their hunger and thirst in sleep.

Clothed in rags that hang from his emaciated body, a man kneels in the middle of the dark, dank barn. Others not too weak, follow his lead, struggle to their knees. It has been days since they have been outside the walls of this prison, so they can only guess they are facing *Qiblah*, the direction of the *Ka'bah'* at Mecca. Kneeling, they assume the position of *Sujud*: body bent forward, hands on the ground, palms downwards, head lowered so that their brows touch the ground. Three times they repeat *"Sobhana Rabbi-yal a'alaa."* Glory to my Lord, the Most High. Save us, our compassionate Lord, from our folly…

Suddenly the barn door is thrown open, flooding the inside with light. Four soldiers stride in, the muzzles of their rifles pointing at the mass of humanity.

One soldier shoves his arm through his gun sling. The rifle hangs from his shoulder and he calls out, reading from a paper: "Ismail Begovich, Amer Landzo, Muhamed Filipovic, Alija Drino, Selam…"

One by one, living corpses struggle to a standing position.

With a finger, the soldier silently counts those who stand. He shouts, "I called fourteen names. I see only thirteen. Which of you is the miserable dog who remains on the floor?"

A weak voice calls out, "Mustafa Topic cannot stand. He is dead."

"Poor excuse," the soldier mutters.

The other soldiers roar with laughter.

The lead soldier waves his gun at those standing. "Outside, you stinking bags of garbage."

Shuffling, picking their way slowly through those sitting and lying on the floor, the 13 whose names are called stumble through the barn door, blinking as sunlight strikes their eyes. The soldiers follow them out. The door is slammed shut.

For 20 minutes the remaining prisoners are silent in the darkness, listening to what they have come to recognize as the metallic sound of shovels striking the ground outside.

Moments after the shoveling has stopped they hear a rapid fusillade of gunfire, followed by screams. Then silence.

Inside the walls of the prison, a murmur starts and grows in volume. "*Sobhana Rabbi-yal a'alaa…*"

CHAPTER 1

April, 1997

Topcoat draped over his arm, Senator Matt O'Brien—make that ex-Senator—stepped out of the VIP waiting room at Andrews Air Force Base into the cool night air. Glancing over his shoulder, he raised his briefcase in farewell to the small group looking on from the doorway, and mounted the steps to the Vice-President's plane. At the top, O'Brien turned and shouted down, "Thanks for the loan of your wheels."

A voice from the darkness yelled back, "Wish I were going with you, Matt. Good luck and safe trip."

O'Brien stepped through the open hatch, almost bumping into the lieutenant who stood waiting just inside the plane. "Welcome aboard, Senator." She reached for his coat. "Let me take that. And I'll stow your briefcase, if you'd like."

He handed her the coat. "I'll hang on to the briefcase. Lot of work to do."

She smiled. "You'll have plenty of time, Senator. It's a long way to Sarajevo."

The door to the cockpit opened and a tall, slender man with eagle insignias pinned to his epaulets ducked through the doorway into the main cabin. He touched his uniform cap. "Glad to have you aboard, Senator. I'll be driving tonight. We'll try to avoid the potholes."

"Thanks Colonel." O'Brien glanced around, nodding slowly in approval at the leather-upholstered lounge chairs bolted to the deck. The perks of being assigned to a Presidential Mission. "I'll miss squeezing into the middle of the three seats across." O'Brien was a shade under six feet, but the pilot towered above him. "How many frequent flier miles do I log on this trip?"

The colonel scratched at his mustache. "Let's see. We're routed over the Pole, come south over Norway, the Austrian Alps, start our descent around Vukovar—."

O'Brien raised a palm. "Sorry I asked. I'll buckle in and be quiet."

Ten minutes later, the plane roaring down the runway, O'Brien opened the notebook on his lap. Its cover read: "*International Committee on Missing Persons in Bosnia.*"

He glanced out the window at the fading lights of the city, his thoughts carrying him back to the day he stood at the podium on the senate floor, pleading with members of his own party—his own party, for Christ's sake—to support his efforts to stop the murder and raping of civilians in Bosnia. Force the release of thousands reported to be wasting away in concentration camps.

Let it go, Matt, they told him. We can't police the world. We haven't got the money. It'll cost you your seat.

But he couldn't let it go. Any more than the hotshot whirlybird pilot who'd plucked *him* out of that mud hole of a VC prison could let it go, ignoring his CO screeching on the horn, ordering him to get the hell out of there, worried his $200,000 government-issue fan would get shot to pieces.

Here he was breathing the pressurized air in a luxury-fitted 707 while that pilot rested in Arlington. No, he couldn't let it go.

And they were right about one thing. It *did* cost him his seat.

O'Brien took from his briefcase a folder the State Department had prepared, briefly reviewing recent Balkan history. He glanced at the opening sentences.

"The Kingdom of Yugoslavia was made up of Slovenia, Croatia, Serbia, Macedonia and Bosnia-Herzegovina. When the Germans invaded in 1941, the Yugoslavian king escaped to England. Croatia willingly aligned itself with Hitler, and all of Yugoslavia was under German occupation for the duration of the war. A guerilla group, the Partisans, refused to submit to the Germans. Led by Josip Broz, the man who called himself Marshal Tito, and with arms supplied by the Allies, the Partisans effectively sabotaged the occupying forces. When, at the end of World War II, the Partisans drove the Germans and Italians out, Tito was the logical person to take charge of the official Yugoslavian government. Although Tito was a communist, he was not a rigid Marxist..."

O'Brien closed the folder and stuffed it back in his briefcase. Nothing here he didn't know.

*   *   *

The jolt as the wheels hit the runway awakened him. He'd been dozing in his seat even though he'd had a good night's sleep in a bunk bed—another perk—followed by breakfast and lunch. After all, this *was* the VP's plane. A moment later the pilot's voice cackled over the loudspeaker. "Morning—or rather, afternoon—Senator, and welcome to Sarajevo where the local time is 1530, temperature four degrees Celsius. Thank you for flying with USAF. Next time your travel plans include..." The voice trailed off.

O'Brien grinned. If his travel plans again included a visit to this part of the world, he was a candidate for Section Eight. He was here because the man in the Oval Office thought a former MIA would be the logical person to look for others. Although his was a different war in a different place and at an earlier time, the tears of a mother whose son was named Milos or Dragan were no less wet, no less salty than those of the woman who'd named her first son Matthew. Besides, here it was April. In a few months he'd be 54, and he still hadn't decided what to do with the rest of his life. Since that day last November when he cleaned out his desk in the Russell Senate Office Building, crating 12 years worth of memorabilia, he'd been tossing a mental coin. Join that mega-person law firm in Columbus, or add his name to the letterhead of the company that figured it would help sell more radar equipment to the government? Peg said as far as she was concerned it didn't matter one way or the other. She'd be happy to get out of the Beltway rat race, but it would have to wait until spring when Brooke and Lesley finished school. "Just let me know which paper to get, so I can start running through the house-for-sale ads," she'd said.

Peg. He could still feel the heat of her anger when he asked her—no, he'd *informed* her, a stupid, thoughtless mistake—that he was going to Sarajevo.

"Bored?" she'd said. "Is that your problem? Not enough action here for you? Need another war? The girls and I finally get to see what you look like after all those senatorial junkets, and now this?"

"Peg, please." He'd tried to quench the fire. "How can I refuse after mouthing off all these years about what's happened to civilians over there?" Peg kept silent, staring at him. He continued. "And I'm not looking for 'action'. The fighting in Bosnia is finished."

In the end, she'd calmed down, accepted his determination to go. But she wasn't happy.

The plane taxied to a berth and stopped. Bundled up in his topcoat, O'Brien clanked his way down the steps. A man at the foot of the stairs stuck out his hand. He seemed to be in his late thirties, a gaunt six-three, sandy-haired, and in spite of the breath-pluming air wore only an unpressed business suit that appeared to have been made for someone a few inches shorter and a few pounds heavier. "Welcome, Mr. O'Brien. I am Al Zee. I will be your aide." His English only slightly accented.

"Zee?" From the name, O'Brien had no clue as to his ethnic background. The Bosnians he'd met were Turkish Muslims or Serbian.

Zee laughed. "Unless you are from here, you'd have trouble pronouncing my real name: Alija Zulfkorpašic. My mother is Serbian, my dad is—was—Turkish-Croatian. I am a little of everything."

Minutes later, they were seated in the back of a chauffeur-driven sedan speeding past farmland where snow covered most of the ground, although patches of brown soil signaled the approach of spring.

O'Brien learned that Zee was from the northwestern Bosnian city of Prijedor. "Your English is remarkably good. Have you been to England or the States?"

Zee laughed. "I learned in school. I've never been farther than Sarajevo, that is about 200 kilometers from my home." His face turned grim. "Except one place."

"Where was that?"

Zee stared out of the car window. "Omarska."

The notorious death camp in northern Bosnia. "You were at Omarska?"

"In 1992. Soldiers came to our home and dragged away my father and me. I was lucky. They just beat me. My father was not so lucky. We never saw him again."

Reports of such atrocities had appeared in the inside pages of the *Washington Post*. Fifty taken from one village, 150 from another. Impersonal reports. Statistics. News that most of his colleagues read, shook their heads, then turned the pages to see whom the Redskins had gotten in the draft. But they hadn't seen the man seated next to him now with stumps of front teeth in his smile. He wasn't a statistic.

They were approaching the city, its skyline a sea of minarets, domes of mosques and synagogues, and steeples of Orthodox and Catholic churches. Intermingled were several modern office and hotel buildings.

O'Brien said, "I want to hear more about it—your experience, but let's save it for later when we have more time."

"Of course. This is your first visit to our country?"

O'Brien nodded. "I visited Slovenia many years ago when it was still Yugoslavia, but never Bosnia-Herzegovina." He grinned. "Unless you count watching the Sarajevo Winter Olympics on TV."

"Yes, 1984." Zee breathed a deep sigh. "I was a graduate student. Those were better times." He tilted his head toward O'Brien. "Slovenia? You visited?"

"My grandparents, my mother's parents, came from a village just outside Ljubljana. You know where that is?"

"Of course. Ljubljana is capital of Slovenia."

"As a high-school graduation present, they took me with them on a visit."

Although it had been almost 40 years ago, O'Brien still remembered his great-uncle's small stone farmhouse where odors of cattle and fresh hay hung in the air. He called up from his memory Uncle Mirko, a tall, leathery-faced man with flowing white moustaches. In broken English, assisted by O'Brien's grandfather's translation, Uncle Mirko had related his World War Two experiences as a Yugoslavian Partisan. He had piled them all into his ancient Yugo and drove them into the mountains, pointing out caves where they had hidden from the occupying German troops, sneaking down at night to Nazi encampments and sabotaging their equipment.

Zee tapped O'Brien's arm and pointed out the car window to a street corner. "Here is where Archduke Franz Ferdinand of Austria and his wife were shot."

O'Brien knew Sarajevo's contribution to history. Those shots had given the world an excuse for war, and the Bosnian Serbs had themselves a national hero, Gavrilo Princip the assassin.

They passed skeletons of buildings destroyed by shells and mortars, standing alongside cranes and scaffolds where restoration was taking place. The car pulled up to the portico of a modern building whose marquee identified it as the Hotel Strand. Zee said, "I think you will be comfortable here. It was just built since the war."

As they walked into the lobby Zee said, "You have meeting with the other members of the committee at 1800 hours. Did you get some rest during your trip?"

"More than I intended. I fell asleep reading my briefing notes. Why don't you run down for me who the others are."

Zee reeled off the four names. The only one O'Brien knew was a Pakistani whom he'd met at a Washington reception several years ago. One of the others represented the International Red Cross. The third was a Dutchman the U.N. had appointed. The remaining member was a Serbian named Bodanovic. O'Brien thought it incongruous to have a guy help look for some people his own government had "lost."

After seeing O'Brien settled in his room, Zee left, promising to return for the meeting early that evening. O'Brien sat in a wooden chair facing the window, propped his feet on the sill, and opened the voluminous notebook he'd carried with him on the plane. Prepared by people in the State Department, it detailed more than 90 concentration camps to which Serbs had taken tens of thousands Bosnians, mostly Muslim, in a program of "ethnic cleansing." Even an approximate number was impossible to determine. After the Dayton peace accord in 1995, which halted the war, the International Red Cross began the task of identifying decaying remains in mass graves.

Immersed in the grisly descriptions of rotting corpses, O'Brien suddenly became aware of a light tapping on the door. He got up and opened it. A chambermaid stood alongside her cart piled high with towels and linens. She motioned to the bed. "For night?"

O'Brien glanced at his watch. Five-thirty. Seemed a bit early to turn down the bed, but she probably wanted to complete her work before going off duty. He nodded and stepped back giving her room to wheel in her cart. Briefly, he watched her remove and fold the coverlet, then returned to his chair and resumed reading. He felt a tap on his shoulder. He whirled around to see the maid above him holding high in her hand a gleaming object. A knife?

He grabbed her wrist and twisted. The object dropped. She screamed.

He glanced down. On the floor was a small, silvered picture frame, its glass cracked by the fall. He released her hand and reached down to retrieve it.

While the maid stood, hands over her mouth, sobbing softly, he studied the picture: A smiling man hugging a shyly smiling woman. He pointed to the woman in the picture. "You?"

She nodded.

He pointed to the man. "Husband?"

Her sobs became a keening. Tears flooded her eyes, streamed down her cheeks. She placed her palms together. "Please, sir. You find."

At five minutes before six, O'Brien waited for the elevator. He was unable to drive from his mind the picture of the sorrowful maid. In broken English she had related a story, not unlike the one he had briefly heard from Zee, of her husband being taken by soldiers in the middle of the night from their home in a nearby village. That was four years ago. The Red Cross had told her that he was probably dead. She slammed her fists to her chest and cried out. "He not dead. I know. He not dead."

O'Brien marveled at the power of her faith. He'd been rescued from his VC prison a mere six *days* after his capture. Had been reported missing in action. He wondered if his own mother would have held on to the belief that he was still alive if he were still MIA after four years.

Another thought struck him: was his presence and mission here common knowledge? Was she *really* his maid, or had she bribed someone to let her use the props to plead her case? Of course, he could check, but why.

Now the elevator door slid open. As the car descended, O'Brien reflected that everybody in this unhappy country had been touched by the war. Back in the States, people sat complacently in front of TV screens, never knowing the terror brought on by bursting shells and bombs of an invading army.

In the lobby Zee sat waiting. They walked quickly to a large, modestly appointed conference room on the second floor. Half a dozen people stood in quiet conversation holding cocktail glasses. A slender, dark-complexioned man spied O'Brien. "Ah, Senator, so glad to see you again. In case you've forgotten—"

O'Brien quickly searched his memory. More than a dozen years of political life had honed his skill at recognition. "Dr. Ahmed. It's been a few years, but my wife still talks about that beautiful reception we attended at the Pakistan Embassy. I was pleased to see your name on the committee roster."

Ahmed stroked his goatee and peered intently into O'Brien's eyes for a moment, then glanced over his shoulder at the others and lowered his voice. "Yes. The committee. We have, I'm afraid, a difficult job ahead of us."

A pudgy man with a mane of snow-white hair, came over in mincing steps. He introduced himself as Maxmillian Van der Velde, the U.N. representative from The Hague. "Come, meet the others."

O'Brien took a glass of wine from the tray of a waiter and followed Van der Velde to the other members and their aides. After trying silently to pronounce the names Van der Velde threw at him—most had more than three syllables and fewer than two vowels—he admitted defeat.

Bodanovic was the last to be introduced. He favored O'Brien with a faint smile and a limp hand, and glanced at his watch. "Perhaps we should get started. We have much ground to cover in a short time."

Bodanovic assumed the role of chairman. O'Brien wondered who'd appointed him, finally conceding reluctantly that as the representative of the host country it might be his prerogative. When the committee members and their aides had taken seats around a table at one end of the room, Bodanovic began.

"We all speak and understand English, no?"

Heads nodded.

"As you all know, our friends in the International Red Cross estimate that more than sixteen thousand people are missing since the war began. Most are Bosnian." He fixed a stare at O'Brien. "Including Bosnian *Serbs*, my own people, and most, if not all of them, are probably dead."

Jesus, what a callous remark, thought O'Brien. If it were true, what the hell was he doing here? Had he traveled 5,000 miles to attend a cocktail party? He was beginning to understand Ahmed's admonition. He listened for another minute while Bodanovic explained that they would meet with the presidents of the republics: Croatia, Slovenia, Bosnia-Herzegovina, Montenegro and Serbia, to learn if files existed so names of those identified as dead could be matched with the names of the missing persons. "I feel confident that we will find few discrepancies, and we will have accomplished…"

Bullshit. O'Brien had heard enough. "Pardon me for interrupting, Mr. Bodanovic, but it is my understanding that some survivors of the Serbian concentration camps—" He stopped to let the words sink in. "—claim that a large number of the missing are still held in secret prisons. I thought we were meeting to either verify or dispute those claims." He glanced around the table. Van der Velde's face had changed color from pink to deep red, and except for Zee, who was trying to suppress a smile, and Ahmed who appeared alarmed, the others were examining their fingernails.

Bodanovic's nostrils flared, his face paled. "My dear Senator. First, let us understand that these people—survivors, you call them, were in refugee camps, not as you put it, concentration camps. This is not Nazi Germany. They were displaced persons because their homes had been destroyed by a war. We won't go into the cause of the war. That is not our function."

"Exactly what *is* our function?"

Bodanovic glared at him for a moment, then flung open the cover of the notebook that lay on the table in front of him and roughly turned several pages. "If you'd taken the trouble to read..." he muttered.

O'Brien *had* read the mission objective, a statement couched in ambiguous diplomatic terms. Vague guidelines that could be interpreted any way the reader wished. He'd lay odds that meeting the presidents and their flunkies would lead to nothing more than soporific press releases.

Bodanovic started to read the paragraph describing the mission's purpose, but O'Brien broke in. "Instead of meeting with the presidents, let's meet with the people who can tell us what went on. Ex-prisoners lucky enough to get out alive. Survivors who claim that others survive and are still imprisoned."

He waited a moment to see if anyone supported him. Is everyone afraid of the Serb, he wondered? Finally, Ahmed timidly raised his hand. "Mr. O'Brien has made a thoughtful suggestion. I for one need some time to reflect on it and perhaps consult with my superiors. Why don't we adjourn for the present, have dinner, and tomorrow come back to arrive at a decision."

The others at the table nodded, relieved.

Chairs were pushed back. O'Brien remained seated with Zee at his side watching the others file out.

After a few moments Zee said, "I like very much your idea."

O'Brien scratched his cheek. "Well, that's two votes."

CHAPTER 3

"How many prisoners were in the camp when you were there?"

Zee stared into his coffee cup, absently stirring for several seconds while he contemplated O'Brien's question.

They were in O'Brien's hotel room the day following his arrival. Zee was staying with a Sarajevan family he had known for many years, and had returned to the hotel at eight that morning to have breakfast with O'Brien.

"Three thousand, maybe more. Serb soldiers every day bring—brought buses filled with men from villages. But not everyone is staying. Every day soldiers took many away from Omarska. Two, three vans full. Some maybe to different camps. Others…" he shrugged.

He heard the pain in Zee's voice. The "others" were the reason O'Brien was here.

"Wasn't Omarska originally a mining camp?"

Zee nodded. "Before the war in Bosnia. They mined iron. Our prison was ten, twelve buildings surrounded with fields."

"Fences?"

"No fences. Guards." With a finger, Zee traced on the tablecloth three concentric rings. "Two to keep us in, one to keep anyone from trying to make rescue."

Was escape possible?

Zee shook his head. "One night while I was there, my friend—at home he was my barber—with two others, they tried to slip past the guards. Two were shot. My friend got through. He escaped to nearby village controlled by Serbs. People from the village tied him up and took him back to camp." Zee fell silent for a few moments, then in a choked voice continued. "The guards made us line up and watch them shoot him. I had to help bury all three men."

Barbarism, inhumanity. It started with Cain and had not ended at Buchenwald and Auschwitz. Beatings were part of the daily life of the prisoners. They'd be whipped with electric cables by guards as they ran a gauntlet to and from the canteen where they were fed a few leaves of cabbage, a slice of bread and beans in tepid water. Every few days Zee's name was called, and he along with three to five others would be taken to an interrogation room where they were beaten with clubs until they signed confessions to an assortment of false accusations: admission that they had fought against the Yugoslavian National Army, or that they had prepared lists of Serbs to be killed by Muslims. "One time they beat me until I confessed to them I stole tools from a store owned by a Serb in village next to my own. *Confess.*" He spat out the word. "I was never *in* that store." He laughed wryly. "I would not know what to do with tools. I was schoolteacher. I am very—what do you called it?" He held up his hands and wiggled his fingers.

"Unhandy?"

"Yes."

O'Brien wondered how he had gotten out.

"One day, after I was in camp about four months, they called many of us out and loaded us on buses. We were taken to another camp, a place called Manjaca. People from International Red Cross came quite often. Conditions were not so bad as Omarska."

Two months later, they were again piled on buses and without explanation taken to a place where they were released to armed soldiers who wore blue helmets and the insignia of the U.N. "I was free."

Although Zee had related his experience quietly, his calmly spoken words rang with passion. Maybe if his ex-colleagues in the senate had heard them, O'Brien thought, his own pleas might have been more effective.

"What a story. Every generation has its holocaust. Will we ever learn?"

Zee slowly shook his head. "For us, I'm afraid it is way of life—hating, killing. And it goes back a long way." His brows drew together. "O'Brien. The name is Irish, no?"

"Yes. My father's side of the family."

"The Irish. They also know of such troubles."

Although for months Sarajevo had been a war zone, to locals it was a time of "troubles."

"As do the Israeli and the Arabs, the Rwandans, the Somali, and on and on. I'm afraid no one has a lock on 'such troubles.'"

"You said you had family in Slovenia?"

"They're all dead now. But yes, several of my great uncles fought with the Partisans."

Zee nodded. "Marshal Tito."

O'Brien said, "As I recall, when Tito was in power, there wasn't much internal opposition."

Zee shrugged. "Look, he was dictator, no? He had ways of taking care of anybody who opposed him."

"Secret police?"

"Of course. You people looked the other way because he had—I forget the word."

"Charisma?"

"That's it. But you are right. He *did* hold our country together."

O'Brien said, "From my reading, I believe Tito's mistake was in not grooming an heir. He knew he wasn't going to live forever."

Zee gazed out the window. "Maybe if he *had* chosen someone to take his place, we wouldn't be in mess like today. After Tito died they tried a system they called 'presidential rotation.'"

"You mean the eight-member council?"

"Yes. Each of the republics elected a member. They took turns to become President of Yugoslavia. Each for a year."

"Eight cooks trying to bake one pie," said O'Brien. "I'm surprised it lasted as long as it did. I predicted it would fall apart. Nineteen-ninety, wasn't it?"

"You have a good memory, Senator. Yes. Slobodan Milosevic, President of Serbia, blocked the Croat who was supposed to become President of Presidency. He controlled four votes. Slovenia—*your* Slovenia—saw that it was impossible to run the country by committee, it voted to become independent from Yugoslavia. A little bit later Croatia did the same. Then the *real* trouble started."

Trouble. An understatement. O'Brien had closely followed the events in the Balkans, but was anxious to get Zee's perspective. "Obviously, Slovenia was important to Yugoslavia—but important enough to start a war over?"

O'Brien's question implied that he didn't think it was. Zee's one-sided smile signaled that he didn't think so either. "It comes down to economics—money."

"Explain."

"Slovenia was richest Yugoslavian state. I am sure you know this already. It sits on northern border, next to Italy and Austria. Goods from Europe had to pass through Slovenian customs. They collected revenue, sent it to Yugoslavian capital in Belgrade."

"How much money are we talking about?"

"For you, an American, maybe not so many dollars. But for Yugoslavian federal budget, about seventy-five percent of all its income."

O'Brien hadn't realized Slovenia had controlled so much of the Yugoslavian economy. Naturally, Milosevic was not going to let Slovenia go without a fight. "Short war, wasn't it?"

"Ten days. Milosevic sent in tanks and men. Slovenia's troops fought back. Chased them out and it was over. The JNA—Yugoslavian National

Army—lost thirty-seven men, and twelve Slovenian soldiers were killed. Milosevic decided it wasn't worth it. Instead, he went after Croatia."

The excuse for battling Croatia, and later Bosnia-Herzegovina, was less about money than about ethnic differences. Croatians were predominantly Roman Catholic, Bosnians mostly Muslims, while Serbians belonged to the Eastern Orthodox Church. The differences were more than religious; customs, dress, dietary peculiarities, even work habits set one group apart from another. O'Brien said, "You told me your mother was Serbian, didn't you?"

"Her parents came from town near Belgrade. But she was born in Bosnia-Herzegovina."

"So really she was Bosnian, right?"

Zee stared at O'Brien for a long moment, another half-smile on his lips. His expression seemed to say, "You may have some Balkan blood, but you've got a lot to learn about us." His answer was diplomatic. "Senator, you must understand that the people in this part of world are very loyal to their, their—" He drew circles in the air with his hands.

"Roots?"

"Exactly. I know families that have lived in Bosnia for generations. But because their ancestors came from Serbia or from Croatia, they consider themselves Serbian or Croatian—and always will no matter how long they live in Bosnia."

O'Brien was playfully goading Zee. Migration and intermarriage had resulted in small enclaves of one ethnic group living in a country populated largely by people of another ethnicity. It had been the same in Croatia where communities of Serbs lived among Croats. "So what we have here is a minority living under rules made by the majority, isn't that so?"

Zee flushed. "Don't you have same in Texas? Mexicans living together among Texans?" His English, O'Brien noticed, became less idiomatic, less grammatical when he spoke passionately.

O'Brien hadn't meant to put Zee on the defensive. "You're right, of course. In my own city, in the state of Ohio, we have large communities made up of people who emigrated from Hungary and Czechoslovakia and Italy." He stopped for a moment. "I think one of the main differences between this country and mine is that United States is made up of people whose ancestors came from somewhere else. Once in the United States, they tend to assimilate. Here, they seem to retain a fierce allegiance to their ancestral country."

Zee said, "Senator, you left out another very important difference. You said something about minorities living with rules made by majority. Before the war I was teacher in gymnasium—what you call high school. The subject I taught was government. I learned that in your country there are laws to protect these minorities."

"That's true. At least in theory."

"Here it is opposite. After the republic began to break up, discrimination was actually encouraged. Whoever controlled guns used their power."

"You mean the army?"

"Not only army, but also police. Police ignored demonstrations against minorities. If you work for government, you must take loyalty oath or you lose job." His lips compressed. "In Kosovo, where Kosovar Albanians outnumbered nine to one the Serbs living there, Serbs controlled the police. Albanians?" He ground his heel in the carpet. "They are like dogs to Serbs—*lower* than dogs.

"I have friend who lives in Pristina, capitol of Kosovo. Was in line for promotion. He comes from long line of Albanians. Did he get promotion? No. It went to a Serb who was much, much less qualified.

"Education, health care, pensions. If you were Serb, you got them. If you weren't Serbian, you had to beg and maybe, *maybe* get some of these benefits."

O'Brien said, "Didn't the same thing happen in Croatia?"

Zee shrugged. "Croats are no better than Serbs. If you were Serb living in Croatia, you were minority. The difference was they could cry to somebody."

"Milosevic?"

Zee nodded. "So when Croatia voted to become independent, Milosevic said, 'I have to send in army to liberate Croatian Serbs.'"

O'Brien had watched it unfold on CNN. JNA tanks parked in the hills above Vukovar and Dubrovnik and for months shelled those Croatian cities killing in addition to Croats, Serbs they were "liberating," until the United States' Sixth Fleet sailed into Dubrovnik harbor. Although the U.S. Navy did not actually engage in the war, its presence was enough to discourage continued military action by the JNA, largely made up of Serbian troops. They withdrew, and the civilians stumbled out of the cellars in which they'd hidden. Croatia had its independence.

Now, with Croatia and Slovenia gone, Milosevic was determined not to lose Bosnia-Herzegovina. Although Orthodox Serbs had lived peaceably alongside Muslims in Bosnia-Herzegovina, a smoldering hatred existed. In December 1991, when Bosnian leaders signaled that they were about to declare themselves independent of Yugoslavia, Milosevic had the pretext he needed to strike. He ignored the fact that Muslims made up a far greater percent of the population of Bosnia than did the Serbs. What ensued was one of the bloodiest wars of the century. Bosnian Muslims were no match for the powerful JNA who imprisoned or killed thousands. Ethnic cleansing.

O'Brien shook his head. "Milosevic. The guy's dangerous. A real charmer, but power-hungry."

"You know him? Milosevic?"

"I first met him in the '80s. He was in the United States representing Beobanka."

Zee nodded. " Yes, I knew he had been a banker before he got into politics."

O'Brien reflected on his own unsuccessful attempt in the late 1980s to warn his congressional colleagues of the potential hotbed brewing in the Balkans. Shortly after Milosevic returned to Yugoslavia, he claimed that in Kosovo Serbs were being repressed by Albanians. Never mind that Muslim Albanians in Kosovo made up 90 percent of the population. His battle cry to the 20th-century Serbs was: "Avenge the Battle of Kosovo." That battle took place in 1369! Turks, precursors of the modern Albanians, had slaughtered the Serbs. Milosevic's strategy worked. Kosovar Serbs mounted a hate campaign against the Albanians while the Serbian-controlled police force looked the other way.

Although Kosovo was a Yugoslavian province, unlike the others, it had been self-governing since the time Tito was in power. After Tito's death, Milosevic rescinded Kosovo's autonomy. With a growing number of intellectuals, writers and educators in the late 1970s, came a hunger for better living conditions. Yugoslavian Serbs, goaded by Milosevic, viewed demonstrations by Albanians as a revolt. In the latter days of the 1980s, tanks were called down from Serbia in the north, and wholesale slaughter of Kosovar Albanians resulted. Now, in the late 1990s, almost ten years later, the action was to be repeated.

O'Brien nodded solemnly. "I'm sorry to say that in the States we paid little attention. If we can offer any excuse, at the time all this was going on we were preoccupied with Iraq and Desert Storm. Only later, when the slaughter started here in Bosnia and Herzegovina, did we notice."

Zee was silent for a few moments. Then looking directly at O'Brien he said, "Yes, the rest of the world, too, said let Bosnians and Serbs work out their problems. But you are too modest, Senator. Your personal efforts to help us—we heard about this here."

O'Brien shook his head. "I wish I could have been more effective. I knew from speaking with people in our government, men like Special Envoy Cyrus Vance and Ambassador Warren Zimmerman, that civilians were being killed, taken prisoner or made homeless. I couldn't get many to listen."

Zee said, "If not for U.N. and your President bringing the two sides together in Dayton to sign the peace agreement, there would be killing still."

O'Brien glanced at his watch. "Nine-forty-five. I suppose we'd better go to the meeting."

As he started to rise, Zee placed his hand on O'Brien's forearm. "By the way, that man at the meeting last night, Bodanovic, I think I have seen him before."

"The head of the Serb delegation?"

"One of the interrogators at Omarska, one of the most vicious. I only saw him twice, that was five years ago. When he was speaking last night, I tried to picture him with beard."

Although Zee was uncertain, O'Brien now had a reason for intuitively disliking Bodanovic. If this *were* the same guy, he should be on trial as a war criminal instead of leading a delegation. Maybe he could get someone to do a background check.

☠ CHAPTER 4

O'Brien gazed around the half-empty conference room. Ten o'clock. Where were the others? He greeted Van der Velde at the coffee urn. "Are we too early?"

"No, the meeting was called for ten. Everyone is here except the Yugoslavian delegation."

O'Brien had the opening he needed. "What do you know about Bodanovic?"

Van der Velde shrugged. "I believe he's an official in Srpska—the Bosnia Serb government. Why do you ask?"

He wasn't about to tell him about Zee's suspicion. Zee *might* be wrong. "Just curious. I like to know who I'm dealing with. In fact, it might be helpful to have a dossier of each of the participants. I'd be glad to provide my own."

Van der Velde smiled. "I don't think that's necessary. I'm sure everyone here knows of your superb record as a member of the United States Senate Foreign Relations Committee. No one in your country spoke out as passionately as you did about your concern for the victims of the Balkan war. I can't tell you how disappointed I was to hear that you had lost your senate seat in the last election."

"Thank you. I have no excuses. I ran a lousy campaign against a bright and ambitious challenger."

"Your country's loss. As for your wish to know more about the delegates, I'll have my aide prepare what information we have in our files in The Hague. It will take a few days."

Ten-thirty. Where the hell are the others? One of the Serbian aides burst into the room, rapped with his knuckles on the conference table and spoke rapidly in Serbian. O'Brien gazed around the room for Zee. He was already at the Serb's side, speaking to him. He turned to O'Brien. "The Serbian delegation has been unavoidably detained. This man says they'll be here within the hour. He asks us to please wait until they arrive before we begin."

'Unavoidably detained?' What the hell did *that* mean? And if the son of a bitch couldn't make it on time like the rest of them, too goddam bad. O'Brien raised his voice. "We all have commitments and schedules. I don't see why we can't start without them."

The leader of the International Red Cross spoke up. "I appreciate your position, Mr. O'Brien, but we are a small group. I think we should all be present at these discussions. I for one am willing to wait."

Ahmed nodded. "Yes, I agree. An hour longer isn't going to inconvenience us."

O'Brien felt heat rise to his face. Losing was getting to be a habit. Probably should save his fights for the battles he was sure of winning. He shoved his chair back. "I'll be in my room. Let me know when they get here."

He stalked out, bought a copy of the *International Herald Tribune* and took it upstairs. He sat with the folded newspaper in his lap. Why couldn't he act like an adult? Just a few weeks ago Peg had remarked that he seemed to be getting more short-tempered. "Just because you lost the election," she'd said, "Don't take it out on your friends and family." That just got him more steamed up. He'd snapped some remark at her, then watched, feeling like a stupid ass while tears welled up in her eyes. He'd suffered through two days of silent treatment before she accepted the roses and bracelet he'd brought to climb out of the hole he'd dug himself into.

The phone rang. Zee, telling him they were ready to start.

"Bodanovic finally showed up?"

"No. He has been taken ill. They sent someone else in his place."

☠ CHAPTER 5

The smiling cherub-faced man who sat at the head of the conference table scanned the faces of the other delegates. "So. We are all in place. I must apologize for keeping you waiting. As you have heard, our colleague Bodanovic was suddenly taken ill. Um, stomach flu or something like that. I am called Jasajovic. Forgive me for not having had time to review what has already taken place."

This guy was deferential, apologetic. The antithesis of his dour, argumentative predecessor. Maybe, O'Brien thought, we can get along. He spoke up. "I'm Matt O'Brien, the United States representative, Mr. Jasajovic. When we left off last evening, we were considering a proposal to hear from ex-prisoners who claim that many of those missing are still alive and are held in secret camps."

Jasajovic nodded. "Yes. I have heard the same rumors. I understand we are to meet with the presidents of the republics to enlist their help."

Ahmed raised a hand. "This is the third time a committee was formed to locate the missing persons from the war. I was a member of the one that met last year. We spoke with the presidents. Nothing came of it. I would not like to go away from this meeting frustrated as I did in the past. I agree with Mr. O'Brien."

Hooray. Finally a point scored. Maybe.

Van der Velde said, "The International Red Cross has been trying for four years to match the names of the missing with those known to be dead. We have two problems: One is locating the graves—mass graves in many cases. The second problem is money. Funding for grave-diggers, forensic pathologists."

Zee, sitting alongside O'Brien, tapped him on the arm. "Can I say something?" he whispered.

O'Brien whispered back, "Sure." Then aloud, "My aide would like a word."

Zee cleared his throat, visibly awed by the prestige of those at the table. "Thank you for listening to me. Locating graves may not be so hard. I and many of my friends helped bury people who were—who died in camps. Most graves are close to places where, before, were the camps. We can show you where they are. Even help—" he paused, dropping his voice, "—digging them up."

"There is still the problem of identifying the remains," said Van der Velde.

"In parts of my country," said Ahmed, "dental records would be used."

Jasajovic shook his head. "I'm sorry to say dental care here is not a priority." He opened his mouth and pantomimed a tooth extraction, then laughed.

O'Brien could see that there were questions not easily answered, but he was determined not to let the matter bog down with specifics. "I've always relied on the advice of experts for things I know little about. Let's ask someone who knows."

"That would be a forensic pathologist," said Van der Velde. "We have an excellent one on our staff in The Hague."

"How soon can you get him here?"

"This is Friday. Probably by Monday." He added, "Dr. Werner. Hazel Werner."

Jasajovic looked around the table. "Agreeable?"

Heads nodded.

He smiled. "Wonderful." Then, apparently determined to have the last word, added, "My government is also interested in locating people who are missing. Don't forget, there was large amount of killing on *both* sides in this war. We do not like to admit it, but soldiers who have been brought up with a hatred for others not of their own religion are hard to control. Some are guilty of cruel and inhuman acts. We have already punished those in our own country who we know have done these terrible things." He smiled. "We hope other republics who fought in the war also punish offenders in their armies."

Quite an admission, O'Brien thought. He wondered if it were true that the Serbian government had tried and punished any of those responsible for the beatings Zee had told him about.

CHAPTER 6

O'Brien gazed out of the car window at the snow-covered fields. Interspersed were stands of pine trees, in the background white peaks of mountains. Too bad he and the driver that had been assigned to him didn't understand each other's language. Although he had a road map open on his lap, he would have liked to know more about the countryside they had passed through since leaving the center of Sarajevo half an hour ago.

Even before they left the city, he had seen few people on the streets. Perhaps because it was Sunday. He welcomed a day away from the boredom of the conference table, looking forward to an afternoon on the ski slopes at Mt. Jahorina, which he vaguely remembered from the TV broadcasts of the 1984 Winter Olympics.

Only two or three cars had passed going in the opposite direction, toward Sarajevo. He had seen a few U.N. military vehicles parked on the streets of the suburb called Ilidza. Even the troops were enjoying a day of rest. He wondered if the black car he had noticed behind them since they left the city also carried passengers on their way to a day of skiing.

The driver pointed out the window toward a clump of trees, made a mock gun with his hand and said, "Bing, bing."

"Snipers?" O'Brien said.

The driver shrugged. Obviously, the word was not familiar but he was probably indicating the place where, O'Brien had read, snipers had attacked a tour bus. That was almost a year ago and O'Brien wasn't worried even though both Zee and Van der Velde had voiced reservations about his day trip out of the city. He told them he would never forgive himself if he had come to Sarajevo and had not skied. He had even brought his ski jacket and wool cap with him. Although he considered himself only intermediate in skill, he loved the sport. In each of the past three years, with Peg and the girls, he'd spent a week of the Christmas vacation skiing in Colorado.

O'Brien's ears clogged as the road became steeper, the mounds of plowed snow on either side became higher. The car motor knocked loudly and with tire chains clanking, they ascended several more miles, finally coming to a lodge built of wood logs. Chair lifts, most of them empty, swayed from their cables, passing each other as they traveled slowly up toward the summit or down to the lodge.

O'Brien got out of the car and stretched, breathing in the clean air, feeling the hair in his nostrils freeze. While his driver parked, he looked to see if the black car had followed them all the way up. Apparently it had turned off.

The young woman behind the counter in the lodge greeted him in good English. "I'm glad that maybe tourists are finally coming back."

Although it was a Sunday afternoon, fewer than a dozen people were seated at tables, some sipping from steaming cups. While he waited for the attendant at the rental shop, he watched a group of ten or 15 young men and women wearing skis, boarding the chair lifts. Quite a difference from the mob scene at the Colorado ski resorts he'd visited.

The boots he rented with the skis and poles had apparently seen a good deal of wear, but they fit comfortably and the release bindings seemed to work.

He rode the chair lift to the summit and stood for a minute admiring the magnificence that surrounded him. The day was clear enough so he could see stretched out beneath him the ski trails, curving white aisles in the dense pine woods. Far down, perhaps three-quarters of a mile, smoke curled from a chimney on the lodge. In the distance, he could make out one of the villages they'd passed. If only Peg and the girls could be there to share the enjoyment with him.

Thankful for the lack of traffic on the slope, he skied cautiously down, testing himself on the gentler trail. But after the first two runs of about three-quarters of a mile each, he became bolder, using the more challenging run, accelerating on the straight-aways, leaning around the bends, even making short quick turns over a few low moguls.

In the late afternoon he took the last lift of the day to the summit. Exhilarated by the day's activity, he skied to the edge of the hill and pushed on to the slope. About a third of the way down, he made a turn and felt one of his boot bindings release. An instant later, the ski flew in the air and he hurtled down the hill, flipping from his back to his belly, now sliding face down. He clawed at the snow, finally felt something crash against his ribs and he suddenly stopped.

For a few seconds he lay still, partially buried in snow, his pulse roaring in his ears. Cautiously moving each arm and leg, he found his parts were intact. He raised his head, saw that the trunk of a tree he was lying against had stopped his slide. The snowdrift in the tree well had cushioned the impact when his back struck the tree. At some point during his fall the binding on the other ski had released, so he was now free of both skis. Using the tree for support, he slowly pulled himself up. He felt a sharp pain in his right knee when he put his weight on the leg, but after flexing and extending the joint a few times the pain diminished. Thank God, nothing worse than a sprained knee ligament. Twenty yards farther down the hill he spotted one ski resting against a tree; the other was out of sight. The ski poles were still held to his wrists by straps.

Gazing around, he saw that he had landed in the edge of a forest about 50 yards to the right of the ski trail. On the opposite side of the trail, the chair lift moved slowly high above the trees. If anyone had observed his fall, they hadn't stopped. Now with dusk approaching, only two people remained on the slope speeding down, but when he tried to hail them, he realized they were too far away and too preoccupied to notice him. Through the trees surrounding him, he could make out the summit but no skiers were on the slope. He thought about trying to climb back to the top and catching a chair lift down— if they hadn't stopped running by the time he got there. With a bad knee? Forget it. No, he'd walk down to the bottom of the hill, a distance of probably half a mile.

Pain knifed through his right knee when he placed his weight on it, but using the ski poles for balance he made himself push through the snow. He kept from falling down by grabbing one tree trunk after another and using the ski poles for support between trees. He avoided the deep drifts, keeping to places where the ground, sheltered by the edges of the pine branches, was covered with only two or three inches of snow.

Watching every step, his attention was focused on the snow at his feet. He glanced up, startled to see someone suddenly step out from behind a tree a few feet in front of him. Tall, husky in camouflaged fatigues, face covered by a ski mask. A man. A United Nations Forces troop? His alarm changed to relief. But where was the U.N. insignia or the blue helmet? The man shouted something in a language O'Brien couldn't understand. As he approached, the man held his arms out from his sides, blocking him. When O'Brien tried to sidestep him, the man moved to the same side.

"Let me by," O'Brien yelled.

The stranger shoved him hard, sending him to the ground on his back. O'Brien felt bile well up in his throat. Images of kidnapped Americans flashed through his mind. He tried to struggle to his feet. He wouldn't be taken without a fight. In an instant, the man was over him, pushing on his chest to keep him from getting up. Pinned down by a guy whose arms felt like steel rods, O'Brien knew it was useless to waste his strength, put up his hands in surrender. The man watched him as he lay in the snow for a few seconds, then roughly helped him to his feet. While O'Brien brushed snow off his jacket, the stranger watched, seemed ready to pounce again if he made a threatening move. Suddenly, the man grabbed O'Brien by the shoulder, turned him to face the depths of the forest and pointed. O'Brien peered into the dark mass of trees. What was he pointing to? Something yellow flashed in his vision. A narrow band of yellow tape tied to a tree fluttered in the gentle breeze. It took a moment before he realized what it was—in the direction he'd been headed.

He turned to the man. "Land mines?"

The man slowly nodded.

☠ CHAPTER 7

O'Brien cursed himself for his stupidity. Of course, he should have known. Bosnia was one big minefield. The guy he thought was trying to attack him was trying to keep him from blowing himself up.

Using gestures, he made the man understand that he had hurt his knee, and was trying to get to the lodge at the bottom of the hill. The man nodded, walked to a tree on which a canvas sack was tied. From it he took a walkie-talkie, made a call, then turned to O'Brien and gestured toward the lodge below. Help was on its way.

O'Brien sat and watched while the man ran yellow warning tape from one tree trunk to another. Apparently he had been replacing tape that had been torn loose by wind when O'Brien had stumbled on him. Looking back, O'Brien saw that the path he had just taken was through the minefield. Only his Irish luck had kept him from blowing his ass off.

Again.

He shuddered, but not from the cold. An image flashed before his eyes. It was 1968 just outside Cam Lo. He was directing a squad on patrol, and had stopped to empty mud and pebbles from his boots. He told Anderson to take the squad and go on ahead, he'd catch up with them. Fifty yards down the trail a VC mine took everything from Andy's right hip down. He never could erase the thought that Anderson had taken the hit instead of himself. The medic said he'd saved Andy's life by stanching with his bare hands the blood that spurted from the stump until clamps could be applied. But there were no clamps strong enough to choke off the guilt that poured out of him, even now.

The ski patrol arrived, consisting of a man riding a two-seat Snowmobile. After thanking his rescuer, O'Brien boarded for his ride back to the lodge.

The young woman who ran the equipment rentals refused his offer to pay for the skis, telling him that one had already been returned. "The other will surely be found. If not now, when the snow melts. I'm just glad you didn't get too badly hurt."

Annoyed that he hadn't been warned about the minefields, he diplomatically said, "I suppose I should have realized the area was mined."

Pointing to a large red sign on the wall behind her, she said, "The warning is posted in five languages, including English."

He hadn't noticed it when he bought his lift ticket, probably because he had been anxious to get on the slopes. "Please come back, and bring others. We need business."

*   *   *

Dr. Hazel Werner, the U.N. staff forensic pathologist was a fifty-ish, stout woman who wore her graying brown hair in a bun. For two days, she had droned on in Dutch-accented monotone, describing the methods used for body identification. O'Brien now sat in a darkened room while Dr. Werner projected slides showing images of gels containing DNA samples.

When the lights came on, O'Brien sat up blinking while she told of the difficulties they were encountering. "We are proceeding already in Vukovar and Srebrenica and other places with large-scale identification. Our progress is slow. But," she turned up her palms, "these poor people have been waiting already for three or four years to learn if their relatives are among the dead. What is another month or year if their minds can be put at ease?"

When O'Brien returned to his room after the lunch break, his phone was ringing. The caller said, "Know where I can buy a house in Washington cheap?"

O'Brien recognized the voice and shouted, "Hank! Where the devil are you calling from?"

"Hi, Matt. I'm just down the street. Holiday Inn. Can't afford the digs you're in. After all, I'm working in the private sector, not for the Uncle."

"You're in Bosnia? Last I heard you were somewhere in Asia."

"Cambodia. I left part of our crew there. The company needed me here. And while we're on the subject, have you decided to come on board?"

Hank Wilson was a radar engineer with Multi-Sensor Technology. One of the options O'Brien was considering after he lost his senate job was joining Hank's company. "Hank, why are we on the phone? Come on over. I'll buy you a beer and we can talk. Room 403."

Half an hour later, he and Wilson, holding glasses of beer, were seated in his hotel room. O'Brien said, "Cambodia, Bosnia. Christ, Hank when's the last time you were home?"

"Four months. Does me good to get away. Relieves the stress."

"Marge?"

Wilson dropped his glance and nodded. A year ago, he'd come home after a month-long field trip to find his apartment in Cincinnati emptied of all but a chair. On it was a goodbye note from his wife of 20 years. O'Brien was thinking the same could happen to him. For the past 12 years his family life had placed second to his campaign treks, senate fact-finding junkets, trips back to his home state, mostly without Peg and the girls. How long can you stay apart from your wife and family and expect to *have* a wife and family? He reminded himself to phone Peg tonight. It had been three days since he spoke to her.

"Any chance you'll get back together, Hank?"

"Nah. She's already got a replacement."

"Marge's remarried?"

"Just shacking up for now, but I hear they have wedding plans."

"What about—is it Randy?"

"Randy's a freshman at Ohio State. Great kid."

Lord, in a few weeks he'd be taking his own daughter, Brooke to look at colleges. Wilson was only a year older than he was, but seeing him today, O'Brien could still picture the carefree kid who'd been his fraternity brother at Miami University in southern Ohio. Even after Wilson had gone on to Ohio State as an engineering graduate student and O'Brien had entered Case Western Reserve Law School, they remained close friends. Each had been best man at the other's wedding. He wondered if he and Hank would have remained closer if Peg hadn't thought Marge a little fast for her tastes.

Wilson brightened. "So, are you ready to sign on?"

"You guys just want me because you think my name will bring government contracts. I'm not sure I want to spend the rest of my life lobbying."

"Come on, Matt. We don't give a rat's ass for your government contacts."

"What do I know about the radar business? I'm a lawyer."

"Right. And a damned good patent attorney, as I remember."

"Know how long it's been since I handled a patent case?"

"When did they last change patent law? Eighteen hundreds?"

Wilson was right. It wouldn't take him long to refresh his knowledge. And, of course, Wilson's firm was in the business of developing radar equipment which they patented. He smiled. "I'm a guy standing on the corner waving a cardboard sign with handmade lettering that reads, 'Will work for beans.' And here I am, arguing myself out of a job."

"Do I take that for a yes?"

O'Brien laughed. "Give me some time. I've gotta talk this over with Peg."

Wilson reached for the phone, handed it to him. "I'll pay for the call."

"Seriously, Hank, you're not here on a recruiting mission. What *are* you here for?"

Wilson drained his beer. "Well, like Cambodia, Bosnia has a problem with land mines."

O'Brien flipped his hand. "Tell me about it."

Wilson's brow creased.

O'Brien pulled up his right trouser leg to show his puffy knee.

Wilson bent over for a closer look. "Come on. You didn't get that stepping on a mine."

O'Brien related his skiing experience. "That's *my* story. Now, what's *your* interest in mines?"

"We're using our ground-penetration equipment to locate them. Then a team goes in and either digs them out or explodes them."

"Wait a minute. Mines are buried in the ground. When I was in the military, radar was used to pick up planes, ships."

Wilson grinned. "We've come a long way since then, Matt. We're working with equipment that uses ground-penetrating radar and pattern-recognition software as well as other sensors. We can program these babies to find a beer can buried in the sand." He let his words sink in, then added, "From a plane."

Jesus, buried objects. Those mass graves—. "Hank, could your radar pick up non-metallic objects?"

"What do you think the anti-personnel mines are made of? They're plastic."

Plastic. Bones. O'Brien gazed at the ceiling for a few moments. "Maybe you and I can work out a deal."

☠ CHAPTER 8

"What did Brooke think of Ohio State?"

O'Brien pressed the phone to one ear and stuck his finger in the other to hear Peg's faint reply, while mentally cursing the phone connection. "Oh, she liked it all right. But she also fell in love with Duke and Brown and—."

"God, Peg. You mean you've been traipsing up and down the coast?"

"Well, someone had to go—."

Damn. That was to have been *his* job. No, not a job. He'd been looking forward to watching Brooke react to the campuses he'd planned to visit with her, seeing the awe in the face of the 17-year-old. His first-born. The child he'd never expected he could father. Not after—. At least she hadn't made a decision yet, and he'd have the chance when he got back.

"Listen, Peg. I ran into Hank Wilson."

"Oh?"

The news obviously did not thrill her. It wasn't that she disliked him. O'Brien knew that she really enjoyed being in Hank's company, his laid-back humor, his zany antics. O'Brien suspected that Peg was jealous of the bond between the two men. He ignored the hint of disapproval in her voice. "He still desperately wants me to join his firm."

"Oh." Brighter. "Did he make the trip to Bosnia just to recruit you?"

"No. But I'm giving his proposition serious consideration. How do you feel about it?"

"Matt, if it's what *you* want to do, and if it will give us a chance to spend more time together, I'm for it." The tone of suspicion returned in her voice. "What *is* he there for?"

He explained Hank's mission of locating minefields, and added that the technique might be applicable to his mission as well. "It should only take two or three days to see if his technology will work for locating mass graves. Then I'm on my way."

"Uh-huh."

He couldn't blame her for sounding skeptical. Couldn't count the times his estimates had been off target. But, damn it, he really meant it.

*   *   *

They were seated on canvas campstools in the bed of a pickup truck, parked on a deserted country road 25 miles southeast of Sarajevo. Facing them in the truck bed were two rectangular metal boxes. The larger one had an oscilloscope display screen and below it several dials. The second had nine knobs on top and a joystick protruding from one side. About 500 feet above, a Schiebel Camcopter—a small, unmanned aerial vehicle—its rotors beating the air, flew at about 60 miles an hour in wide circles.

The day was cold but clear, the sky deep blue. He and Wilson both wore padded ski jackets, wool watch caps and gloves.

His body tingling with exhilaration, O'Brien watched as Wilson made small movements on the joystick, and the helicopter changed course and flew out of sight behind a hill. Wilson pointed at the green display screen. "Looks like we're getting some hits. Here and here."

O'Brien saw what appeared to be a series of irregularly depressed waveforms. "Mines?"

Wilson shrugged. "We'll have to analyze the raw data later. Separate it from ground clutter. Bosnia's got a lot more iron in the soil than places I've worked before. Remember, this is just a trial run to calibrate our instruments."

O'Brien gazed up as the eight-foot-long helicopter came back into view. "That thing weighs less than a hundred pounds?"

"Uh-huh. 'Course that's without the on-board instruments. The sensor payload weighs at least half again as much."

"You mean your ground-penetrating radar?"

"That and the IR and—"

"Infrared?"

"Right. Also a few other sensoring devices. How technical do you want me to get?"

"You can stop right now. I'm already on brain-cell overload. In fact, I'm not convinced you don't have a thumb-sized man up there piloting that helicopter."

Wilson laughed. "That unmanned crate does quite a job by itself. Of course, it needs a little goosing from my joystick here, but sure beats me having to log all that flight time." He maneuvered the joystick and the small craft performed a graceful roll. "Watch this, Matt." The camcopter glided down until it was barely a foot off the ground, and accelerated toward the truck.

Certain the helicopter was about to crash into them, O'Brien ducked. At the last moment, Wilson tweaked the control and the craft went into a loop missing the truck by a handbreadth. "Jesus, Hank you trying to kill us?"

Wilson grinned. "Not to worry, Matt. Learned that watching the Blue Angles."

"But if that thing crashes you've lost a few thousand bucks."

"A *few* thousand? Your house in Georgetown probably cost less."

"Impressed the hell out of me. You didn't bring all this equipment to Bosnia by yourself, did you?"

"I had a technician with me. He helped set it up. He had to fly back to Aviano, the Air Force Base. He's helping them with some radar repair work."

"Italy?"

"Uh-huh. Just a short hop over the Adriatic."

O'Brien watched as Wilson maneuvered the helicopter to a smooth landing alongside the truck. Together they disassembled the small craft, unhooked the sensor pack and loaded all the parts aboard the truck.

As they drove back to Sarajevo, O'Brien said, "I know you're interested in locating minefields, and I am too from a humanitarian standpoint. But we were going to see if we could adapt the technique for finding gravesites, remember?"

"I haven't forgotten, Matt. I'm having our engineers develop an algorithm. We should be ready to run tests in two or three days." He grinned. "Hey, are you cleared for this grave-robbing caper?"

"Huh?"

"I thought you were supposed to be sitting around conference tables, drinking coffee and wine and shooting the shit with other big shots."

"First place, I'm no longer a big shot. My former constituents took care of that last November. The President tossed me this bone to keep food on my table until I get a *real* job."

"Don't give me that. I read the newspapers. You've been making noise in the senate about the Balkan atrocities for a couple of years."

"Well, okay. I can't stand around and do nothing when I have the chance to be of help."

"Just a minute, Matt. Under your seat you'll find a violin. Mind rendering a tune?"

"Drive, dammit."

Wilson snickered. "Sorry to ring your bell, old buddy. Didn't mean to touch you where you're sore."

O'Brien couldn't suppress a grin, then broke out in a guffaw. "I should know you by this time. Anyway, I started to tell you that I did call Washington. Spoke to the President's chief of staff and told him I'd like to do a bit of fieldwork while I was here. He said it sounded all right to him. If there was any problem after he'd batted it around with the boys at State, he'd get back to me. I haven't heard anything so I assume I'm cleared."

"I guess in Washington a 'maybe' is as good as a 'yes.' Incidentally, have you arranged for the—uh, test materials?"

"Ready to go." O'Brien had made arrangements with a slaughterhouse to provide him with several cow and goat shanks. They planned to bury them at various depths and see if Wilson's instruments could locate these simulated "corpses."

The truck rounded a curve. Fifty yards ahead a wooden barricade and two police cars blocked the road. Four men in police uniforms stood alongside the cars. The policemen held assault rifles.

Wilson braked the truck, leaned out the window. "What's going on?"

A policeman came alongside, said something and Wilson shook his head. He turned to O'Brien. "I don't suppose you speak the language, do you?"

"No, but from the way he's gesturing with that rifle, I think he wants us out of the truck."

A second policeman stepped to the side of the truck. "*Aussteigen, Bitte.*"

Guy probably figured everyone understood German. Wilson put his hand on the door latch. O'Brien said, "Wait a minute, Hank. I'll show him my ID." He reached for his wallet in the back pocket of his jeans.

Both policemen instantly raised their guns, aimed them through the window and shouted an order.

Reaching back like that, O'Brien thought, was probably not a bright idea. "Maybe we'd better do what they want, Hank."

CHAPTER 9

Wilson said, "What's funny?"

They sat in tandem in the cell, too narrow to sit side by side. O'Brien was seated on the single wooden stool, Wilson on the straw mat on the cement floor.

Wilson's clothes were disheveled and he had a one-day stubble. "What the hell do you have to grin about?"

"I was just thinking, this is one of the best prisons I've been in."

Wilson rolled his eyes.

"No shit, Hank. The one the VCs had me in was a pit in the ground. Over the top were bamboo slats. They'd toss down hunks of bread, then howl as they watched me fight the cat-sized rats for the food."

"Yeah, I'm sure it was no picnic." Wilson pulled one of his shoes off and used it to hammer an inch-long roach scurrying across the floor. "But this keeps up, I'm calling the manager to change my room." He looked up at O'Brien. "Hey, Peg ever complain about your snoring?"

"It couldn't have been me. I didn't get more than fifteen minutes sleep last night."

"Maybe it was one of our other roommates."

"You mean one of these roaches? That's about all that can fit into this shoebox." O'Brien yawned. He glanced at his wrist before remembering that the police had taken their watches. "Wonder if they made that call to the U.N. last night."

"I'll ask our concierge." Wilson, who was seated closest to the cell door, turned sideways and kicked the bars.

A guard appeared a few seconds later, scowled and shouted something.

O'Brien turned up his hands. *"Sprechen sie Deutsch?"*

The guard shrugged. Shook his head.

Wilson said, "Wish that guy who booked us in last night would show up. At least he understood a little German."

The corridor door clanked open and another guard appeared outside the bars accompanied by a man in a well-fitted business suit who was carrying a briefcase. He appeared to be in his early forties, small mustache, dark- complexioned, black hair.

One of the guards unlocked the cell door and, after the visitor squeezed inside, he relocked it. The odor of cologne that emanated from the man was a pleasant change from the uriniferous stink of their cage. He offered a hand to O'Brien. "Mario Santori, *signores.*" His speech was tinged with an Italian accent. "We receive your message at U.N. headquarters, and of course we are in distress at—." He swept his gaze around the cell.

Wilson struggled up from the mat. His eyes, red-rimmed, were narrowed to slits. "How about getting us the hell out of here. These bastards are treating us like we're criminals."

O'Brien felt as crummy as Wilson looked and both were starving. Since they were jailed yesterday afternoon, their only meal had been a tin cup of watery soup and a slice of bread. They needed help and Santori was all they had at the moment. He didn't want Wilson scaring him off with tough talk. "Hold it Hank. Thanks for coming Mr. Santori. We have a language problem and have no idea why they arrested us."

Santori nodded. "Yes. So. I will certainly try to be of help. As I am sure you know, the Dayton Peace Agreement provided for division of Bosnia into ethnic compartments. Unfortunately, you wandered into a zone that is under the control of the Serbian government." From his briefcase he extracted a map and pointed. "Sarajevo is here at the easternmost edge of the Bosnian sector. You were here, just east of that line. Clearly, it is under Serbian jurisdiction."

Wilson said, "Look, Mr. Santori, we weren't trying to invade—?"

Santori raised his hand. "Please, let me go on. Apparently the Serbian police have found some damaging evidence in your truck."

"What fucking damaging evidence?" Wilson shouted. "I'm here to keep their asses from being blown away. Is that a crime?"

O'Brien put a hand on Wilson's chest to keep him from advancing on the man. "Mr. Santori, we had no idea we were in the Serbian sector. We were not doing anything illegal. In fact, we were trying to locate mines left here during the war. You know as well as we that mines don't discriminate. They've maimed and killed Serbian farmers as well as Bosnian." He suddenly felt stupid. Why the hell was he making one of his senatorial speeches? "Look, Mr. Santori, what can you do to get us out of here—and quickly."

Santori dug into his briefcase. "The magistrate handling your case will be seeing you in a few hours. He requires you to sign some papers before he agrees to releasing you."

O'Brien stole a glance at Wilson who was seething. "Let me see the papers."

Santori handed him two sheets. "I haven't had time to have it translated, but I can summarize for you what it says."

"Yes?"

"It is a confession that you were flying in Serbian airspace."

Technically, it was probably true that they had conducted the test flight of the unmanned helicopter in Serbian territory. Wilson had cleared the flight with Bosnian authorities, but O'Brien had misjudged the location of the test site.

Wilson said, "I'm not signing any goddam phony confession. I demand we see the American consulate."

Santori shrugged. He placed the papers back in the briefcase. "Your privilege. However, I must advise you that it will take some time before we can arrange to have the consulate here, and I suspect that the United States consulate will have even less influence than we at United Nations. If you don't sign, it will delay your release indefinitely."

"Matt, you must have some influence. Christ, you're a senator."

"*Ex*-senator, Hank. But I *am* on a Presidential mission. Mr. Santori, how can I get word to the White House?"

"I can try after I return to Sarajevo."

Wilson threw up his hands. "All right, I don't want to spend another day in this hole. Let's sign. When we get out of here I'll get my company's legal department to quash the confession. We're making it under duress."

O'Brien could live with that. Santori went back into his briefcase, handed him the papers and indicated where he and Wilson should sign.

Santori motioned to the guard standing outside the cell that he was ready to leave. Suddenly he turned back. "Oh, I have some other unpleasant news. The Serbian government has temporarily confiscated the equipment from your truck. They plan to have it examined by their experts. If they are satisfied that it poses no danger to them, they will return it."

CHAPTER 10

The technician stood up, took a handkerchief from his back pocket and wiped his brow. "I've never seen such messed-up equipment."

Shortly after O'Brien and Wilson were released from the Serbian jail near Pale, the technician had returned from the Air Force Base at Aviano, Italy. Now they were in a small concrete block building on the outskirts of Sarajevo. Wilson had rented it to garage his truck and mine detection equipment, and also to serve as a laboratory where he could synthesize by computer the raw data he collected in the field. On a table stood one of the control consoles they'd had on the truck when they ran the test. Its metal cover was off and lay alongside surrounded by a small sea of screws. To O'Brien, the open contraption was a spaghetti tangle of wires in a rainbow of bright colors.

Wilson said, "This is their idea of an inspection? They must have torn it down and had a cageful of monkeys put it back together." He turned to the technician. "What do you think, Sam? Can it be patched into shape?"

He shook his head slowly. "I don't know, Mr. Wilson. I've got the spec sheets and I'll sure give it a try. Might be simpler to sent for a replacement."

O'Brien said, "How long would it take to get another one?"

Wilson shrugged. "Week, ten days. Sam, see what you can do. Meanwhile, I'll phone the plant, tell them to ship one over air express. Worse comes to worst, we'll have two."

Having two units might not be a bad idea. Could cover more ground.

*　　　　*　　　　*

"I'm fine, Peg. I really am."

"Did they beat you?"

"Of course not."

"You're just trying to put me at ease. I know you, Matt O'Brien."

He laughed. "Honestly, Peg. The Ritz Carlton it wasn't. But—"

Her sighed swished into his ear. "How much longer do you expect to be there?"

"Our committee meets with some former prisoners and relatives this afternoon. Hank Wilson expects to have his ground-penetration gizmo fixed in two days. I'd like to see it in action before I head back home. My guess is I'll be home in another week, ten days tops. How's Lesley coming with her riding?"

"She's out at the stables more than she's at home. She has that big show in a few weeks."

"Put her on. I'd like to speak with her."

A few moments later, "Hi, Daddy. Gee, it's so good to hear your voice."

His eyes misted and he heard the hoarseness in his voice. He pictured the 11-year-old, twisting a curl of her blonde hair with an index finger while she talked on the phone. "Hi, sweetie. I can't tell you how much I miss you—all of you."

"Taffy too?"

"Who? Oh, *Taffy*. Yeah. How's the cute pony?"

"Daddy, you should see her take the jumps. She can make two rails, sometimes three."

"You be careful, now."

"Don't worry, Daddy. I'm practicing for the spring show. You *will* be back for it, won't you? Please, Daddy? Huh?"

"I wouldn't miss it. When is it, three weeks?"

"Uh-huh."

Peg's voice was back on the line. "Please be careful yourself, Matt. And hurry. We miss you, I can't tell you how much we miss you."

"No more than I miss you and the girls. Love you."

He put the phone down slowly. For sure, this time he was not going to blow it.

*   *   *

O'Brien couldn't have spelled Hassan's last name if he'd had a dictionary. He was a Bosnian Muslim with piercing black eyes, a leathery face as creased as a relief map, and a permanent five-o'clock shadow. He could have been in his twenties or fifties. Like most of the Balkan men, he was over six feet tall. Gaunt rather than slender. His dark hair came over his ears but was neatly combed. He wore a wrinkled black suit and a white shirt buttoned at the collar without a tie. Like the others who had spoken before him, he was seated in the Hotel Strand conference room at the head of a long table, a translator alongside him. The committee members sat on either side of the table listening intently to his recitation, which, by pre-arrangement, was limited to 20 minutes. Not once during that time did O'Brien see even a faint smile on Hassan's face. But, again, there was nothing for him to smile about. Hassan's story was similar to those told by the other four who were appearing before the committee this afternoon. Through the dispassionate voice of the interpreter he told of being beaten daily, seeing other prisoners being taken out of the building in which they were kept and shot.

"I would stand in line, my eyelids clamped together, my fists clenched, my knees shaking. Praying to almighty God: Please don't let them take me.

"On three occasions, packed in with others, I was shipped in trucks from one camp to another. I did not know why I was moved around."

While he spoke, O'Brien could see from the edge of his vision, Zee seated alongside him, nodding gravely or slowly shaking his head, no doubt in silent remembrance of his own experiences.

Hassan had helped bury more than 30 other prisoners who had either died following beatings or succumbed to sickness. Other prisoners were called out of the barracks and never returned. At one of the camps—he couldn't remember whether it had been at Omarska or one near Srebenica—a guard, a man he'd known in his village, told him that there was a camp where the prisoners received "special treatment."

Ahmed said, "Did the guard tell you where this camp was?"

Hassan shook his head.

"Did he mean the 'special treatment' was better or worse than the way you were treated?"

"It couldn't be worse."

Jasajovic said, "Tell us, please, the name of this guard."

"Sretko Jeftic."

Although the others who had appeared before the committee during the long afternoon had heard from other prisoners of a "special camp," Hassan was the first one who could produce a source. Perhaps they could verify his story.

Jasajovic beckoned to one of his aides and said something O'Brien couldn't understand. After the aide left, Jasajovic addressed the others at the table. "I will find out where Jeftic is, and have him come here to tell us what he knows."

O'Brien would give odds that Jeftic would not be found.

So far, the committee had been hearing of atrocities committed on Bosnian Muslims. The last two men to appear were Bosnian Serbs. So, thought O'Brien, we're about to hear from the other side.

Miro Damjanovic, a tall handsome man in his thirties with sandy-colored hair and a bushy mustache, had lived all his life in the Bosnian village of Gornji Malovan. He bowed slightly, then sat in the chair at the head of the long table. Jasajovic asked him to tell the committee his experience in a prison camp. "We had ninety men in our village. Forty were Serbs, the others Muslim." He waited while the interpreter translated into English, then continued. "Soldiers of the Croatian army came one night, took we Serbian men—not the Muslims—to a nearby farm that had been owned by a Serb family who left and abandoned their property when the 'trouble' started.

"We were kept in the barn, twelve to fifteen men crowded into each of the horse stalls. No straw, bare cement floors. There was not enough room for all of us to lie down at the same time, so we took turns sleeping. Every day the Croats took a few of us out and beat us with clubs. For the first two days we had nothing to eat or drink. Some of the men would catch their urine in their hands and wet their lips."

After they'd been there about two weeks, they were marched to a nearby forest where they were ordered to kneel in line on the ground.

"I saw the soldiers gouge out the eyes of many of my friends. They cut off their ears, broke their arms and legs. Then shot them. I was one of the last in line. Before they got to me I got up and ran into the trees. The soldiers shot at me. I expected to be killed, but I would rather die quickly than go through the torture like my friends. One of the bullets went through my shoulder." He started to remove his shirt, but Jasajovic stopped him, saying, "We believe you."

Damjanovic continued. "I ran and hid in bushes in the forest. I ate leaves from the trees and drank water from a muddy pool for two days until the soldiers had stopped looking for me. I crawled through the fields back to my village at night, and went to the house belonging to one of my friends. He was one of those who had been tortured and killed. His wife took me in, bandaged my wound, and hid me in the cellar until the soldiers left the village. I was the only Serbian man left alive."

The daughter of the woman who hid him smuggled him out of the village in a hay cart. "If the Muslims had known I was still alive they would have turned me over to the soldiers."

Did he know anything about secret camps where the missing men might still be held?

"I have heard such fairy tales. It is wishful thinking by the women who think their men are still alive. No, they are casualties of the war—just as our men are."

O'Brien had read that the Bosnian Serbs had been subjected to torture, rape and murder not only by the Muslims but by the Croatians. Now he was hearing it from the mouths of the victims. Although 30 years had passed since Vietnam, he had not forgotten that inhumanity of one group toward another was not confined to any religion, sect, color or race.

The last speaker, 26-year-old Nenad Herak, had grown up in Polimac, about 50 miles east of Sarajevo. Although in Bosnia, the village was close to the border with Serbia.

"Most of my schoolmates were Muslim but we all got along without trouble until June 1992." Muslims who belonged to a group called the Bosnian Territorial Defense dragged out all the Serbs, men, women and children, and burned their houses. Herek had gone to Belgrade a few days before the raid. He remained there until after the Dayton Peace Accord had been signed in 1995 and it was safe to return to his village under U.N. protection. "They were all gone. My father, mother, three brothers and two sisters."

Dead?

Herek turned up his palms. "I still had some Muslim friends in the village. They showed me places where the ground was covered by young weeds. They suspected these might be gravesites and helped me dig. Three places turned out to be shallow graves each with two or three bodies."

Herek rubbed his eyes. "Even though the bodies were rotted, I was sure none of them were members of my family. I know I cling to a straw but I cannot let go of the hope that they are in a prison somewhere."

O'Brien stole glances at Zee while the two Serbs were telling their stories. His gaze was fixed on the carpet, his face impassive. There seemed to be no reason to disbelieve any of the people. Again he was reminded that bestiality was not a monopoly of either side in this war, any more than it was in his own war. For Gornji Malovan or Srebenica, read My Lai. O'Brien knew the argument. Like kids in a schoolyard scrap, each side would point to the other: "He started it."

He asked Herek, "What makes you think they might be alive?"

"We know only of the few bodies we found. Yet there were more than sixty Serbs in the village before the attack. If they are all dead, where are the other bodies?"

Probably there were other graves that hadn't been found. He needed Wilson's little plane.

☠ CHAPTER 11

Zee drove the small rented Yugo carefully, negotiating the twists and turns around construction crews repairing sections of the road still gouged by shells. O'Brien waited until they were well clear of the city traffic before he engaged in more than casual conversation. Finally, he said, "Those Serbs who spoke at the committee meeting yesterday, can they be believed?"

Zee kept his eyes on the road, but smiled. "I wondered when you were going to ask. Yes, I am sure many of these things they said were true. I know of some of my own people who belonged to BTD—Bosnian Territorial Defense. They believe in principle 'an eye for an eye.' A small number but as wicked as the other side." Zee added, "The Croats also had their terrorists—Ustashis."

Muslim BTD, Croatian Ustashis, Serbian Chetniks. Everyone in this crazy land had a label. You were either a guerilla freedom fighter or a terrorist. You needed a scorecard to keep them straight.

Zee read his thoughts. "All our republics have these ultranational-ists—your newspapers call them 'fringe groups.' Serbian Chetniks killed my grandfather on my father's side just after World War II. He was Muslim, lived in village in southern Serbia. The Chetniks wanted to make the place only for Serbs."

"Ethnic cleansing?"

"Yes."

Zee glanced at him, a mischievous grin on his lips. "You forget the Partisans. Weren't they what your Western movies call the 'good guys'?"

"Sure. They were on the same side as United States, fighting the Nazis. I'm curious, Al. Were you better or worse off under Tito?"

Zee thought for a long moment. "For many of us he was cruel, but when he was head of government we had jobs, schools, health care. Except for his secret police, people did not kill each other as they did after he died. At least not so much as recently."

"Are you saying you were better off under Tito?"

"For me, yes. For many others, no."

"Spoken like a true diplomat."

Zee laughed. "I think we are finished with our history lesson for today. We are here now."

"Here" was the snow-covered field of an abandoned farm off a dirt road about 30 miles north of Sarajevo, near the city of Dastansko.

Zee opened the car trunk and stepped back, holding his nose. Crammed into the small space, wrapped in a blood-soaked canvas tarp were a dozen assorted animal legs: cow, goat and sheep. O'Brien had gotten a cold stare from the Muslim slaughterhouse proprietor when he asked him to put "a few pigs' legs in as well."

O'Brien handed Zee a pair of work gloves and donned a pair himself. "Lord, these things stink. I wonder what would have happened if we'd been stopped and searched by the police."

Zee laughed. "Probably put you back in jail."

They hauled the tarp and its contents out of the trunk and dragged it about 50 feet into the field. Zee went back to the car and from the back seat brought a pair of shovels. He scraped snow from the ground and drove his spade into the soil. Below the frozen surface crust, the earth was surprisingly soft. "This isn't as hard as I thought it would be."

"That's the reason I asked you to find a field that had been cultivated," O'Brien said.

After digging for 40 minutes, O'Brien's arms felt leaden. He rested on his shovel and watched Zee, deep into the second hole he'd dug. O'Brien was still working on his first. After a minute, somewhat revived, he resumed his digging, but with each shovelful he could hear himself grunt. When he again stopped to rest after a few minutes, Zee paused long enough to glance at him and grin.

Two hours after they had started, they had dug four holes about four feet deep, placed from one to three of the animal legs in each, and refilled each of the "graves" with soil. They marked the sites with short wooden stakes topped by small red flags.

O'Brien sank into the car seat without bothering to brush the dirt from the legs of his jeans, and took a long swig of bottled water. "I haven't worked this hard since I landscaped my first house."

Zee seemed fairly fresh although he had worked more rapidly than O'Brien. He mopped his face with a handkerchief. "I had much practice digging graves."

"Omarska?"

Zee nodded.

"Well, the next step is to see how accurate our instruments are at finding and identifying the things we've buried."

Zee grinned. "I have at home a dog who can do that—and costs much less than your fancy instruments."

"I understand they *do* have dogs that are trained for this sort of work. Trouble is they tire easily and they're not discriminating enough. They'll find all kinds of things. Wilson tells me that his instruments can be programmed to detect objects that match the sizes and shapes of human corpses and will screen out garbage. Also they can cover a wide area in a short time."

Zee, an anxious expression on his face, had been looking off in the distance toward the main road they had taken from Sarajevo, the road from which they had turned off to gain access to the field. O'Brien followed Zee's gaze. A black sedan was parked by the side of the main road about 500 yards away. Although too far off to see the car's occupants, the lowering sunlight glinted off an object in a side window. Binoculars? The field in which they had planted the animal parts was well away from any habitation, was screened from the main road by a row of trees, so unless someone were specifically looking for them, they would not have been seen. No cars had come into the access road they had taken, and only an occasional farm truck or tractor, had passed on the main road.

"Was that car following us?"

Zee shook his head. "I didn't see cars behind us after we passed through that village about 5 kilometers from here."

"Drive over. I'd like to see who that is."

Zee started the car but before they had driven 100 yards, the black car sped off, heading away from Sarajevo. By the time they reached the main road, the black car was out of sight. For a fleeting moment, O'Brien had considered giving chase, but after reflecting on the size of the other car, he realized the Yugo would never be able to catch it.

On the drive back to Sarajevo, O'Brien remained silent much of the way, questions spinning around in his brain. Who was watching him? Why would anyone be interested in his activities? Could the black car be the same one he recalled having seen behind his when he drove to Mt. Jahorina? In the future, he'd have to watch his back more carefully.

☠ CHAPTER 12

Wilson drove his pickup to the hotel entrance and opened the door for O'Brien. "Howdy, cellmate."

O'Brien climbed in and laughed. "This time we stay far from trouble. Gear all fixed?"

"Yeah. Tech's a wizard. I'm only sorry he can't stay here with us instead of ferrying back and forth to Aviano."

"Found any mines?"

"Matter of fact, we have. Spent the past three days in recon. Backcountry's full of the goddam things. Hope the bones you buried are as easy to locate."

"Do you use the same radar as you did for the mines?"

Wilson nodded. "Yeah, the GPR's the same."

"GPR?"

"Ground-penetrating radar. That and some other sensors. But we've developed different algorithms than we use for the mines. Ones that should let us identify the stuff you've buried."

"I'd ask what an algorithm is except I'd never understand the answer."

"It's a set of instructions for solving a problem. You tell the machine to just look for an item such-and-such a size, and having such-and-such density and ignore everything else."

"Sounds easy. All you need is a graduate degree in physics." He gazed at the sky. Snow had fallen intermittently during the three days since he and Zee had buried the animal legs. "Glad the snow's stopped. Looks like it's going to stay clear and dry today."

Arriving at the field, O'Brien saw that the fresh snow had covered the burial sites as well as the stakes and flags they had placed as markers. Wilson set up the equipment and sent the unmanned helicopter aloft. It flew back and forth in a pattern that covered the field of 60 or 70 acres in about 15 minutes. Wilson glowered at the monitor screen, adjusting knobs, shaking his head.

O'Brien kept silent, not wanting to break Wilson's concentration. From his expression and muttered oaths, it was obvious things were not going according to plan. "Something wrong?"

"You're sure we're at the right place?"

"Positive."

Wilson slapped the top of the monitor. "Then this goddam thing goes back to the shop. We're not getting the signals we should."

Another disappointment. O'Brien had been so sure that this was going to work, he'd pushed back his departure for home so he could watch and formulate plans that could be continued after he left. "Want to give it another try before we head back?"

Wilson shook his head. "Nah. I've tried all the combinations." He landed the helicopter and with O'Brien's help, stowed the equipment. He started the truck. "I'll get hold of the tech and see if he can work out the bugs. Can't understand it. The terrain maps out fine. There are voids out there that can be graves. Just can't get signals from your 'corpses.'"

Something tugged at O'Brien's brain. He grabbed Wilson's forearm. "Wait. Got a shovel?"

"Yeah. In the tool box behind the cab."

O'Brien jumped out, retrieved the shovel and hurried to the part of the field where he had buried the animal legs. Although he was sure he had refilled the graves after depositing the legs, he now found four distinct depressions in the snow-covered ground. The depressions corresponded in size to those of the burial sites. With Wilson looking on, he dug into the soft dirt of one of the pits, finally catching a glimpse of a red object. One of the flags he had attached to a marker stake, but the stake itself was gone. He continued to dig until he was sure he had reached the depth at which he had buried the legs. The odor of decaying flesh rose from the dirt in the pit. No question, this was one of the burial sites. Empty.

He dug into the second depression, uncovered another red flag and found another empty grave. Once more the fetid odor confirmed the location. He found the third hole, and the fourth. All empty graves.

Weary, he turned to Wilson. "Nothing wrong with your machine, Hank. Let's go home."

CHAPTER 13

"Well," said Wilson. "I can think of one good thing about this trip."

"Yeah, what's that?"

"We didn't end up in jail."

O'Brien was still wondering who could have dug up the animal legs and why. Someone apparently trying to block his efforts. He hadn't discussed with other members of the committee his project with Wilson of attempting to locate mass graves. No point in saying anything until he had something positive to report. He ran through a mental list of people with whom he'd come into contact since coming to Sarajevo, but could think of no one who would have knowledge of what he was doing. Or if they did, no one who might try to stop him from locating the graves. Even the Serbian representatives had said they were as anxious as the Muslims to find their missing people. The only possible source of trouble might be the person or persons who had spied from the car parked in the road when he buried the animal legs. Well, no point worrying about it. Nothing he could do about it except keep his eyes open. "Hank, could we just go ahead and try to locate burial sites in areas where we suspect they might be?"

"You mean forget about the test runs?"

"Uh-huh."

"Sure. The only drawback is if we came up empty we wouldn't know if there really were no burial sites in the places we were looking, or if we weren't properly programmed for them."

"Let's take that chance. I can't afford to waste any more time here."

"Okay," said Wilson. "When you know where to start looking give me a ring."

*   *   *

The large map was spread out on the bed in O'Brien's hotel room. Zee was marking with a red pen places where detention camps had been located. He pointed to one of the red Xs. "Here, for sure, there are at least a dozen graves."

"Isn't this near the field where we buried the animal parts?"

"Yes, about thirty kilometers north of Dastansko. Some soldiers burned out a village there. None of the people are left—alive."

*   *   *

Two days later, O'Brien and Zee were crammed into the cab of the pickup alongside Wilson who drove. They had passed through several villages but saw no people on the streets. Many of the houses had been destroyed, leaving only isolated brick chimneys pointing like red fingers toward the sky. The only traffic they encountered during the ride consisted of a few dilapidated automobiles and half a dozen farm trucks.

Every few minutes O'Brien checked the sideview mirror, but they were not followed.

As they approached a dirt road, Zee said, "Turn here."

For another four miles, the truck bumped over a rutted trail cut through a forest, climbing a hill and finally descending to a valley through which snaked a narrow creek.

Zee pointed to a row of charred wooden studs protruding from the ground. To some were attached remnants of joists, giving the appearance of crude crosses. Memorials to what had been perhaps 20 houses. A crumbled mass of stone topped by fragments of red tile may have been a small mosque. "This is the village—what is left of it."

What probably had been surrounding cultivated fields were now meadows of tall weeds that protruded from the snow.

O'Brien swept an arm in the vicinity of the meadows. "You think the graves are around here?"

"I have been told that is so. But exactly where…" He shrugged.

Wilson was already in the truck bed removing the tarp that covered his equipment. "Okay, people. Give me a hand with my little pigeon. We'll send it up to map the terrain, then overlay that with a grid and start the survey."

O'Brien was hunched over Wilson's shoulder examining the display on the screen of his control console. Wilson pointed a gloved finger at a green splotch. "That's subsurface electromagnetic conductivity contrast."

"Give it to me in English."

"We're detecting contaminant plumes. Could be decaying corpses."

O'Brien looked up at the small unmanned craft, its rotors beating as it flew back and forth over the field. Wilson explained he had added some sensors to its packet since their last outing. "They measure changes in groundwater and gases that seep up through the soil."

"How long would seepage like that go on?" O'Brien asked

"Centuries. We've found buried hazardous waste that had been placed in the ground ten, fifteen years before. This looks promising. Let me check the grid, see where it is."

Mumbling to himself, he turned dials, flipped switches and fiddled with the joystick controlling the flight of the helicopter. The small craft changed course and was now making turns over a stand of trees about 300 yards away.

"Watch how close to the tree tops I can maneuver this craft," said Wilson. "Pinpoint control."

O'Brien marveled at the sophisticated display of technology he was witnessing. "Don't the trees interfere with the signals?"

Wilson shook his head. "This baby's got foliage-penetrating capability." His face brightened. "Hey, I think we've got confirmation."

"Meaning?"

"Maybe your buried treasure. Let's go look."

He grabbed a shovel from the tool chest.

O'Brien and Zee followed Wilson loping over the snow-sprinkled field. He came to a halt under the hovering helicopter. The site was a clearing in the woods about 30 yards in diameter. He stood studying the ground, covered by patches of low weeds and bare, damp dirt.

"Interesting, Matt. No snow."

O'Brien followed Wilson's gaze. A rough rectangle of the ground about 15 feet in one direction and eight feet in the other was devoid of snow, although it covered the rest of the surrounding area. "The ground must be warmer. Snow's melted."Wilson started digging.

Zee said, "Please. May I have shovel?"

Wilson gave him the shovel. Zee picked up piece of fallen tree limb about five feet long. "Here's how we simple people do it." With the back of the shovel, he hammered the wood into the ground. After only six inches protruded, he worked it back and forth until it was loose and extracted it. He held to his nose the bottom end of the stick, then offered it to O'Brien, "Smell."

The fetid odor was unmistakable. "Phew! Paydirt."

Fifteen minutes later, they watched as Zee uncovered a partially rotted hand. Wilson's face paled. He turned and walked a few paces from the other two. "Excuse me guys. I think I'm going to throw up."

"Hold it, Zee," O'Brien said. "Let's mark this spot, and turn the job over to a forensic team." His stomach had begun to churn as well, and he was glad for an excuse to quit.

*   *   *

Wilson was recalling the small helicopter in preparation for landing, when a large khaki truck, its bed covered by a hooped tarp, rumbled up the dirt road. It braked behind their vehicle. The tarp flap was thrown back, and two men in camouflage fatigues, carrying rifles leaped down and stood silently with muzzles pointed at the three men. A stocky man similarly clad rolled out of the driver's side of the cab. He was unarmed, obviously their leader. He spoke rapidly. Serbian, O'Brien thought.

Zee interpreted. "He says we are in a restricted area and must come with him."

Wilson stood in the bed of his truck, appeared ready to jump down. He fumed. "Who the fuck is—"

O'Brien put an arm on Wilson's shoulder. "Hold it, Hank." Turning to Zee, he said, "Ask him to show us some identification." Unwilling to risk being jailed again, he had carefully checked their position on the map before starting out. He was certain that they were not in an area controlled by the Bosnian Serbs. He wondered who these men represented. Sure as hell not the Bosnian government. But whose?

After listening to Zee relaying O'Brien's message, the leader's face turned red. A spray of spittle accompanied his shouted response.

"He says he does not have to show us anything. He wants to know what we're doing here."

O'Brien expected as much. He could see they'd only get into more trouble arguing with this bull. Besides, they had accomplished all they had intended here. His main concern now was to avoid being taken into custody. "Okay, Zee. Tell him we're leaving."

The leader listened to Zee, then shook his head and gave a lengthy response.

Zee said, "He says we must come with him to explain why we are here."

Wilson's fists were balling. "This is a fucking shakedown. Let's see how much they want." He started reaching for his pocket.

O'Brien pictured them being tossed into another roach-infested cage—or worse. Trying to bribe this gorilla might make matters worse. "Wait, Hank. We'd better play this by the books."

"You mean go with them?" Wilson jaw was set. He looked determined to take on an army.

O'Brien wasn't sure if any of these guys understood English, but he had to rein in Wilson. He spoke quietly. "Hank, stay here in the truck bed. Zee, tell them we have to get our helicopter down and put our equipment away. Then we'll follow them. I'll drive."

After Zee had delivered O'Brien's message, the leader gazed at the helicopter circling above them, thought for a moment, then gave a single nod. He spoke to one of the armed men.

Zee said,. "One of these men is coming with us to make sure we follow."

Zee climbed into the truck bed alongside Wilson. The man who was to accompany them waited alongside the leader.

O'Brien nudged Wilson and shot a glance skyward. Quietly, "Hank, it's Blue Angel time."

"Huh?"

"Pin point control? Show me."

Wilson stared at him for a moment, then grinned. "Roger that."

He moved the joystick and the helicopter dove for the three in uniform like a hawk after a sparrow. They hit the ground, the little craft barely skimming over their heads. The men started to scramble to their feet, but the craft went into a tight loop and plunged at the men sending them to the ground again. O'Brien jumped down from the truck bed and leaped into the driver's seat. The ignition caught. He yelled back, "Hang on!" A sharp U-turn over the field, and he was back on the dirt road behind the army truck. From the corner of his eye he could see the helicopter swooping down again. Gunning the engine, the spinning wheels sent up a cloud of dust. He yelled over his shoulder. "How're you doing back there?"

Wilson shouted back, "Great. Hold 'er steady. I'll make one more pass at the bastards."

In his rear view mirror, O'Brien could see the small craft buzzing the three soldiers. They remained on the ground.

A quarter of a mile ahead, O'Brien could see the main road leading to Sarajevo. A few moments later they were on it speeding toward the city, the small helicopter soaring above them. No sign of the khaki truck.

*   *   *

O'Brien swallowed a swig of beer. "I'm still wondering who these guys are. Zee says he's sure they aren't troops of the Bosnian Security Force."

O'Brien was seated on the bed in his hotel room after returning from the field where they had discovered the gravesite. They had left Zee off at the U.N. building to see if he could learn anything about the men who had confronted them. Also, he was to make arrangements for a team of forensic investigators to exhume and identify the bodies.

Wilson said, "They didn't try to follow us, so chances are they have no official standing." He grinned. "My little pigeon sure scared the shit out of them."

"I loved the way you handled it."

"Yeah, those years I put in the Air Force Reserve finally paid off."

O'Brien set his beer bottle on the coffee table. "Okay, Hank. Let's talk business."

Wilson was lounging in the room's only chair, his feet up on the edge of the bed. His forehead creased. "Business?"

"You still want me, don't you?"

"You mean—?"

"I'm yours. I talked it over with Peg, and it's okay with her."

Wilson leaped from his chair, and grabbed O'Brien in a bear hug. "Fantastic, Matt! I've been waiting to hear this." He suddenly pushed himself away. "Hey, what's it gonna cost us?"

"How bad do you want me?"

Wilson shrugged. "Look, pal. It was up to me you could ask for the moon and I'd throw in the stars. But I've got a board full of bean counters looking down my pants."

"For starters, my salary—."

"Hold it, Matt. Give us a figure and I'm sure we can work something out." He grinned. "I haven't forgotten you'll be double-dipping."

O'Brien knew Wilson's company would take his senate pension into consideration in cutting a deal. "My salary won't be a problem for your people. But there are a couple of issues we've got to negotiate."

"Okay, let's hear 'em."

"First, I don't start working with Multi-Sensor until after my mission here had been completed."

"That's a given, Matt."

"Second, Multi-Sensor supplies the equipment and your services without charge, for up to one year.

"Third, the company holds in escrow an additional $500,000 to be used to help defray labor costs for grave diggers and forensic pathologists."

Wilson threw his arms in the air. "Five-hundred thousand?

"O'Brien nodded. "As in half a million."

"Jesus, Matt. You're talking about a million-dollar package."

"You've got the math right."

Wilson gazed at the ceiling and tapped on his knee. "When I said we'd give you the moon and the stars, I was using a figure of speech. I didn't expect you to take it *literally*."

O'Brien had decided he was going to hold firm. "Those are my terms, Hank." He grinned. "After all, some kid fresh out of high school gets a two-million dollar signing bonus for throwing a baseball around—and might not even make the team."

Wilson smiled and shook his head. "You're a tough nut, Matt." He reached for the phone. "Let me run it by the guys with the keys to the vault."

CHAPTER 14

"Gentlemen, I may have found a solution to our problems. With your permission, I'd like to introduce someone…" O'Brien did not wait for their approval, but beckoned to Hank Wilson who stood waiting at the doorway of the conference room.

"Mr. Wilson is an executive of Multi-Sensor Technology. He is in Bosnia-Herzegovina at the request of the government, to locate buried mines. It turns out that the same equipment used to find hidden anti-personnel mines can be easily modified to locate gravesites." He turned to Wilson. "Hank why don't you explain, in lay terms, how this is done."

The other members of the committee sat in silence around the conference table while Wilson described how the unmanned hovercraft and its sensors could detect gravesites even long after corpses had been buried.

When he had finished, Van der Velde said, "Thank you for a fascinating presentation. I'm sure all of us would be pleased to have you apply your techniques here. One thing concerns me, and I'm sure we all have the same question. What are the costs involved and who is going to pay them?"

Wilson said, "I've anticipated your question. I contacted my company. Were pleased to report that we will fund the project—call it our humanitarian contribution."

O'Brien suppressed a grin at Wilson's display of altruism. It had taken Wilson half a dozen phone calls to Multi-Sensor before they had grudgingly accepted O'Brien's terms. The haggling, O'Brien knew, was for show. Multi-Sensor Technology's accountants would write the whole thing off, saving a bundle in taxes. And there was no way to put a dollar value on the publicity the company would get.

After Wilson had finished detailing the contribution, Ahmed clasped his hands together. "I'm overwhelmed, sir."

Even Jasajovic sat mouth agape for several seconds, then bowed slightly and murmured, "Thank you."

*   *   *

"I can't very well go back on my word after they agreed to my terms, Peg. It's just another two weeks, and then I'll be home forever."

"Two weeks? Last time what was it, a few days? Next time a few months?"

"I just wanted to be sure you understand—."

"Oh, I understand all right. I've been understanding for the past twenty years."

He was pressing her to the limit. "You'll get no disagreement from me on that. I couldn't ask for a more understanding, devoted—"

"Spare me the Blarney, O'Brien." A deep sigh. Then, "Well, wear a red carnation in your buttonhole when you step off the plane, so the girls and I will recognize you."

He laughed. "You'll recognize me. I'll be the guy who grabs and hugs you. And tell Lesley that I haven't forgotten about the horse show. I'll be there if I have to fly the plane myself."

*   *   *

O'Brien, standing at the edge of the field, watched Zee stride from a pit where one group of gravediggers was shoveling, to another. O'Brien had counted six teams of men digging in the large field. They were at Omarska where Zee and his father had been taken in 1991. At the periphery of the field were relics of buildings that had once housed prisoners. Three teams had unearthed corpses covered by tattered clothing. Lying alongside the pit from which they had been exhumed they looked like piles of rags.

His face drawn with anxiety, Zee would peer down at a body, frequently brushing with his hand, dirt from its partly decayed face, then turn to inspect another.

Suddenly, he fell to his knees alongside one of the bodies. O'Brien saw him frantically brushing clotted dirt from the corpse's face. His father?

His pulse racing, O'Brien hurried to Zee's side. He gazed down into the remnants of a bearded face. More than half of the tissue was gone, exposing underlying bone. Even with a handkerchief pressed to his nose, O'Brien found the odor unbearable, yet Zee didn't seem to notice and continued to wipe away the dirt. A wave of nausea engulfed O'Brien, but he clenched his teeth, swallowed and willed himself not to vomit. He gripped Zee's shoulder. "Is it him? Your father?"

Zee sat back on his haunches staring at the corpse's face. For a few moments he sat silent, his eyes closed. Finally, he shook his head slowly. "His brother. My uncle."

O'Brien helped him to his feet, and with his arm around Zee's shoulders they trudged to the car they had rented.

For ten minutes Zee stood leaning against the car, gazing into the sky. Occasionally, he swiped at his eyes with his sleeve. O'Brien stood a few paces away, not wanting to interrupt, not sure whether Zee's grief was caused by the realization that his uncle was dead, or disappointment at not finding his father's body. Probably, he concluded, some of both.

He reflected that his own father would be 76, if he were alive. A hard-drinking, free-swinging bricklayer, Pat O'Brien had risen through the ranks to head the state branch of his union. Matt credited his father for his inheritance of his political genes, as well as his willingness to use his fists if need be. He'd always suspected that his father was more puffed with pride when Matt had come home with a fat lip and bloody nose after brawling with a couple of bigger kids who were tormenting Mark and Luke, his younger brothers, than he was when he was elected to the senate. Pat O'Brien had died four years ago sitting at a bargaining table, fighting for his union to the bitter end—literally.

Zee had started walking back toward the gravesites. While O'Brien waited, he searched for another half-hour before coming back to the car with his head bowed.

Quietly, he said, "We can go now." He touched O'Brien's arm. "Thank you."

*   *   *

A week later, O'Brien was butt-sore from the bouncing he'd been taking in pickups traversing potholed back roads.

For two hours today he watched a technician whose jeans were dirt-caked push an apparatus that looked like a cross between an old-fashioned lawn mower and a metal detector, over a field. In the distance were the buildings that could have been remnants of barns, which in fact they were. Except it had been years since these barns held hay or cattle. More recently they had held humans. Captives. Records of this detention camp, designated in official documents of the International Red Cross as G39, could not be located by any of the former Yugoslavian governments.

Earlier in the week, airborne ground-penetrating sensors had returned subsurface reflections from four distinct sites in the field, indicating the presence of objects whose densities differed from those of the surrounding strata. Infrared scanners which detected minute temperature changes in the same sites, confirmed these findings.

Suspecting that the temperature changes resulted from decomposition of underlying bodies, field technicians from the Sarajevo office of a geological exploration company with headquarters in Florida were now probing the sites.

The technician, a young redheaded Bosnian named Milan stopped and, wiping perspiration off his forehead walked over to O'Brien.

"Tough work," O'Brien said.

"Da." He smiled. "Yes. I forget you don't speak our language."

O'Brien reached into a portable ice chest he'd carried from the pickup, took out two bottles of cola, uncapped them and handed one to the technician. "I've seen these magnetometers before, but none quite like this one. What do you call it?"

"Pay-Pay."

"Huh?"

Milan laughed. "You not engineer. Yes?" He pronounced it "enya-neer." He pointed his chin at the machine. "This is proton procession magnetometer."

"I saw you filling it with a liquid. Smelled like petrol."

"Kerosene. Has many hydrogen atoms. You know hydrogen?" He mimed pouring liquid from a pitcher. A demonstration for the simple-minded.

O'Brien nodded. He'd heard about hydrogen.

"Inside machine is coil with small battery. Hydrogen protons turn." He made rapid circles with his finger.

"Spin?"

"Exactly, spin."

"Then it measures the difference in magnetic field from that of the ground under your machine?"

Milan smiled at him appreciatively. "Exactly. If something buried, spin is faster." He tilted the bottle into his mouth and chugged down the cola, wiped his mouth with the back of his hand and handed the bottle back. "Good. Now I go back to work."

Five minutes later, he called to O'Brien from an area of the field he was surveying. Pointing to a dial mounted on the long handle, he said, "See?"

A needle wavered in the red zone. Milan called to his superior, a lanky Texan in his late thirties named Tim Lawton. A field technician, he had been sent to Bosnia by Global Surveys, the company that serviced the equipment. Lawton, seated in his green van, looked up from the clipboard on which he was writing, strolled over and inspected the dial. He nodded, went back to the van and returned with a handful of wooden stakes.

Milan slowly scanned the ground with the magnetometer, and read off the dial. Lawton explained, "What we've got here is a section of ground where the electromagnetic conductivity is different from that of the surrounding earth."

Lawton marked the section, a rough rectangle about eight by twelve feet, with stakes.

O'Brien said, "Graves?"

"We'll soon know."

High tech appeared to have supplanted Zee's "stink test."

Lawton put two fingers to his lips and whistled to three grizzled, bearded men in loose clothing and wool caps who squatted alongside the van. Slightly apart from the men stood two Bosnian women, dressed in their traditional black dresses and black head shawls. They all trooped over, the men carrying shovels.

Milan said, "They are from village not far from here. During trouble in 1992, JNA soldiers came."

"Yugoslavian National Army?"

"Yes. Burned up many houses. Took away all men."

He went on to explain that the men had been imprisoned in the G39 detention camp. These three were among the few who had eventually been released and returned to what remained of the village. The women were relatives of men who were never seen again.

Milan spoke to them, pointing to the staked area, and the men began digging. Twenty minutes later, one of the diggers shouted. O'Brien, peering into the hole, now about two feet deep, spied in the depths a black object. Milan handed the digger a large whiskbroom with which he brushed dirt from the object. Gradually a human head covered by black hair came into view. Some of the skin over the forehead and nose was rotted away, exposing bone.

O'Brien caught a whiff of fetid odor, felt the ground under his feet tilt, his knees buckled and he grabbed Milan's shoulder.

Faintly, he heard someone say, "Put head down." Felt a hand pushing his neck down.

He took a deep breath, but when he lifted his head, the world began to spin and colored balls danced in his vision. Slowly, his dizziness abated. He found himself sitting on the ground, Lawton's grinning face peering down at him. "You okay now?"

He nodded.

"Don't feel too bad. Happened to me too, first time. Used to it now."

Damn it. He was going to have to get used to it, too. It wasn't as though he hadn't seen dead or maimed bodies before. Lord knows, in Vietnam he'd watched as men he knew had their body parts splattered over the countryside. Was it because he was more concerned with getting them, or what was left of them, the hell out of there? In those days, he didn't have the luxury of getting sick.

By the time O'Brien arose unsteadily to his feet, the diggers had unearthed the fully clothed body. They gently placed it on a canvas litter and lifted it out of the grave.

A wail suddenly broke the silence. One of the women stared down at the corpse, her hands to her cheeks. Milan put his arms around her shoulders and spoke to her softly while she rocked back and forth, keening. He walked her back to the van and helped her into one of the back seats, then returned to the gravesite.

O'Brien said, "A relative?"

"Husband."

The diggers had now exposed the boot of a second corpse. O'Brien watched, but with a handkerchief over his nose to filter out the odor. He said, "Doesn't the smell bother them?"

Lawton shook his head. "They're too engrossed in what they're doing."

By the time approaching dusk forced them to stop working, the exhumed bodies of three other men lay covered by canvas tarps alongside the shallow pit. The women recognized all as former fellow-villagers. Except for the first body retrieved, their wait until their own relative would be discovered was not over.

Over the next three days, O'Brien visited four places identified by aerial survey as possible gravesites. One turned out to be a false reading. The other three were mass graves containing three to 12 bodies.

As Zee had predicted, relatives of missing persons willingly worked alongside forensic pathologists and their technicians. They sifted through the dank soil searching for a fragment of clothing, a distinctive button or belt buckle, anything that might allow them to relieve their uncertainty about the fate of a loved one.

*   *   *

Dr. Hazel Werner, the forensic pathologist on the staff of the U.N., extended the steel tape measure over a bone that lay on the table in front of her. "Left femur, 42.5 centimeters."

O'Brien watched a white-coated forensic pathology technician write the figures down on a clipboard,

They were in a large room that occupied the entirety of a cement-block building in Sarajevo, and served as a makeshift morgue. Bones of assorted sizes and shapes lay on most of the half dozen tables in the room.

Dr. Werner said, "This one is female." She glanced up at O'Brien. "You were at the gravesite, no?"

O'Brien nodded. "That was the biggest one yet. They counted at least twelve bodies—or I should say skeletons. How are you going to make identification from the little that's left of these people?"

"Well, in most cases we've got enough tissue for DNA analysis. We can even use hair, you know. The root cells. We match the DNA of the corpses with that of the relatives."

O'Brien had seen in the center of a village near the gravesite from which a dozen bodies had been exhumed, a parked house trailer outfitted as a lab. Fifty or more black-clad women in single file had slowly shuffled up the ramp leading to the trailer's only door. There was no conversation between the women. On each creased face was a tight-lipped anxious expression. Some dabbed at their eyes with handkerchiefs. A few sobbed silently. The women were the sisters and mothers of missing men. They were waiting to have their blood drawn for DNA analysis.

"I had the impression from the lecture you gave that DNA analysis was quite time-consuming," said O'Brien.

Werner laughed. "That was a somewhat abridged version. I saw a lot of drooping eyelids in the audience. No, we use a method called polymerase chain reaction. PCR is an inexpensive and rapid way to produce many copies of DNA molecules. So, even if we have only a very small amount of DNA to work with we can produce samples than are adequate for our tests."

O'Brien glanced at his watch. "Well, I've got to go back to the hotel. I still have packing to do."

"I will see you this evening at our farewell dinner, I'm sure."

"Certainly, I'll be there. I don't leave for two days. In fact, tomorrow I'm accompanying Hank Wilson to the mountains near the Bosnian-Serbian border. I wanted to get in another survey before I take off for home."

Werner smiled. "I admire your dedication. Van der Velde has told me how much the committee appreciates all you've done."

O'Brien murmured his thanks. The six weeks he'd spent here had been a rewarding experience for him, but he was ready to turn over to others the work that remained. *More* than ready. He had never been away from Peg this long. The fact-finding trips he'd taken without her had lasted no longer than a couple of weeks. She'd always accompanied him on the campaign trail. And he'd needed her. Politics was a contact sport with no holds barred. Without her at his side to rein in his temper, war hero or not, he doubted he would have been elected to *any* office, let alone two terms to the House of Representatives and two terms senator. Now the tone of her voice was sharper than he could ever recall. With each phone conversation he could feel the chasm between them growing wider. Peg resented her role as single parent—particularly now that he no longer could justify his absence as being due to his responsibility to his constituency. Sure, he'd been given a humanitarian mission. But it was one she thought he should have refused. He'd already forfeited his pledge to take Brooke on a tour of college campuses. Peg had taken over and now Brooke had narrowed her choices to two. She wasn't interested in seeing more. He was left with guilt that clutched at his throat. But no more. He'd make it up to Brooke somehow. And to Peg. The one thing he was *not* going to miss was Lesley's horse show.

*   *   *

Led by Van der Velde, the committee members raised their glasses in a toast to O'Brien. "You, sir, have helped us immeasurably to accomplish what we have unsuccessfully been attempting for two years.

"Let me summarize: Fifteen gravesites identified, most containing several bodies. Forty-seven bodies exhumed.

"Although the committee is now officially disbanded, thanks to your efforts in organizing the search and arranging for financial help, the work you started will go on. We are much closer to our goal than we were a few short weeks ago when we came together."

O'Brien was touched by the tribute, but determined to keep it light. "You are too generous," he responded. "This is not the one-man show you make it sound like. I don't believe I've ever worked with a more dedicated and unselfish group of people. My only regret is that you can't vote in my state."

*   *   *

Wilson drove the pickup to the entrance of O'Brien's hotel. They had just returned from a mountainous area 40 kilometers southeast of Sarajevo where they conducted an aerial survey hunting additional gravesites. After dropping O'Brien off, Wilson would take the raw data they had collected and stored on his computer disk back to his garage/lab for processing. "Well, Matt, this time tomorrow you'll be hugging your wife and daughters. I envy you."

O'Brien grabbed Wilson's hand. "Hank, I can't begin to thank you—."

Wilson cut him off with a wave. "Let's not get weepy, old buddy. Have a safe trip. I'll be seeing you back at the office in a few months."

O'Brien got out, waved a farewell and went up to finish packing. The job of locating bodies was far from finished, but the International Red Cross would supervise the operation he had organized, and now it was time to put his personal life in order. At eight this evening, he'd be at the airport boarding the Vice-President's plane, Air Force Two.

He snapped closed the catch on his valise when the phone rang. Wilson's excited voice came over the line. "Hey, Matt. Glad I caught you. Thought you'd want to hear this before you left. I've just gone over the data we pulled today and came up with the screwiest thing I've ever seen."

O'Brien glanced at his watch. Six o'clock. The car that would drive him to the airport would be along shortly. "Screwy?"

"There's a signal—. Well, I can't really describe it, but it's huge. Much larger than anything we've seen. Listen, you remember where my lab is? You know, the garage? Where I keep my pickup?"

"Yeah. But, Hank, I'm being picked up in an hour."

"Okay. This place is on the way to the airport. You've got to stop off, even for just fifteen minutes. This is something you've got to see."

"Can't you tell me what it is?"

"I'm not sure. But I'll explain when I see you. You *will* stop, won't you?"

"Okay. I'll have Zee pick me up as soon as I can reach him."

Wilson gave him the address and directions.

*   *   *

O'Brien recognized the windowless gray cement-block building. "This shouldn't take long," he told Zee when he had parked. "How much time do I have?"

"I can get you to the airport in 30 minutes."

He would be the only passenger on the plane, and undoubtedly had some latitude. But the pilot did have to file a flight plan and follow airport departure procedures. That gave him just under half an hour to see what Wilson had discovered.

The garage door was up. Approaching the entry, he could see inside the large room. It was unlit. The pickup was gone.

CHAPTER 15

"Hank!" O'Brien shouted from the doorway. His voice echoed in the cavernous empty space. No response. His pulse raced. He cautiously crept into the garage. On a side wall he found a light switch and flicked it on. The worktable lay on its side. Tools strewn on the cement floor. He scanned the room. Hank Wilson gone. For the moment, he felt relief. At least Wilson was not lying somewhere on the floor in a pool of blood, or worse, dead.

*   *   *

O'Brien paced in front of Wilson's garage. For the sixth time in the past minute he checked his watch. Shit. What in hell took the goddam police so long to get here? The bastards who did this had torn the phone out of the garage, and the area was too remote to find another. It'd been half an hour since Zee had gone to get the police. He tried to recall how long ago it was that he'd had the phone conversation with Hank. If the police sent out an alarm, maybe they could pick up Hank's truck before whoever had grabbed it got too far away. And if Hank wasn't in it, at least they'd nab the person driving it. Tear out his fingernails until he told them where they'd taken Hank. But first they had to get here. He scanned the street. Still no sign of them. Or of Zee. Shit.

The thought struck him suddenly. *The computerized data.* What Hank had called him about. What he had come here to see. He dashed back into the garage. On the desk where the computer had been, there was only the imprint of its rubber feet in the dust. The whole damn thing including the monitor was gone. He searched around the floor and all the cabinets looking for backup floppies or tapes. Nothing.

He went back outside and gazed up and down the street. No police yet. What could be taking them so fucking long? He didn't know what he was going to do about his plane ride home. He'd stall them as long as he could. At least it wasn't a scheduled airline. There was little question this business would not be resolved before his scheduled departure time. He'd have someone at the consulate call the Vice-President for permission to postpone—. Great! There they were. Finally. A blue and white car pulling up. Behind them, Zee drove the Yugo he'd rented. Zee bounded out of his car, but the two cops remained seated in theirs. O'Brien ran up to the police car. He leaned into the window. "Are you gonna sit there the whole night?"

The policemen stared at him, but made no move toward getting out.

Zee leaned into the window of the police car and shouted something at them. Slowly, they opened the doors on either side and lumbered out. One cop was tall and skinny, the other tall and fat. O'Brien felt his fists clenching until his nails dug into his palms. He wanted to shove sticks of dynamite up their asses. The cops stood gazing at the garage building until Zee, speaking rapidly, pointed to the inside.

The two policemen walked slowly toward the garage entrance, each had his hand on the grip of his holstered revolver.

O'Brien pushed them aside and hurried into the garage. He turned and faced them, his arms outstretched. "Look, you idiots. There's no one in here." They looked at each other and shrugged. He turned to Zee. "Tell these stupid bastards to radio an alarm to pick up Wilson's truck. You remember the make and color?"

Zee nodded, then talking rapidly accompanied by vigorous hand gesturing, he conveyed O'Brien's message. The tall cop went back to the police car, picked the handset from the dashboard and spoke into it. The fat one wandered into the garage and inspected the overturned workbench and the tools scattered about the floor.

O'Brien could see that there was nothing to be gained by his staying around here. He'd just eat a hole in his gut watching these two bumble around. By now Hank, his truck and his abductors were long gone. If the police managed to locate them, it would be a miracle. He had to make a few phone calls. "Zee," he called. "Would you take me back to the hotel?"

*   *   *

Peg's voice shouted into his ear. "Darling! Where are you calling from? Andrews? Did your plane get in early? I wasn't expecting you until this evening."

Sweet Jesus. This was going to be even harder than he expected. He spoke quietly. "Peg. I'm still in Sarajevo."

He thought she might have hung up. There was no sound from her end during the time it took him to relate what had happened. When he finished, he waited for some response. There was none. Finally, he said, "Are you there?"

Her hoarse voice hissed into his earpiece. "Yes. I heard." Pause. "I'm sorry about Hank."

Until he could see some effort being made to find Hank, or, God forbid, his body, he had to stay in Sarajevo. Not only was the guy like a brother to him, but there was little question that he was abducted because of the job Hank was doing for *him*. No, there was no way he could just walk out on him now. But he wanted desperately to have Peg's approval. "What do you think I should do?"

"I don't give a damn *what* you do."

"Please, Peg. I'm as disappointed as you are. All I want to do is make sure they start an investigation." It would be senseless to try to estimate how long it would take. And he already had emptied his bag of excuses.

"Fine. You do that. Call me when you get back in the States—if you think of it." Bang. The sound of the hang-up stung his ear.

He stood for a moment with his head bowed, the phone in his hand, then tried to call her back. She didn't answer. He knew she wouldn't, but he had to try.

*   *   *

Howard Shaw, the attaché from the U.S. Consular office in Sarajevo was in his mid-thirties, slim, blond and soft-spoken. He stood alongside O'Brien and Zee outside the garage entrance the police had blocked off with yellow tape last night. Other than isolating the crime scene, the local police had made no progress in the investigation of Wilson's disappearance along with his truck and equipment. Now two Sarajevo police officers stood at the garage entrance talking, joking with each other.

"Senator, we're as concerned as you are," said Shaw. "This is a very sensitive matter. We can't just take it out of the hands of the local police. They have assured us that their investigation is proceeding as rapidly as possible."

The local police knew shit about investigating. Zee had gone back to the crime scene last night, and reported to O'Brien that he had watched while a detective had fumbled around in the garage, finally coming up with the astounding deduction that there had been a struggle and Wilson apparently had been abducted. O'Brien tried, without success, not to let his boiling temper show. "Damn it, Shaw, there's *got* to be a more efficient investigative unit here—like our FBI. These clowns obviously can't handle it."

Shaw looked around nervously. He seemed worried that someone might overhear. "Sir, with all due respect, you've got to realize this is a country with limited resources. They're doing the best they can with what they've got."

Resources? Bosnia might not have many, but the U.S. certainly did. And O'Brien's view from the senate floor had shown him that his country could piss away resources on investigations a lot less important than this. "Well, what they've got is obviously not good enough. Before they blow any leads how about calling in some private investigators?"

Shaw shook his head. "We have protocol for cases where an American citizen is kidnapped in a foreign country and we're following that line." He glanced at his watch. "Now, I have to get back to my office. We'll be on top of things, I assure you. I'll inform you if there is a development."

Bullshit. O'Brien watched him get into his car and drive off. Instead of standing here in Sarajevo on a cool, cloudy day with his thumb figuratively up his ass, he should be in the living room of his home in Georgetown. He'd cancelled his return, of course, and sent the plane back.

The Vice-President wasn't much help either. He said they'd have to turn the matter over to State. Let them handle it through the consulate's office here. All that brought him was Shaw, for all the good that seemed to do.

Zee said, "Would you like me to take you back to hotel?"

"Let me have another look around the garage."

He ducked under the tape, but immediately was stopped by one of the policemen who guarded the scene. Although he argued, the policeman just kept shaking his head until Zee threw up his hands. "He has orders not to let anyone in."

At the hotel, O'Brien tried to decide how to proceed. He was back in the same room he'd been in before he'd checked out. Although his anxiety about Wilson's safety was uppermost in his mind, he could not curb his curiosity about Wilson's cryptic statement on the phone: *This is something you've got to see.* The guy had always been cautious in his evaluations. Whatever he'd found in the data they'd collected this time had gotten him excited.

Something else tugged at his thoughts: how did anyone know that Wilson had found something of importance? Since that experience when the three men had confronted them after discovering the first gravesite, they'd taken extra precautions to be sure they weren't followed. In fact, Wilson, observing him constantly checking the road behind them, had chided him on his paranoia.

The phone. *Wilson's phone call.*

He knew nothing about bugs, but he would bet the consulate people did.

From a phone in the lobby, he called Shaw. "I think my phone is bugged. Would you send someone over to check?"

*   *   *

O'Brien answered the soft knock at his door. A young man carrying a briefcase stood in the doorway his finger on his lips. He held out a slip of paper on which was written: "U.S. Consulate. Communications Technology. Don't speak."

The technician walked directly to the phone, set his briefcase on the floor and unscrewed the cover from the mouthpiece. After examining the inside, he shook his head and replaced the cover.

O'Brien opened his mouth to ask whether he'd found anything, but the tech held up a finger for silence and shook his head.

From the briefcase he removed a small black box with wires attached and carried it slowly around the room, watching the instrument. O'Brien could see on its dial face a small panel with a needle. The tech stopped in the center of the room, gazed up at the smoke detector fixed to the ceiling, then moved a chair under it. Standing on the chair, he carefully removed the cover from the smoke detector and shone the beam from a penlight around its base. He smiled, nodded and after replacing the cover climbed down from the chair, beckoned O'Brien to follow him outside the door.

"Yeah. You guessed right."

"Any way of finding out who did it?"

"Simplest way is to give them a message—something only someone who's listening would know."

O'Brien thought for a moment. Maybe he'd already done that. He recalled that morning in his room, right after Zee had told him he thought he recognized Bodanovic to be a former prison guard, the guy took "sick" and was replaced. He wondered too if they'd overheard his conversations with Wilson discussing where they were going on the test run that ended up with their arrest, as well as the time Wilson's dive-bombing camcopter saved them from being captured. Bastards. He probably should have been more careful. But in his own defense, how was he to know that any of the conversations that took place in this room were of a sensitive nature? In fact, he *still* didn't know what was said that would warrant the raid on Wilson. Nor was he sure if the Serbian government was responsible, or if was a faction outside the official organization. And what could he do about it anyway? Accuse them? They'd laugh him off. No, now that he knew he had no privacy in his room, he'd have to act accordingly.

CHAPTER 16

Sam Powell, Multi-Sensor Technology's technician, wiped his hands on a rag. After Wilson's disappearance he'd returned from the USAF Base in Aviano, Italy, and arranged for the company to ship replacement for the stolen equipment. "I think we're ready to go for it."

O'Brien climbed into the passenger's seat of the pickup he'd rented. Although he saw no results from the police investigation in the five days since Wilson's abduction, he had no choice but to leave it in their hands. The State Department's Bureau of Diplomatic Security had distributed fliers offering a "substantial" reward for verifiable information on Wilson's whereabouts and condition. They did not stipulate the amount of the reward, in accordance with policy, but in any case, there had been no takers as yet.

The surveillance gear was now loaded in the bed of the pickup. He and Powell were headed for the mountains where Wilson had collected the data that appeared to have led to his abduction. If Wilson and his abductors had considered it so important, O'Brien was determined to resurrect the data in the hope that they might produce clues leading to his rescue. He refused to concede that Hank was dead.

In order to be sure they were not followed, on the way out of Sarajevo they took a circuitous route, making several false turns, then returning to the main road. They had driven about two hours when they came to a dirt lane leading into the woods. "This is the road we took," said O'Brien. Powell steered the truck down the lane for about five miles until they came to a clearing. Ahead about 500 yards were the skeletonized remains of several buildings that, on his previous trip here, Zee had identified as a former prison camp. "Here's where we park," said O'Brien.

He helped unload the small helicopter, watched Powell attach the sensor pack and send the craft aloft. He described for Powell, as well he could recall, the flight path on which Wilson had sent the plane and watched as the hovercraft disappeared around the side of the mountain. On the display screen of the control console, he could see wiggly lines appear as data were collected by the plane and sent back to them on the ground. "Mean anything?"

Powell shook his head. "Can't tell until we process the raw data back at the lab."

"Wish I'd known more about what Hank was seeing. Maybe…"

Powell grinned. "I'll try to explain, but unless you have some background in this technology, it can be confusing."

"Okay. Give me the 101 version."

"Well, what we've done is send a variety of sensor signals into the ground through several antennas, IR lenses, acoustic couplers all mounted on the helicopter. Then we collect the return signals from buried objects to a receiving antenna also on the helicopter. We got it set up to filter out a lot of the crap—pardon me—clutter that's in the soil and rocks and stuff. The data collected we store on a computer disk.

"Back at the lab, we run software that reconstructs the raw data into images that are recognizable."

"That sounds simple enough."

"Maybe I've oversimplified it. There's really more to it. For instance—"

"Hold it. You told me all I need to know."

Powell was gazing at the sky. "Holy shit!"

O'Brien looked up. White puffs dotted the sky. Anti-aircraft fire. The helicopter had not returned from its last pass around a mountain. They waited ten minutes but it hadn't reappeared. Meanwhile the AA fire had abated.

Powell said, "That little chopper should be back by now. I think some sons of bitches shot it down."

O'Brien considered the options: wait a while longer, drive in the direction the helicopter had gone, turn tail and get the hell out of there. "Think you can make something out of the data you've got?"

Powell shrugged. "Won't know till we see what it is."

As much as he hated to abandon the project, O'Brien realized that without means of protecting themselves, the danger was too great. If it had been he alone, he might have investigated the source of the gunfire, but he would not put Powell's life in jeopardy. "Okay. Let's split."

*   *   *

Back in his hotel room, O'Brien, for the third time that day, called his home. The previous two times, either Peg was out or wasn't picking up. In the five days since Wilson's disappearance, although he'd phoned half a dozen times, he'd managed to reach her only once. On that occasion, the conversation was entirely one-sided—his side. He started to tell her how the investigation was going, but she'd cut him off saying, "Look, I'm busy." Then hung up.

He'd spent each night tossing in bed, debating whether it was worth what this might be costing him to stick around here in what appeared to be a fruitless search. Nothing, absolutely nothing, was worth losing Peg. Only one other time in their 20 years of marriage had he been this seriously worried that he might. They'd only been married two years when he'd gone off to Caracas, against her wishes. His law firm had asked him to check out the patent of a South American client. Peg was eight months pregnant with Brooke, went into premature labor and drove herself to the hospital. He showed up when Brooke was two days old. How could he have done it, he asked himself over and over? Had he forgotten so soon the weight that had been lifted when Peg came to him with the news that she was pregnant? Lying in the hospital bed with the infant at her breast, tears streaming down her face, she'd told him that she'd stay with him because it was a better option than going through life with a fatherless child. Fatherless child. Childless father. He almost told Peg then, the secret he'd buried in his memory. Instead, he'd told her he couldn't imagine going through the rest of his life without her, and meant it. But Adventure and Challenge were a pair of jealous mistresses. He was able to resist them—most of the time. Now, almost 18 years later, he was going through the same anguish. In the darkness of each night he would decide to chuck it, let the consulate and Sarajevo police handle the investigation. He'd grab the next plane out. Yes. But by morning he'd resolve to give it just one more day.

He was about to hang up when a small voice said, "Hello."

"Lesley! It's Daddy. How are you, sweetheart?"

"Oh Daddy." He heard her sob. "Daddy, where *are* you?"

His throat tightened and he couldn't speak for a few seconds. How do you tell an 11-year-old angel that you're a couple of thousand miles away, too busy solving the problems of the world to see her and her pony perform in the most important event in her young life? "I'm—.

"Les, remember Uncle Hank?"

"Uh-huh." Her sob turned to a giggle. "*He's* funny."

"Well, he's here, but someone kidnapped him."

"Gross!"

"I'm trying to find where they've taken him."

"Wow!"

He paused. "I'm so sorry I missed the horse show. How'd you do?"

Lesley's voice bubbled with pride. "I got a second in the jumps."

"Wonderful! I'm so proud of you. Look, sweetie, I'll only be here a few more days, then we'll all be together again. Let me speak to Mom."

"She's not here."

"Brooke there?"

"She's still at school." A pause. "Daddy, Mom cries a lot. She tries to hide it, but…"

"I know. She's disappointed that I haven't come home yet. But I have to try to find Uncle Hank."

"Can't you call the police and tell them?"

"I have, and they're trying too."

"I miss you Daddy. Please come home soon."

"I will, honey. Real soon.

"I love you Daddy."

He choked on his response.

CHAPTER 17

"Barton here."

Finally. O'Brien had been on hold, listening to 15 minutes of silence, waiting for the U.N. guy to pick up. Now he knew what his senate aides had to go through when he would mindlessly tell them to get someone on the phone for him.

"Mr. Barton, you may have heard about our surveillance hovercraft being shot…"

"Just one moment. Who *is* this?"

Shit. Did he have to go through that lengthy explanation again? "This is Matt O'Brien. I'm the U.S. representative on the Missing Persons Committee. Our surveillance plane was shot down outside Sarajevo."

"Oh, yes. I know who you are now. You want us to investigate the area where the plane was lost?" Clipped accent. Not British. He couldn't be sure of the nationality.

He felt the heat rising in his neck, in his face. It was all he could do to keep from screaming into the phone. "Not 'lost,' Mr. Barton. *Shot down*. And I'm certain whoever *shot it down*," Let the son of a bitch chew on that thought for a moment, "—is also responsible for the kidnapping of Henry Wilson, the radar engineer who was here to locate land mines."

"Yes, I'm familiar with that incident. Of course, that's not a U.N. concern. Your consulate will be handling it."

"Look, anti-aircraft fire shot that UAV down. It is my understanding that it's the U.N.'s job to control hostile activity here. Shooting down a plane is hostile activity. Kidnapping is hostile activity. All I'm asking is that you send a team into the area where the plane was shot down. Investigate. Maybe find a clue that will lead us to Mr. Wilson."

He heard an exasperated sigh at the other end. "Mr. O'Brien, we are well aware of our mission here. And as for sending a team in, our Weapons Control people are quite busy at the moment. You may have heard of Iraq. I'm afraid your request will have to wait its turn."

*   *   *

"You don't really expect us to call for a retaliatory air strike because of an attack on a model plane, do you?" The U.S. Air Force colonel to whom O'Brien was speaking on the phone sounded indignant. From a telephone in the hotel lobby, he had called the base at Aviano, hoping to get some help in locating the source of the anti-aircraft fire. No doubt whoever was responsible for the attack on the helicopter was connected to Wilson's disappearance.

"Colonel, we're talking about rescuing a kidnapped American citizen. And this isn't a model plane. It's an unmanned airborne platform for surveillance…" Why was he wasting his time spelling it all out to this idiot? "Now listen carefully. This is Senator O'Brien. I'd like to talk to your superior." Maybe word hadn't reached Italy that he'd been voted out of office.

"General Anderson is not available. Leave your number and I'll see if he'll get back to you."

O'Brien slammed down the phone. He was getting no help. The consular official, too, had said he could do nothing. The area in which the helicopter had disappeared yesterday was a designated "no-fly zone."

Meaning that the Dayton peace accord, in order to protect Bosnians in the area from air attacks, had ruled that all aircraft must keep clear of the zone.

To add to his annoyance, he had to use a lobby phone. Even though he had changed his hotel room because of the bug, using the pretext that the old room was too drafty, he was wary of trusting the phone in his new room. He doubted that the hotel management was responsible for planting the bug, but it would be easy for someone to gain access to his room and hide an electronic listening device.

A bellman approached him as he stood near the phone contemplating his next move. "Someone is waiting for you at the door."

That would be Sam Powell. The radar tech was picking him up to take him to the hideaway Powell was using as a computer workstation. He was anxious to see what had turned up in the data they had collected before they lost contact with the helicopter Although the garage was no longer in police quarantine, he did not feel it was secure, and had commissioned Powell to find another place.

*   *   *

"What we have here is a large void space in this mountain very close to the border between Bosnia and Serbia." Powell was pointing to a computerized reconstruction on the screen. Shades of reds and greens produced an abstract effect, reminding O'Brien of a Jackson Pollock "drip" painting. The colors, Powell explained, represented different amplitudes of the radar reflections that had been relayed to the ground control unit by the sensors on the helicopter before its signal was lost.

"This must have been what Hank saw when he called me. What do you think it is?"

"Could be a cavern."

"Large cave?"

"Possibly."

"Would that be unusual? After all, aren't caverns present in mountains?"

Powell shrugged, pointed to the map that lay open on the workbench. "There are other mountains in this scan. None of them show the same hole." He drummed his fingers on the table, gazed at the ceiling. "There's another thing. If I didn't know this was in a remote location, I'd think it was fairly densely populated."

O'Brien felt the skin on his neck prickle. He didn't know Powell well enough to judge his competence, but Wilson had a lot of respect for his ability. "What makes you say that?"

Powell hit some keys on the computer. Another color photo appeared on the screen. "This a Spaceborne Synthetic Aperture Radar image of the area. We assign colors to different radar frequencies and polarizations. For example, the green is L-band that's transmitted horizontally—"

"Hold it, Sam. You're talking to a radar illiterate. How does this differ from the last picture you showed me?"

"Sorry. The screen I showed you first was a reconstruction from the data sent back by our own craft. The image you're looking at now was picked up from one of the orbiting satellites. We license the software from the government to access it. We're looking at a 20-kilometer swath in this mountainous area. It should be all vegetation, right?" He pointed to a small orange-red splotch surrounded by numerous shades of green. "This is something I'd expect to see if there was a village here. Now let me show you something else." He typed several keys. The image was overlaid by an aerial photograph map. "This is a detailed satellite-generated photo of the area. No villages. No towns. Not even farmhouses."

"How recently was that made?"

Powell grinned. "Yesterday."

O'Brien chewed on the information he'd gotten. There was no question in his mind now about what needed to be done. It was clear that whatever authority existed here showed no interest in following up on the loss of their UAV. And except for the offer of a reward, Wilson's disappearance had provoked only stifled yawns. That left the one person who *did* care.

This was going to take some planning.

☠ CHAPTER 18

O'Brien was driving the rented Yugo, Zee was seated alongside him. Three days had gone by since the surveillance craft had been lost, presumably shot down. Three days during which O'Brien had been busy making preparations.

Zee said, "I would like to go with you."

"Not a chance, Zee. I appreciate all you've done, but the only reason I've let you in on my plan, is in case anything goes wrong, I want someone to know what I'm doing."

Zee pointed to the corner they were approaching. "This is where my friend is picking me up."

O'Brien pulled to the curb and braked. "Remember, 72 hours." Three days should be all the time he needed. He had written an explanatory note Zee was to give Shaw at the U.S. Consulate if he hadn't returned by then. What the consulate could do, he hadn't a clue. But at least they could notify Peg.

Peg. He was strangling on his guilt. His long absence was bad enough, and now he was going on this insane mission that could leave her a widow with two daughters. But, damn it, this was war—of a sort. He was once again a front-line soldier as he had been 30 years ago when he signed up in the Marines. He'd finished a year of law school, saw the war heating up and, rather than be drafted, decided to choose his branch of service. In Vietnam at least he knew who the enemy was. Here he had no idea who he was up against. He also was well aware that he was captivated by the prospect of a thrilling and dangerous adventure.

Zee reached down to the floor of the car and brought up a small, paper-wrapped package. He handed it to O'Brien.

"What's this?"

"What you asked me to get."

O'Brien felt through the wrapping. A gun. "Thanks. Where did you get it?"

Zee smiled, shrugged and shook his head.

O'Brien decided not to press him. "Beretta?"

"Nine-millimeter. Semi-automatic. Also a spare clip."

O'Brien didn't know under what circumstance he might need it, but having it gave him a sense of security.

Zee opened the car door to get out, turned and extended his hand. "Be careful, my friend."

*   *   *

Powell was waiting at the corner where they'd arranged to meet. He got into the passenger's side and directed O'Brien to his workstation on the outskirts of Sarajevo.

Powell said, "I've got the equipment ready for you. The only thing I don't have is the gun."

"That's okay. Zee got one for me."

O'Brien was wearing camouflage green and khaki fatigues, an outfit he'd picked up in a Sarajevo army-surplus store. Over it he had his ski jacket. Fur-lined gloves would keep his hands from freezing if it turned cold. In his pocket he had a wool ski mask. On his feet were parachuter's fatigue boots. He was ready for anything he could think of.

Inside the building, Powell took from a closet a khaki backpack. "I'll show you all the gear that's in here and make sure you know how to use it."

He began to remove the contents of the backpack. O'Brien noticed the USAF stenciling on several of the items. "How'd you get all this stuff?"

"Well, you know I'm a technical radar consultant for the Air Force Base at Aviano. They ferry me back and forth in their planes, and I get the same survival equipment they give their flying personnel." He grinned. "In case I'm shot down."

Most of the objects required no explanation: Swiss Army knife, compass, penlight, small field glasses, matches, spare wool socks, AA batteries, six sealed plastic packs of water, iodine water-purification tablets. Powell held up a rectangular black plastic case about four by three inches. "This is your GPS, global positioning system. Runs on two AA batteries. There are a couple of spares in case it goes dead. GPS can tell you where you are in the world to within ten yards of your position."

"How?"

"Lines up to three satellites and triangulates. Takes about five minutes to make its calculations and reads out in latitude and longitude to three decimal places."

"That's great. But what do I do with the information?"

Powell took out a small two-way radio. "This is already set to Guard, a search and rescue channel. All you have to do is press this button on the side and call for help. When a search plane answers, tell him your position. They'll send a chopper to pick you up."

O'Brien shook his head and smiled. "I just say, 'Bring around my car, James.'"

"'Mayday!' might be more in order. Remember, the radio works by line of sight. So, if you're behind a hill or mountain, your signal might not be heard. Ever read *Return With Honor*?"

"No."

"Great book. Story of Captain Scott O'Grady. One of the F-16 fighter pilots from our base at Aviano—1995, before I got there. He was patrolling for NATO when a Serb SA-6 missile shot him down over Bosnia. Tells about his survival and rescue."

"Oh, I know who you mean. I was still in the senate when he came back to Washington. President gave him a citation."

"That's the guy. You ought to get the book. Reads like a manual for survival technique—only more suspenseful."

O'Brien glanced at his watch. "Unless I can read it in twenty minutes, it'll have to wait until I get back." *If* I get back, he could have added. And he knew a bit about survival technique. He wondered how much it would have changed in the 30 years since he'd survived his capture.

Powell removed from the backpack a large folded piece of heavy paper. Unfolded, it was a topographic map of Bosnia, measuring perhaps five by three feet.

O'Brien shook his head. "That's too damned big and heavy. Forget it. I've got a small road map."

"Mr. O'Brien, this may be one of the most important items in this pack." Powell pointed to the margin of the map. "Here are some first-aid hints, and these pictures are plants that are edible. Take it. The whole chart is made of a waterproof plastic material. You can even spread it out and lie on it or use it as a shelter."

"Feels like roofing paper."

"Actually that's one of its uses. A heavier version, of course. Called Tyvek. Really, I think you should take it."

"Okay. But if it weighs me down I may deep-six it."

Powell repacked the knapsack and handed it to O'Brien. "You're not planning to take out that anti-aircraft battery with this gear, are you?"

O'Brien laughed. "Hell no, Sam. I'm an *old* dog, not a *hot* dog. This is just a look-see trip. If I see something worthwhile, I'll come running back for help."

"I sure hope you know what your doing."

O'Brien slapped him on the shoulder. "So do I."

CHAPTER 19

At dusk, around 6:30, O'Brien left the outskirts of Sarajevo. He had driven in a haphazard route after leaving Powell, checking in his rearview mirror for anyone who might be following. Now there was only a farm truck behind him. Half a mile farther, it turned off to a dirt lane and the road behind was clear.

O'Brien was thankful that in the three days since he'd been here last, the weather had turned warmer. The snow had mostly melted, present only in patches. Even though the sun had now set, he found the ski jacket too warm, and while he was in the car he took it off.

He had carefully studied the road map before starting, and although the road was unlit, by checking his odometer he knew his location. Three times, he turned onto side roads and parked with headlights off for five to ten minutes just to be sure he wasn't tailed. On one of the times he was parked, a car sped by on the main road from Sarajevo, but other than that no other cars were headed in the direction he was going.

Shortly before midnight, he reached the side road he had taken with Wilson and later with Powell. He turned on to the road and parked in pitch-black darkness. He'd brought along a ham and cheese sandwich, and ate it washing it down with a can of Pepsi. This meal might have to last him a few days, although he could fall back on granola bars he'd stuffed in the pockets of his jacket.

He got out of the car and taped dimmers over the headlights. He'd fashioned them out of a pair of black wool caps he'd bought that afternoon in Sarajevo. He had cut slits in the caps which left barely enough light to see the edge of the road, but he didn't want to chance the full beam of his headlights. Back in the car, he drove slowly along the dirt lane bordered on both sides by forest, checking the odometer as went. When he had gone five miles he stopped, turned off his headlights, sat in the car until his eyes had accommodated to the darkness, then got out to check his position. Ahead was the clearing where they'd parked both times to send the helicopters aloft. A short distance beyond that, he could see the ruins of the deserted prison camp Zee had pointed out the first time he'd been here.

Although the weather was almost balmy, a shiver went through him from anticipation of—he wouldn't attempt a guess.

He drove the small car off the lane into the pine forest, skirting around and between trees until he could go no farther. Where there had been snow on the ground before, it was muddy and he prayed the tires would not get mired down in muck. He was now about 30 yards off the road. If he went in much farther, he might not be able to get out. It took him eight minutes to maneuver the car around so, if he needed to, he could drive out in a hurry. He smiled to himself. Ever the optimist, he was assuming he'd be back this way again.

Okay, O'Brien, end of the line. Here's where the fun starts.

☠ CHAPTER 20

The dirt lane on which he started hiking ended just beyond the remains of the deserted prison camp. Using the large topographical map, he calculated that the mountain toward which he was heading was 18 miles to the southwest. He followed a narrow footpath in the woods, frequently flicking on his penlight to keep on the path. Rustling he heard in the underbrush on either side, he assumed were small animals—at least he hoped they were small. Although he'd kept in shape working out once or twice a week in the senate gym, the walk tonight carrying a pack was fatiguing. After an hour he stopped.

Seated on a boulder munching half of a granola bar, he began to wonder what in hell he was doing here. Instead, he should be sitting in an easy chair at home, listening to Peg and the girls chat on about how they'd spent the day. Now that he had time to reflect, he realized that his decision to start on this venture—this walk in the woods—was impulsive. And foolish. He'd been frustrated with the way the investigation of Hank's disappearance was being handled. He slapped the boulder on which he was seated. *Get up and turn back, O'Brien. Now.* He'd catch the first plane he could get, and try to patch together what had come unglued between himself and Peg. And yet. And yet. If there was the slightest possibility that finding the source of the anti-aircraft fire that had shot down the helicopter would lead him to Hank, shouldn't he take that chance? He gazed down at the rucksack. All that preparation. Was it to go to waste? Christ, he felt like a lawyer arguing both sides of a case. What finally decided him was the fact that he'd already come more than halfway. He stood up, shouldered the rucksack and headed in the direction from which the helicopter had disappeared.

When the path veered off due east, he left it and walked through the woods, sticking to his plan of heading southeast. Good chance to use the global-positioning system. He switched it on and waited, checking its LED screen periodically. Five minutes later, the instrument had received signals from three satellites and computed a latitude and longitude reading.

Hooray for technology. The thing really worked.

He copied down the GPS reading. If he ever wanted to come back to where he had left the path, he could plot the coordinates on that big map.

Now that he was off the path, in the darkness he ran into low bushes and stepped into shallow holes. The thought of stepping on a land mine made a knife stab at his chest. He fought to drive the thought from his mind. Mines were used to protect populated areas. *Why would anyone mine a dense wood? Of course not.*

Every five minutes he stopped to listen. Heard only the rustling of branches from the gentle breeze. He sniffed at the air. Pine. Change the scenery to tropical, the weather to humid, the underfoot to swampy, and he was back 30 years and a few thousand miles from here, on a night patrol. Then as now, his senses were alert to something, anything that had as its goal his destruction. One difference: Here he was alone. No one to account for but himself. Back then, as a 25-year-old second lieutenant, he'd had the responsibility of seeing that his 41-man rifle platoon came back in one piece. Even after all these years he was still filled with remorse when he recalled the times they didn't. There was Anderson, of course, who'd lost his leg to the mine. And then the time he'd been captured. If there was any solace to that incident, it was that he was the only one the VC had grabbed. He had pushed far back in his mind the unspeakable torture he'd been through. Even now, light-years later, he refused to let it surface for fear it would cause the hand-wringing despair it did at the time.

Now, he was suddenly out of the woods and stumbling into a mud-filled ditch. He picked himself up, wiped mud off his gloves and jacket, and found that he was on a narrow, dirt lane bordered on either side by trees. It consisted of parallel ruts made by the wheels of a car or small truck. Because of the overhanging tree branches, the lane probably would not be visible from the air. *Maybe that was the idea.*

The wheel tracks appeared to originate from the general direction as the main road from Sarajevo and headed southeast. Would this have been the route taken by the truck someone had heisted from Hank? The thought gave him reassurance that the decision he'd made to keep going was the right one.

He decided to follow the tire tracks and see where they led.

To offset the possibility that the trail might be under surveillance, he walked parallel to it rather than on it. Anyone these days could have night-vision field glasses. He wished he did.

Another hour and the backpack felt as though it were weighted with rocks. *Time to get some rest.* On a small plot of level ground a short distance from the lane, he found a bed of pine needles where he could curl up.

Powell had been right about the large map. Unfolding it, he found that although it was somewhat stiff, he could wrap it completely around himself. It kept the damp earth from penetrating through his clothing. In addition, the padded ski jacket and wool ski mask were more than enough to keep him warm, and the rucksack functioned as a pillow.

*   *   *

A rhythmic tapping awakened him. Startled and disoriented, he opened his eyes puzzled to find himself lying on the ground, his arms pinned to his sides. It took a moment to realize where he was. The tapping was rain dripping from the tree under which he lay, onto his Tyvek blanket. Daylight. He struggled to free his arm and read his watch. Six-ten. He pushed up the ski mask and listened, heard only dripping. A faint odor of smoke alerted him. A light drizzle made the air misty. Through the trees he could see perhaps 20 yards in any direction. He licked rainwater off his lips, put out his tongue to catch drops, wet his mouth. Although he still had several packets of water in his bag, this would help conserve his supply.

O'Brien crawled out of his wrappings, stretched to work out the kinks, drew in a deep breath. Again he smelled smoke. *Where there was smoke, there were people.* Time to move on.

He folded up his makeshift shelter and stowed it in his backpack. He carefully examined the ground on which he'd made his bed, making sure there were no signs of his presence. Thirty years ago he hadn't been so careful, and the trail of garbage he'd left while on patrol in Vietnam had led the bad guys to his bivouac. Four of them jumped him. The others in his platoon had escaped, radioed for help and were picked up by rescue choppers. To this day, he could feel the prodding of the gun barrels in his back as he was shoved with his hands and ankles rope-bound, past villagers gaping from their hootches. On the village outskirts, they kicked him into a pit and covered the top with bamboo. For two days, his captors toyed with him, shooting down into his prison, as though he were a rat in a barrel. Lucky for him, they'd missed. For the first few hours, he was afraid he would die. A few hours later, he was *sure* he would die, and was no longer afraid. It was when they dragged him out of the pit for questioning that he prayed for death. He found it painful, even now, to recall the sickening torture they'd put him through. At the end he could only scream his name and serial number to all their questions. The VC gave up on him only after he'd lost consciousness. They'd let their intelligence people work on him at the main prison for captured Americans—the one the prisoners had nicknamed the Hanoi Hilton. Before they got around to transferring him, one of the villagers reached a Marine patrol unit and told them, in exchange for the standard monetary reward, where they could find an American prisoner. Two days later the CH-45 came for him. The pilot and a Marine charged out of the chopper, guns blazing like Rambo. The Army captain who was in charge of the unit remained in the helicopter. Spotting a group of VC soldiers running up as reinforcements, he got on his walkie-talkie and yelled to the rescuers, ordering them to abort and get the hell back. The pilot ignored the warning, pulled O'Brien out of the pit, and with the Marine, dragged him back to the chopper. He remembered the vow he'd made to himself lying on the deck of that rescue helicopter. He'd been given a second chance at living. A rebirth. He'd use whatever power he had to see that anyone in the same straits he'd been in, would somehow get the same chance. It was the reason he accepted this Bosnia assignment. It was the reason he couldn't give up on Hank Wilson.

Two weeks after O'Brien's rescue, that pilot, on another mission, went down with his plane in flames. Every May 30th since, O'Brien had placed a wreath on his grave in Arlington.

This time he would leave no trail of breadcrumbs. He swept pine needles over the ground where he had lain.

He was still trying to detect the source of the smoke when he heard the labored sound of a car or truck motor.

When the sound had faded, he walked back to the lane. Fresh, deep tread marks scarred its muddy surface. The drizzle had abated, and although the air was still misty, now in daylight he could look around and get his bearings.

There it was. Rising out of the haze about two miles ahead: a small mountain. Covered in pine, the mountain looked no different from others in this part of the country. What could be so important about this one? A cavern? Certainly other mountains contained caverns. Yet Wilson was abducted, his data stolen and the camcopter was shot down when Powell sent it back up to reconstruct the stolen data. *This mountain, he was sure, was linked with Wilson's disappearance.* With his gut tingling, he headed for it.

He had been trudging under the heavy backpack for about 30 minutes when he heard the faint sound of a motor coming from the direction in which he was walking. He quickly withdrew into the forest. He peeked around the side of a tree as a large khaki-colored truck with a canvas cover came into view, bumping along the trail. A troop carrier? Supply truck? As it drew abreast of where he stood, he heard it brake. The truck stopped.

CHAPTER 21

O'Brien's heart thumped so loud he was sure it could be heard out on the trail. Had he been spotted? Voices speaking a foreign language. Slapping. He could imagine feet hitting the ground as someone— maybe more than one—jumped down from the truck. He tried to remain still, but his knees begin to tremble, so he slowly moved his hand down to steady them. He pressed his eyelids together, not daring to look around the edge of the tree. The voices suddenly stopped. Were they coming after him? Then, what sounded like water hosing the ground. He almost laughed aloud. *They'd stopped for someone to take a piss by the side of the trail.*

A moment later he again heard voices; someone laughed. Then creaking, someone getting back into the truck. The motor revved, and he heard it start to rumble out. He peeked from behind the tree, but could see only the flapping tarp on the back of the truck.

Was this was the same vehicle he'd heard earlier, returning from the mountain? Have to be more careful now. There was traffic on this lane.

An hour later he reached a clearing, an open field covered by waist-high weeds in a valley that stretched in front of him perhaps a quarter of a mile to the base of the mountain. The truck tracks continued on through the field in the direction of the mountain, but he could walk no farther in the daylight without exposing himself.

At the edge of the forest he lay prone scanning the pine-covered mountain through field glasses. He searched for sign of habitation, for smoke. Nothing. The truck tracks disappeared into the forest on the other side of the clearing. He couldn't see whether it wound around the mountain. To follow the truck tracks he'd have to cross the clearing, but not until dark.

He withdrew into the trees, ate two granola bars and drank a packet of water. Seated on the waterproof map and with his back padded by his ski jacket, he leaned back against the trunk of a tree. If he were home now, he and Peg could be going out to dinner. In his mind's eye he saw her, seated in front of the boudoir mirror to finish putting on her makeup. He'd watched her do this a thousand times before: apply her lipstick, then press her lips together to distribute the coloring. Fluff her hair. Turn her head this way, then that. Her movements were a series of pictures he carried in his head.

The sound of voices drifted into his ears and he was instantly alert. He remained motionless, his pulse hammering in his ears. The sound grew louder; they were coming toward him. Now he heard the cracking of twigs. His hand crept to his Beretta. Wait. By the time he got it out, they would already have reached his position. If they had rifles, he'd be outmatched. Going for his gun would create enough noise and movement to take away surprise. Okay, forget the gun, hope they'd pass him by. In his camouflage fatigues, he must blend into the scenery. Should have used camouflage paint on his face, but that was one thing he hadn't brought. He lowered his face, burrowing it as best he could into his chest. Then he noticed his backpack on the ground. Shit! *It must stand out like a beacon*, but nothing he could do anything about that now. He slid his glance to the direction of the voices. Two men. Peaked khaki caps. Rifles. Hunters? More likely soldiers. One smoking a cigarette. If they kept walking in a straight line they would pass behind him, behind the tree that was his backrest. If they spotted him, he was caught. He'd have no chance to put up a defense.

Intent on their conversation, they shuffled through the pine needles, passing less than ten feet from him.

When the men were well by him, he sucked in a deep breath and stole a glance at their backs. They wore holstered sidearms. Definitely not hunters. Peripheral security patrol? If so, their vigilance sure as hell wasn't high. For a fleeting moment he considered following them at a safe distance. But what was safe? Any rapid moves he made could create noise. If they turned and looked back while he was flitting from tree to tree, or turned around and *came* back, he was dead. No, his best bet was to stay put, then follow the trail as soon as it became dark, another hour or so.

Now that the danger of his being discovered was no longer an immediate concern, he realized that he had neglected to prepare a cover. Nothing he could think of sounded plausible. Just don't get caught.

Six-thirty. Daylight was fading rapidly. Time to start across the clearing, toward the mountain. For the next quarter mile he would be exposed, protected only by darkness. He tried, without success, to drive from his thoughts the possible dangers: spotters, sensoring devices in the trail, mines. Take the chance and go on, or turn back now? He reminded himself that it could lead him to Wilson. Yes. Hank would do it for him. Taking a deep breath, he crept out of the woods in a crouch.

CHAPTER 22

For the next half hour he kept low, slinking across the quarter mile of open field, his stomach knotting, until he reached the forest at the base of the mountain.

Now the trail became steeper. He sat on the ground to rest, and felt pounding transmitted through his body. *Come on, O'Brien. It's the drumming of your own pulse.* To prove it, he touched a finger to the artery at his wrist. His pulse was racing. But the pounding he sensed was half that rate, sure as hell not coming from him. But where? He placed his hand on the ground next to where he was seated and felt a rhythmic beat. It had to be transmitted through the ground. Reminded him of something. A pump motor? Generator, that's what it was. Transmitting its vibration, but from where? He'd have to wait until daylight to see where the machinery was located. Well, at least he could be sure of one thing: he'd come to the right place.

Giving himself a ten-minute rest, he got up and followed the tire impressions winding up the side of the mountain. The higher he went, the less dense were the trees and the more exposed he was becoming. Rapid movements would be more noticeable, so he walked in slow motion, stopping frequently to listen. He also kept feeling the ground for the generator pulsations. They'd neither lost nor gained intensity.

The pulsations *had* to be coming from inside the mountain. From the cavern Powell had shown him on the computer screen.

He checked his watch. Two-fifteen. One day of his three-day allotment had passed. He wondered if Peg might be trying to reach him. Although she hadn't returned his phone messages, her irascibility usually had its limits. In fact, he was counting on it to get himself back in her favor again. But, after not hearing from him for a couple of days, she might worry enough to call *him*. And become panicky if she couldn't reach him. He could picture her phoning the consulate's office in Sarajevo demanding they locate him. Hell, Shaw couldn't give her any information. Zee and Powell were the only ones who knew where he was—and he had sworn them to secrecy. All he could hope for was that she was still pissed enough to let him hang in the breeze. Because if she knew what he was doing at this moment, she'd be racing off to a divorce lawyer's office.

What he *was* trying to do was find out what happened to Wilson. Although he might be geographically closer, the specific answers were not yet in sight. He was betting that a truck or some vehicle would come this way. They'd have to follow the trail; there was no other way to go. Better conserve his strength by waiting and watching.

He needed a place where he'd be concealed. Trouble was, the pine forest here on the upslope of the mountain was less dense than the one on the other side of the valley in lower ground. He needed a bush, but here there was no undergrowth, at least none he could see in the dark. Suddenly he stepped into a hole, dropping to his knees onto a bed of pine needles. He felt around him and found he'd stumbled into a depression about ten yards to the right of the truck trail. Perfect. Now he could lie flat in the depression and see over the edge, his own little foxhole.

Lying on the ground, he could feel the pulsations through his heavy jacket. He was confident the truck, when it returned, if it returned, would lead him to the source.

A low rumble. He had been dozing when he heard it. Then the sound of a truck motor. Field glasses pressed to his eyes, he peered through the blackness waiting for the lights to appear. There was no way they could navigate the narrow trail without headlights. The motor sound grew louder. Still no lights.

Wait. The sound was coming from the other direction.

He'd been looking *down* the trail—the way he'd come up. He swung around. There they were. Double slits of light. Dimmed headlights. The distance, maybe the length of a football field, 100, 150 yards.

Suddenly the lights were gone. The motor sound muffled, fainter. He waited for lights to reappear. One minute. Two. No lights. The sound of the truck motor was gone.

He climbed out of his hole. Somewhere off to his right was the way into the mountain.

The backpack and all it held was too bulky to wear sneaking around. He stripped it off. The sack would stay here in the depression, but a few items small enough to fit in his jacket pockets, he'd carry with him. The Beretta was holstered and strapped near his left armpit. He felt around in the sack until he found the second clip of bullets and the Swiss Army knife. These he shoved into his pocket. If he ever needed the pack again, he wondered how he'd find it. Looking for landmarks in the dark was a waste of time.

The GPS. Powell said it could tell him his position within ten yards.

He retrieved it from the backpack turned it on, waited until he had a fix on his position, and after committing the figures to memory, jotted them down in his notebook. He jammed the GPS into his jacket pocket. Even without the map, knowing the coordinates might help.

Placing the backpack in the ground depression, he kicked pine needles over it and stuck a branch in the ground near it as a marker.

Three-thirty. About two hours until dawn. He felt his pulse speeding as he started following the truck tire impressions toward where he had seen the headlights.

Bent in a crouch, he crept along the trail. Every muscle in his body was tight as a wound rubber band. He counted his paces. At one hundred, he stopped, looked around, listened, sniffed the air. Nothing. He moved on. Fifty paces. Nothing. Fifty more. *Where had that goddam truck gone?* Using his shielded penlight, he saw the tire impressions. Maybe he hadn't gone far enough. He walked another 50 paces.

It couldn't have been beyond here that the truck lights disappeared from view.

What had he missed?

He followed the tire marks for 20 yards when, suddenly they turned in toward the upslope of the mountain, perpendicular to the trail. Another ten yards, they vanished. Gazing upward, he saw a solid rock face, bare of trees rising toward the summit of the mountain. *Unless that truck could climb at a 90-degree angle on the face of that rock, it had disappeared into the mountain through an opening in the rock.* He crossed over to the rock and ran his fingers over the rough irregular surface. There had to be a seam, but where? He shone the beam of his penlight on the rock, moved to the right then left, but there was no break in the continuity. Where the tread marks ran into the base of the rock, he bent and felt for a space between the ground and the rock face, but the rock continued below the ground surface. Frustrated, he slapped at the rock, and the sound that returned was low-pitched, hollow, not what he expected from a solid rock. He moved to his right while tapping the rock with the back end of his penlight, like hunting for a stud behind a wall. The hollow sound persisted for about five feet, then changed. He'd hit solid rock. At the interface, he examined the rock surface with the beam of his penlight. No change in color. No break or crack. Dammit, there *had* to be a seam. He rested his palm on the rock face—*and felt his hand slowly rise. The rock face was moving upward carrying with it his hand.* He leapt back, yanking his hand away, his pulse roaring in his ears. Was it something he'd done? Had he caused the rock to move? At that moment the ground beneath his feet shook. A rumbling sound, coming from behind the rock.

Earthquake?

He backed away, staring at the rock while a ten-foot wide section continued to slowly move upward. A long, narrow slit of light appeared at the base of the rock, and gradually expanded. The section of rock face was sliding up like a garage door opening leaving a hole large enough for the body of a truck.

CHAPTER 23

O'Brien's feet were rooted to the ground, his heart hammering in his chest. A rhythmic beating came from the depths of the hole. Beyond the opening, a dim light shone, but he could make out nothing inside the cavern. The sound of voices stirred him to movement. *Get out of sight.* In back of him and to either side were trees. Their trunks were too narrow to hide his body, but he had no choice. He ducked behind the nearest tree, hoping that the darkness was his friend.

His curiosity forced him to peek from behind the tree. A pair of slitted headlights appeared at the mouth of the cavern. A truck slowly climbed up from the depths of the hole on what seemed to be a ramp that led down. When the truck reached ground level, it moved out of the cavern and turned to the right on the trail, opposite to the direction from which he had come.

That's the way to Serbia.

The truck stopped momentarily. An arm extended from a window of the cab, pointed an object at the opening and, as the portal gradually slid down, the truck moved down the trail.

O'Brien watched the opening in the hillside slowly close. He was ten yards away. Still time to dash across the trail and duck under the slowly closing portal. He began to spring forward. Felt his feet glued to the ground. A sign flashed in his brain. Ten-foot high letters that read: Okay, you get in. Then What. Go it alone? Insane.

He remained behind the tree for another minute, watching as the portal lowered until there was no longer light visible under it. Once again a solid rock wall. If he hadn't seen it open, he would have no clue as to its existence. An amazing piece of camouflage.

For another two minutes he waited behind the tree to see if anyone appeared. Finally, the sound of the truck motor faded out of hearing, and the woods were once again quiet. He returned to the depression, retrieved his pack and, staying well back in the trees, lay prone so he could watch with his field glasses where the mountainside opening had appeared.

He remained in his foxhole, his eyes trained on the opening. Four a.m. Five-thirty. Nothing. Several times he dozed off, but with the approach of dawn, his vigilance increased.

Vigilance. He'd learned the hard way. At Officer's Training School in Quantico he'd been warned how quickly combat troops can become complacent. For the first few weeks after they'd landed at Da Nang, he'd jump when a twig cracked underfoot. But soon, he was no better than the grunts on their second or third tour. Their feeling of immortality was contagious: Something bad might happen to the guy next to you, but not to you. Until something *did.* Lying in that mud-filled pit after he'd been captured, hearing the ping of bullets ricocheting off the pebbles near his head, he had plenty of time to remember the warning: keep your guard up. He'd carried it with him for 30 years.

He was now into the last of the three days he'd allowed himself to carry out this mission. He'd have to head back or Zee would alert a rescue party. And that would mean notifying Peg. He was determined that was not going to happen. He wouldn't put her through what his mother had suffered when they told her that he was missing. Poor Mom. At least she'd never have to go through any more suffering. The cancer had taken care of that.

At 8:15 he heard the approach of a vehicle, and three minutes later a truck appeared in the east. Brown canvas tarp arched over the back, like a troop carrier. How many trucks were in that cavern? Or was there only one going back and forth? From his hidden position, he watched as it went by. Two men, a driver and passenger. From what he could see of their upper bodies through the truck window, both wore military jackets and peaked caps. If anyone was in the back, he was unable to tell. A mud-caked license plate hung from the chassis, too obscured to see numbers. He thought it looked like the license plates he'd seen on vehicles in Sarajevo, but without numbers there was no way to check its registry. When the truck approached, the hidden portal slid up. Probably responding to a remote control. He trained his lens on the inside of the cavern, but could not make out details in the dim light.

While the truck waited, a jeep appeared, carrying two men besides the driver, all in khaki uniform. The passengers held rifles pointing skyward.

The jeep stopped behind the truck, the two armed men got out, one heading up the trail away from him, the other down to where he lay. He nestled down in his lair, his heart pounding. All he could do was lie quietly and listen. Twigs crackling underfoot, motor sounds. The odor of gasoline. Voices. He fought the temptation to lift his head and see what was going on. He checked his watch. Ten minutes, 15. Finally, 18 minutes after the truck had come into sight, he heard the portal close, then silence. He cautiously raised his head and peered over the edge of the depression. The truck and jeep were gone. Although the soldiers were no longer in sight, he wasn't sure if they gone into the mountain or were still patrolling.

O'Brien lay in his shallow pit chewing on what he had seen. What the trucks had been carrying? Troops? Supplies? He was reminded of pictures he'd seen of paramilitary operations in the wilds of Wyoming and Montana. Conducted by groups calling themselves survivalists. Guys who were convinced factions in the government were plotting to make them powerless. Take away their guns. Repeal the Second Amendment.

Was that what he was witnessing here?

Except for stretching his legs every few minutes while he lay prone, he remained at his watching post all morning with as little movement as possible.

At noon, a plane flew overhead—too high for him to see it through the trees. He thought it might be one of the U.S. Air Force. planes from Aviano, attached to the U.N. and NATO forces. He had learned they patrolled the no-fly zone. He switched on his radio and heard chatter in English. But like most of the radio airplane conversation he'd heard in the past, the communication was unintelligible to him. It was the first English he'd heard in two days, and gave him a feeling of comfort knowing that somewhere up there he had friends.

Mid-afternoon the portal rumbled open and two rifle-carrying sol- diers strode out. One activated a remote control that brought the door down. They walked down the truck trail toward the field he had crossed yesterday. No doubt the early evening perimeter watch. Before they passed from his view, they stopped; one scanned in a circle with field glasses. O'Brien pushed his body into the ground and prayed. The sol- diers, apparently satisfied, moved down the hill out of his sight.

At dusk he decided to pack it in, and made his way down the mountain to the valley, stopping at the edge of the tree line. While he waited for darkness to set in before crossing the open field, he recapped what he'd seen: trucks—how many he couldn't be sure. A jeep—or were there more? One going east toward Serbia. Another, maybe the same one, coming from the same direction. There was a hole in the mountain large enough to accommodate trucks. Some kind of motor was continually running inside the cavern. Probably a generator powering the lights inside. Uniformed men patrolled the area. Soldiers? Which army? Anti-aircraft guns that had shot down Powell's camcopter were somewhere, possibly in the cavern. Whatever was going on in the cavern was secretive enough to warrant guards.

When darkness fell, he entered the field in a crouch. He had not seen the two soldiers who left the cavern hours before. They were no doubt long gone from this area. It took 20 minutes to traverse the quarter mile, but once on the other side, he ducked into the trees and breathed freely. He could now walk erect and under cover of the trees once again felt protected.

"*Halte.*" The shouted order seemed to come from his left and close enough so that he could hear raspy breathing.

Christ. The soldiers. He froze, then ducked and started running zigzag into the forest, stripping off the backpack and dropping it to the ground as he ran. A shot and a whoosh as a bullet passed over his head. His heart raced. "*Halte.*" Now from farther away. A bullet ricocheted from a tree whizzing past his ear. He reached for his weapon. No good. If he fired he'd be giving his position away. A bullet thudded into a tree trunk directly ahead. Close. The shooter must have night-vision goggles. He glanced back, saw muzzle fire at the same time as he heard the bullet strike the ground at his side. He was racing now, from tree to tree, but never in a straight line. He could barely make out the trees through the inky blackness, catching sight of them only when they were directly in his path. Low branches scraped his face and thicker ones slowed him, making him back off and duck underneath. He stopped for a moment, heard the cracking of twigs behind him. The guy had stopped shooting long enough to give chase. Good. His adrenaline rush would give him the advantage over someone running while carrying a rifle. The footfalls behind him grew closer. He made a 90-degree turn left, heard a grunt and felt the warmth of a body. He'd run into someone's chest. A pair of arms wrapped around him and a whiff of foul breath assaulted his nostrils.

CHAPTER 24

There had been two of them. The one he'd run into wasn't carrying a rifle, probably dropped it off to make himself more mobile. He now had O'Brien in a bear hug. Freeing a hand, O'Brien shoved it to the man's face, felt goggles and tore them off. He drove his knee into his captor's groin. Another grunt and the man released his hold, bent forward holding his stomach. O'Brien heard a crashing to his right; in the darkness could make out a rushing silhouetted figure, a rifle at hip level. The one he had groined was still bent forward at the waist. O'Brien grabbed his shoulders and swung the man in front of his own body, a shield. The soldier with the rifle couldn't shoot for fear of hitting his partner. He turned his gun around, grabbed it by the barrel, and swung it at O'Brien's head. O'Brien ducked, shoved the other soldier in its path. The gunstock thudded into the guy's head. He sank to the ground. O'Brien grabbed the rifle butt and twisted, wresting it out of the second soldier's grasp. Those twice-weekly sessions in the senate weight room were paying off. Now unarmed, the soldier backed away. O'Brien pointed the gun at his chest. Even in the dim light, O'Brien saw the face of a frightened teenager. "Over fifty, kid, but I still remember what they taught me. On your knees," he yelled.

The young soldier remained standing, raised his hands. Of course, the poor bastard doesn't understand. O'Brien fired over his head. *That* he understood. He dropped to his knees, covered his head with his arms. O'Brien circled around and prodded him in the small of his back with the barrel. "*Legen sie!*" Maybe he understood German.

For emphasis, he pushed the gun barrel into the guy's back until he lay face down. Pressing the gun barrel into his neck with one hand, O'Brien reached down with the other and felt for a sidearm. Finding none, he stripped the guy's goggles off and slipped them on himself. The world turned green, but now he could see more clearly. He spied the other pair of goggles on the ground and crunched them with the heel of his boot. For good measure, he reached down and flung them deep into the forest. *Try to find them.* The condition they were now in, they wouldn't do anyone much good.

Not wishing to push his luck, O'Brien slowly backed away. For all he knew, others were on patrol and might have been alerted by the gunfire. The soldier whom he'd disarmed raised his head and O'Brien fired a shot into the ground next to his shoulder. That got his attention; he promptly dug his face into the dirt . With his foot, O'Brien rolled the other man over, heard a moan. Satisfied the guy was in no shape to get up and give chase, he took off running.

The night-vision goggles made the going easy. He had a momentary pang of regret over leaving behind the backpack along with the radio, but he was not going back for it. Besides, he had no idea where to start looking.

After trotting for five minutes, O'Brien was winded. He stopped, sat on the ground, held his breath and listened for the sound of anyone following, but heard only the stillness of the forest.

He flicked on the GPS, and five minutes later had a fix on his position. Headed west, good. But south of where he wanted to be. Back on his feet, he took off in the general direction of his car.

After 15 minutes he found the heavy rifle an unnecessary burden. He wasn't going to shoot anyone, so he flung it into a bush.

The goggles, even though they narrowed his field of vision, helped him to walk much faster than he did on his outward trip. Checking his position by GPS every 15 minutes, he found the path that led to the deserted prison camp and when the skeletons of the buildings came into sight, he took a deep breath and mouthed a silent prayer.

His watch read 3:15 when he dragged himself to the car he had hidden. Weary as he was, he was anxious to get as far away as he could from the area. He drove back to the paved road, thinking how good a warm meal would taste about now. Still 40 miles to Sarajevo. But this wasn't the States where he'd find a fast-food joint open somewhere on the highway. Even in Sarajevo, everything would be shut up tight.

His eyes felt as though they were full of sand and he had trouble keeping his lids open. No good. He'd end up in a ditch or with the front end of the car hugging a tree. He turned off on the next dirt lane and drove a couple of hundred yards to a copse, where he parked, stretched out in the back seat and immediately felt as though he were floating on a cushion of air.

*   *   *

He opened his eyes and thought he was looking at the lining of a coffin until he realized he was in the car. His mouth felt like the inside of a sewer. The last time he could recall aching as much as he did now was in OTS at Quantico after a zillion-mile run with full backpack.

By noon he arrived at his hotel. While the tub was filling with hot water, he phoned Zee to assure him he was alive and reasonably well. He also checked in with Powell, thanked him for the equipment he'd given him and apologized for losing much of it.

"Oh, well," said Powell. "That's where your tax dollars go. What did you learn?"

O'Brien was about to tell him about the cavern, then remembering the bug in his last room, pulled up short. "Tell you all about it when I see you."

Peg hadn't called while he was gone. He wasn't sure whether that was good or bad. One thing he *was* sure of: he was still entrenched in her doghouse. Should he call her? It was still early morning back home. No point to disturbing her sleep. Besides, he needed time to decide what to say.

Should he end his search and start home?

That would mean leaving the fate of Hank Wilson in the hands of others.

What others?

The U.S. Consulate? They felt their duty ended when they offered a reward for information about his whereabouts.

Wilson's company? Multi-Sensor Technology might hire someone to trace him, but Sarajevo wasn't someplace you thumbed through the Yellow Pages for a list of private investigators. And sending someone over from the States would cost a bundle, if—a big if—they could get someone to take the job.

The Bosnian government? They had problems of their own, and finding Wilson wasn't one of them.

The Sarajevo police? Their attempts so far had been fruitless. There was nothing to indicate they'd be any more successful in the future.

He could think of no other choice but himself.

Then there was the matter of the mountain cavern and its secret contents. He couldn't erase from his thoughts the idea that there was a connection between Hank's disappearance and what was hidden inside that hole. He'd put his own ass on the line trying to find the answer. Was all that time and effort to go to waste? What was he to do with the information he had collected? The U.N. had already indicated they had no interest in sending a team of weapons inspectors. The U.S. Air Force wasn't about to call an air strike. As much as he'd like to find out for himself, he didn't think the Matt O'Brien Army had enough manpower to conduct an invasion.

Finally, there were Peg and the girls. He'd already been away much longer than he had intended. Didn't his family come before anything else? Before the fate of Hank Wilson? Before the secret of some remote mountain?

Yes.

He'd devoted more than half his life to fighting causes for others. In Vietnam, it was for a republic he knew nothing about before he went. In the law firm he'd joined, he argued for patents on behalf of clients whose inventions were mysteries to him. In congress, he fought for constituents of his district; people with diverse—and often opposing—interests. In the senate, he fought for the party line until some of his party's issues conflicted with his conscience. That was where he had drawn the line. And the rug was pulled from under him. Well, screw 'em all. The time had come to devoting himself to his family—while he still had one.

While he was calculating what the time would be in Washington, the phone rang.

Peg's voice. "Matt." Somber.

Oh, God. Something's happened. "Peg!"

"Lesley…riding…missed a jump, thrown…unconscious…Georgetown General."

He felt the blood leave his face. "Peg. Oh, Peg. Hang in there, honey. I'm on my way. Anything I can do from here before I leave?"

"No. Got to go. Got to get back to her."

His mind raced. He'd have Shaw arrange for him to be on the next flight out of here.

He punched in the consulate's number, and stood at the window gazing mindlessly at the mountains in the distance while he waited for them to answer. Little Lesley. He could still feel the warmth of her body through the swaddling blanket when he held her the first time in the hospital nursery. A weightless bundle.

A stabbing pain shot through the right side of his chest. He was suddenly unable to breathe. He heard the sound of tinkling bells. Or was it breaking glass? The room became filled with a sea of colored lights. They grew dim. Then dark.

CHAPTER 25

He was dimly aware of white-coated figures hovering over him. Of something hard covering his face. Of being bounced around. Of every bodily movement setting fire to the right side of his chest. Of being stuck with needles. He was living in a frame-by-frame movie.

He opened his eyes, found himself in the lower berth of a sleeper from Washington to Columbus. Or was it Columbus to Washington. Why did he take the train instead of the plane? When he got back he was going to introduce a bill to fix the damn roadbed. This train bounced around more than he could remember. The porter was seated next to his berth. O'Brien heard himself mumble, "Time to get up?"

The porter said—why was the porter in a white jacket? The porter said, "Stay. Not to get up."

Foreign porters? Have to get busy with civil rights issues. What happened to ERA? "Where are we?"

"Ambulance. For transfer."

"From where?"

"Hospital."

"Transfer?"

A nod.

"Transfer to where?"

Shrug.

"Hey. What are you sticking in my arm?"
"Quiet!"

*   *   *

He awoke in pitch-black darkness and stretched. The knife-like pain that cut through his chest took his breath away. He reached under the covers to rub the place that hurt, and felt something rough stuck to the skin of his chest. Tape. He tried to sit up, but the sharp pain in his chest forced him to remain down. Where was the goddam bedside clock? *Need to find a light switch.* No lamp? He cautiously reached out to the bedside table where he kept his watch. If he moved slowly, he could minimize the amount of pain. *What happened to the bedside stand? Hey, this isn't my hotel room.* Where in hell was he?

"Hello. Anybody." He heard his voice. Faint. A whisper. Tried to shout, but the pain in his chest prevented it.

Footsteps. Snap of a lock bolt. A dim light from the far end of the room, then an overhead light blinded him. A giant with a beard clopped up to where he lay. Wearing khaki fatigues, carrying a tray, on it a tin cup and a soup bowl.

"You sit. Eat now." Gruff voice. Some kind of accent.

"Where am I?"

"I leave food. Come for dish later." The bearded man placed the tray on a small wooden table in the center of the room and walked out, leaving the light on. The bolt snapped. It had happened so quickly, O'Brien's head was somewhere in the clouds. He thought of the things he should have asked: where he was, why, what day, what time.

He gazed around the room. About eight by ten. No window. A naked bulb, maybe 20 watts—if that—hung overhead. A fan, its electric cord dangling beneath it, mounted on the far wall. No pictures on the rough gray cinderblock walls, like an unfinished basement. No furniture except a Goodwill-reject wicker chair and the scarred wooden table on which the food tray had been placed.

He lay on a narrow canvas army cot. Only a thin wool blanket covered him. Cracked linoleum on the floor. In a corner was a pail. The toilet, he supposed.

He struggled up from the cot, holding his chest. Looking down, he found he had on a wrinkled white hospital gown. He played his fingers over his ribs. God, he'd lost weight. Feet were bare. On his face he felt a stubble that could be four, five days, maybe a week old. Had he lost that much time?

Suddenly he remembered standing in his hotel room, and being stabbed in the chest. No. Not stabbed. Shot? But how and by whom? The shot must have come through the window.

A light-blue plastic band encircled his wrist. Letters typed in a clear space read: "O'Brien, Mathew/Dr. Dancic." A hospital identification tag, but where was the name of the hospital? And who was Dr. Dancic?

Wait. *Lesley* was in a hospital, not him. Peg said Georgetown General. No, that was a dream.

He slapped his face. It stung. No dream. And Lesley was somewhere unconscious. *And he had to get to her. NOW.*

He shuffled to the door. Locked. He pounded at it. Again and again. Exhausted, he slipped to the floor.

He lay panting. Why didn't someone come?. He rose, dragged the chair to the table and sat. The tray held a tin cup of water and a metal bowl of clear soup. He was very thirsty. Had the water been doctored? He touched his tongue to it. Metallic. He drank a small mouthful. Waited a moment to see if he would drop dead, then drained the cup. He tipped the bowl and tasted the soup. Salty, maybe nourishing. He finished it.

He slowly paced the floor, but soon his legs felt wobbly, so he sat on the edge of the cot. Questions swirled around his brain, but thinking was too much of an effort. He'd lie down for a bit and close his eyes. Just for a mome—.

*   *   *

"Welcome, Mr. O'Brien."

He hadn't realized he'd been asleep, but the voice awakened him and he opened his eyes. He tried to focus on the blurred figure that stood next to his cot. Bald-headed man, stocky, dark business suit.

"I see you're getting stronger, no?"

Accent. O'Brien struggled with his memory. "We met before?"

Smile. Shrug.

O'Brien glanced at his wristlet. "Dr. Dancic?"

A coarse laugh from another part of the room. O'Brien slid his gaze toward the laugh. Tall man with a beard leaning on the closed door. Guy who'd brought him a tray of food. Yesterday? Last week? Month?

The bald one said, "Doctor who?"

Obviously not Dr. Dancic. "Where am I?"

Baldy smiled. "All in good time, Mr. O'Brien. But first I have some questions for you. Or would you rather wait a few days until you are stronger?" His English was heavily accented with Slavic inflections.

"What day *is* this? I'm not answering any questions until I know why I'm being kept here."

The man waved a dismissive hand. "It does not matter." He walked to the door, turned and said, "I will be back."

The bearded one followed behind him. The bolt clicked.

O'Brien stared at the closed door for a few moments. That was it? The bald guy hadn't pressed him for answers. Who the hell was he? Something about him looked familiar, although O'Brien was sure he hadn't seen him before.

First Wilson, and now him. They had both tried to find out what was going on inside the mountain.

He fought through pain to get out of bed and paced the small room. He felt like a caged animal. A declawed tiger. Of course, he would be missed. Peg would be trying to reach him. When she found she couldn't, she'd march into the goddam White House and demand action. Even though he was no longer on Uncle Sam's senate payroll, he had *some* influence. Wasn't he the President's emissary to Bosnia? They'd set up a search and rescue effort and he'd get out of this mess. Sure. And the rescue team would consist of the Easter Bunny and the Tooth Fairy and Santa…God damn it. With a fist he pounded the rough wall. Ouch! Cement blocks. The ceiling was the same.

A grate-covered vent, about a foot square, was high on the wall in one corner. He dragged the chair to it, but was unable to see inside the grate. Not even large enough to crawl through if he had some way to remove the grate, which he didn't.

The room air smelled stale and he looked for an electric outlet in which to plug the fan, but found none. If the fan were ever used, it probably was connected through an extension cord to a double socket at the ceiling light.

Once again he lay back on the bed, thinking. Rescue was almost out of the question. The only way he was going to get out of this prison would be to escape. *Think, O'Brien, think.*

Forcing himself to stay awake was difficult. In spite of the chest pain he suffered from movement, he paced his cell until his legs refused to support him. He tried to sleep, but he was so dry his tongue stuck to the roof of his mouth. Thirst occupied all his thoughts. He dragged the chair in front of the door, and sat waiting for the guard to return.

Finally, the bolt clicked. The bearded giant entered carrying a tray, and on it a tin cup of a liquid. He made a grab for it. The guard pulled back, the cup fell to the floor. O'Brien fell to his knees and tried to scoop up the water. The guard cursed in a language O'Brien didn't understand and kicked him away, his heavy boot hitting O'Brien's chest. He screamed in pain and watched in anguish as the guard splashed his dirty boots on the wet linoleum, like a child in a gutter after a rainstorm. When O'Brien started to crawl toward the water, the guard kicked him in the face.

Bastard. O'Brien made a grab for his leg.

The guard swung the empty tray, hitting him on the head. Momentarily dazed, O'Brien remained sprawled face down on the floor. He heard the door slam, the bolt click. He wanted to beat the floor, but didn't have the strength.

He mopped what little water remained on the floor with the bottom edge of his gown, wrung out the gown to catch the few drops of water in his mouth, then sucked dry the moisture that remained in the cloth.

The image of Lesley lying unconscious flashed in his mind. He *had* to get out of this prison. Either find a way of unlocking the door or overpowering the guard. Even uninjured and in his best condition, he had as much chance of overpowering that hulk, as he had of growing wings. But if he had a weapon…He scanned the room searching for something, anything. His eyes came to rest on the fan bolted high on the wall in a corner of the room. That useless fan. Maybe not so useless after all.

He dragged the beat-up wicker chair to the wall under the fan and cautiously stood on the seat, hoping it wouldn't give way. It sagged but held. The fan was standard: three metal blades under a heavy wire-mesh guard. He tugged at the fan, but bolted to the wall, the goddam thing wouldn't budge. Nor could he wrest off the guard that was secured to the back plate with four screws. Those he could deal with, but he needed something he could use for a screwdriver. Of course, they hadn't left him a knife or fork.

He scanned the room for anything that might serve the purpose. Nothing. Wait. He spied the electric cord dangling from the fan. At the end of the wire was a male plug. European type, three prongs.

He yanked on the plug until it came loose in his hands. But when he tried to fit the end of a prong into one of the screw slots, he found it was too thick. Improvisation time again.

He sat on the floor, and using the cement-block wall as a grinding stone, honed the end of one of the prongs until it was thin enough to fit the slot of the screws. Even standing on the chair, the fan was bolted so high he had to reach up to work the screws. Goddamn chest pain. Reaching lit the fires of hell. Every few seconds he had to bring his arms down and rest. When, after an hour of grueling work, one of the screws finally turned, he would have yelled a cheer if he'd had the strength. Then he heard the door bolt click.

💀 CHAPTER 26

O'Brien dived to the floor, muffling the scream brought on by the pain that shot through his chest. From a corner of his eye he saw the boots of his jailer walking into the room, stopping inches away from his face. Although he did not look up, he could imagine the guard staring at the bared ends of the electric cord dangling overhead or spying the black plug peeking out of his clenched fist. *Don't let him notice. Please don't let him notice.* When he felt a boot nudging him, pushing him over on his back he opened his eyes and moaned, convincingly he hoped. The guard stood above him holding a tray. In a deep guttural voice he said. "Water?"

Relief washed over him. The guard hadn't noticed. O'Brien nodded weakly.

Looking up, he saw yellow teeth framed by the beard of the grinning guard who was holding out a metal cup. O'Brien reached up. The guard tipped the cup emptying it, pouring water down on O'Brien's face. He opened his mouth to catch it, but much of it went into his throat, choking him. He coughed and the pain that knifed through his chest brought tears to his eyes. The guard let out a bellowing laugh, and placing his boot against O'Brien's face, shoved hard.

"All right, Dodic. Enough."

O'Brien looked up at the smiling face of the bald man.

"Strong enough to answer some questions now?"

O'Brien grunted.

"Get him off the floor and make him sit, Dodic."

Christ. *The chair is right under the fan and the dangling cord.*

The guard roughly pulled him to his feet—and dropped him down on the edge of the bed.

Baldy said, "What were you doing at Mount Piva? What were you looking for?"

So, that was it was called. They knew about his little excursion. "Mount what?"

"Come now, O'Brien. No games."

"I have no idea what you're talking about."

Baldy's lips curled in a one-sided smirk. "Maybe we would do better if we asked Margaret. Isn't that her name?"

What the hell was he getting at? He *couldn't* mean—.

"You are puzzled? You call her Peg, no?"

Shit! He started to leap up, ignoring the searing chest pain. Dodic reached out a huge hand and shoved him back on the bed. His voice came out a hoarse whisper. "Listen, you bastard. I know nothing about any Mount—whatever you called it. I am here looking for gravesites."

Baldy stared at him for a moment, then turned. "Come, Dodic. We will give him time to think of the right answer."

As soon as they disappeared outside the door, O'Brien buried his face in his hands. The threat to his family ripped into his heart. Where and how did they get the information? How much did they know about his family? Could these bastards somehow get to Peg and the girls? His resolve to break out of this place—and fast—was now re-doubled, in spades.

He clambered back on the chair and tucked the bared ends of the electric cord behind the fan. He went back to work, loosening the screw. Within minutes, his arms were like lead weights. At this rate, he wondered if he'd get it done before someone returned. He finally had the first screw loose enough to remove when he heard voices outside the door.

He scrambled down from his perch, tucked the plug under the blanket on his cot, and sank into the chair just as the door opened.

Baldy was back. Behind him came Dodic carrying a paper sack, and last in line a thin man with whose black hair was pulled back with a rubber band into a ponytail. On top of his shoulder he bore a video camera like a TV newsman.

Baldy smiled, held out a sheet of paper. "I have something for you to read. Aloud."

O'Brien scanned the typed message:

"I am well and am being treated humanely. I am being held because I have performed some illegal and immoral acts…"

He stopped, looked up and threw the paper at the man, watched it flutter to the floor at his feet. "This is ridiculous. I'm not reading this for your propaganda campaign. I don't care what you do to me."

The bearded guard dropped the sack and rushed at him, his arm cocked. O'Brien ducked and threw his own arm in front of his face, but the blow never came. He raised his head, saw Baldy restraining the guard. "Wait, Dodic. Listen to me, O'Brien. We are trying to show your wife and your two daughters that you are alive and well. You would be wise to cooperate so you can go home to them."

O'Brien tried to conceal his concern.

The man went on. "Let us see how much your family and country values you."

Of course. He was being held for ransom. That's why he was being kept alive. "What assurance do I have that you'll release me if I confess to this—this bullshit?"

Baldy chuckled. "Really, O'Brien, do you have any choice?" His eyes narrowed. "Or perhaps you think more clearly when your mouth is dry."

The bastard. *This* is why they had him groveling for water. "How much ransom are you asking for?"

A shrug. "What does it matter?"

His mind churned. If he read the lie for the camera, they might keep him alive until they collected the ransom. If he refused…Either way he was a dead man. His only hope was to stay alive until by some miracle he could escape. He picked the paper off the floor, nodded and pointed to the flimsy, filthy gown that hung from his body. "Okay, I'll read it, but nobody's gonna believe I'm well-treated seeing me dressed like this."

Baldy snapped his fingers at the guard and gave an order.

Dodic removed a pair of trousers and a checkered work shirt from the sack and handed them to O'Brien. They appeared to be too large, so he put them on over his gown. Still barefoot, his tender soles wouldn't get him very far very fast, if he ever got out. "What about shoes?"

"You will not need shoes."

Of course, the video would show him from the waist up.

He felt his head; hair covered the tops of his ears. His beard now had to be about two inches in length. "I look like hell. What about a shave and haircut?"

"Later."

Left unsaid was: in the unlikely event that you're still alive.

A small red light winked on top of the video camera, and he started to read in as an unconvincing a monotone as he could manufacture. After he'd finished, he balled the paper up and flung it across the room. As the three man started to leave, he demanded, "What have you done with Wilson?"

The bald man turned. Stared at him for a few seconds. "Who is Wilson?" Then smiled, turned back and walked out without waiting for an answer. The others followed. At least they had left him with clothes.

He waited, then put his ear to the door. They were gone. He went back to work removing the other three screws. But the fan guard remained firmly fixed to its backing plate. Welded? Was all this work wasted? No. The paint behind it was acting as a bond. This he easily broke, using the blade of his makeshift screwdriver as a wedge, and the fan guard clattered to the floor with a gong-like sound.

He held his breath. No one appeared at the door. He puffed out a deep sigh.

Back to work. Just one of the fan blades. That's all he would need. He grasped it, pulled, and it snapped off in his hands.

CHAPTER 27

The waiting was the hard part. Once again, O'Brien rehearsed in his mind his plan. Rechecked the props he'd so carefully arranged, went over each movement again and again, until they were as automatic as breathing. He would have only one shot at it. No second chance. Could he pull it off? Wait. That was negative thinking. Of course he could, would.

He glanced over to the cot. The bulk under the blanket wouldn't fool anyone who gave it a close look, but what the hell, all he had to work with was the slop bucket laid on its side, the wire fan guard and his balled-up gown. He tried to convince himself that it did look a little like someone lying in bed. Thank God they hadn't taken away the trousers and shirt they'd given him for the video. At least he had clothes on his back.

He had no doubts about the knife—okay, the fan blade. The edge he'd honed down on the wall was razor sharp. And the inch-wide strip of adhesive tape he'd torn from the wide band over his chest wound and applied to the dull edge of the fan blade helped him get a firm grip on it.

The light in the room was subdued enough, thanks to another slab of the adhesive he'd taped over the naked bulb. He'd debated whether or not to turn off the light at the switch, but decided that would arouse suspicion. If Dodic saw the room dark when he opened the door, he might just back off. No, there was just enough light so he could see something in the cot, but not enough to recognize it as phony.

The chair was positioned just right; behind the door with enough room so he could stand on it. Dodic was at least three inches taller than he. He'd need that extra height to take him from above and behind. For the past day—he guessed it was a day—he'd watched Dodic's movements. Walk in. Gaze at him lying in the bed. Kick the door shut with a backward thrust of his boot—a good guard never takes his eyes off his prisoner. He no longer carried in a tray. They'd stopped feeding him after making that video yesterday. No point wasting food. Dodic would stroll over to the bed maybe to make sure he was still alive. Cuff him on the head once or twice until he moaned. Well, this time the son of a bitch wouldn't get beyond the door.

Nothing to do now but wait. And listen. As he'd been doing for what seemed like half a day, but more likely was only a couple of hours. Trouble was, the guard came in to check at irregular times.

A slight noise outside the door sent his pulse racing. In a second, he was standing on the chair, knife at the ready, poised for a lunge. D-Day, H-Hour. Every muscle tensed. Seconds went by, then a minute. Still nothing. He gave it another minute, counting to 60 slowly. False alarm. Back to the waiting game.

*   *   *

It happened so quickly it all fused into one seamless motion. One moment he was standing on the chair, the next he was over Dodic's prostrate form on the floor, trying to stay clear of the twin jets of carotid arterial blood, watching the death throes as the bastard's life ebbed away. The only sounds were the scraping of Dodic's boots as his body slumped to the floor and the hissing of blood spurting from the man's neck. With his windpipe slashed open, the air remaining in his lungs sighed out noiselessly. O'Brien's preparations had paid off; his actions were mechanical.

O'Brien stood over the body for a minute, reflecting. He'd never killed a person in hand-to-hand combat. In the war his shots had been at long range, aimed at faceless targets. This was someone he knew. A poor slob doing a job. Maybe had a wife, children. Enough. It was me or him.

The ankle-high work boots and socks came off first. They were too large, but better than having to go barefoot. He had an odd sensation when he felt the man's still warm body as he went through his pockets. He fished out a ring of keys and a penknife, slipped them into his own pocket. He took the few bills Dodic had in his wallet since he didn't know where he'd be going once he got out of the door. Dodic's shirt was wool, or some heavy fabric, and even though the upper part was blood-soaked, he might need it for warmth, so he removed it and put it on over the thin shirt he was wearing, shuddering as he felt the wetness seep through his own shirt. His original plan had been to put the body in the cot, but the guy was heavy and now that his adrenaline rush was subsiding, O'Brien decided to save his strength and leave him where he lay. He couldn't hide the body. Besides, the walls and floor were so blood-splattered that anyone entering the room would know in a moment what had occurred. He hoped to be long gone before that happened.

Time to roll. He retrieved his makeshift knife from the floor. Dodic's penknife might be easier to handle, but its blades were too short to do much damage, and the edge of the honed fan blade was sharper. He turned out the room light to make his silhouette less visible, took a deep breath and put his hand on the doorknob.

He cracked the door ajar and peered into a dimly lit room that he guessed was the basement of a building. At the far end was a staircase. Cautiously, he stepped out of his prison cell into the basement. There was only one way out. The stairs.

Even putting his weight slowly and carefully on each step, they squeaked as he ascended. No light came from under the closed door at the head of the stairs. He put his ear to the door, but heard nothing. The keyhole was not one that he could see through. He watched his hand tremble as it reached for the doorknob. His pulse was roaring in his ears as he slowly turned the knob, then pushed. Locked.

Three of the dozen keys on the ring he'd taken from Dodic looked as though they might fit the lock. The second clicked the bolt open. He held his breath and took a firm grip on the fan blade. He pushed the door open an inch and peered through the crack.

He first thought he was looking at a huge, high-ceilinged airplane hangar or warehouse. Then he saw the bars, and beyond them, cells. They lined the walls on all sides. Above the ground floor was another tier of cells with a catwalk encircling the upper tier. Years ago he had toured the State Penitentiary at Joliet. The scene before him was a miniature copy. Without prisoners. The cells were empty. No guards.

O'Brien slowly pushed open the door. He scanned the steel scaffolding for TV cameras, but whoever ran this operation hadn't reached that level of technological sophistication. His boots made a clicking sound on the cement floor, but there was no one around to hear.

Where next? There appeared to be only two doors on the ground floor: the one from which he had entered and another across from where he stood. He inched along the lower tier, gazed into the cells. Mats on the floor, two or three in each cell. Clothing strewn on floors: a sock, a cap, a tattered shirt. Recently occupied.

He arrived at the second door, put his ear to it and heard the sound of sloshing liquid. For a full minute he stood waiting. Finally, he decided he had no choice. He was not going back down to the basement. He slowly turned the knob. Locked, of course. He was sorting through the keys, when the door suddenly swung open.

☠ CHAPTER 28

A blast of warm air hit his face. Before him, a wide-eyed woman, one hand on the doorknob, the other holding a large wooden spoon.

She opened her mouth, drew in a breath to scream and he lunged at her. With one arm wrapped around her neck, he pushed the blade in front of her eyes.

He spoke quietly. "Scream and you lose your face." The words had hardly left his lips when he realized she probably didn't understand his language. But she understood the knife and stifled the scream. He took in the room with a glance. Black stove. Steaming kettle. Wooden table. Refrigerator, and above it, close to the ceiling, a small barred window. Daylight. The first he'd seen in days—or was it weeks?

Gripping her, he could feel the heat of her trembling body. He pushed her down to the floor. She appeared to be in her forties, plump, light-colored hair stringing down her face. She began whimpering. He spoke quietly. "I won't hurt you unless you do something stupid. Understand?"

She stared at him, terror in her eyes.

He said, "Speak English?"

No response.

"*Sprechen sie Deutch?*"

She nodded, and in a voice barely a whisper said, "*Ja. Ein bitschen.*"

Fine, she spoke a little German—except his was a dim recollection from a college freshman course.

She cautiously peered behind him. "Dodic?"

He was not about to tell her what he'd done with Dodic. He shook his head. "*Nein.*" Let her interpret that any way she wanted.

In fractured German he asked where the others were. The men.

"*Bei der arbeit.*"

He wasn't sure who she meant was at work, and was trying to figure some way of asking, when she said, "*Der Gefangener.*"

He didn't understand the word, but thought she might mean the prisoners. He turned to look back toward the cells.

She nodded. "*Ja, Ja.*"

So this was a prison camp. Probably slave laborers. They'd been taken out to work. Apparently Dodic stayed behind as the lone care-taker. She was the cook. He looked around for a way leading outside. "Door? *Ausgang?*"

She pointed to the door he'd come in. That one led to the cells. He shook his head. "Way out. *Ausgang.*"

She nodded insistently. "*Ja. Ja.*" She struggled to her feet. He held her firmly with one hand on the back of her neck while she led him out the door, then past a row of cells to a steel door in a corner of the large room. He hadn't noticed it when he entered from the basement.

Pressing her face against the door, he tucked the blade into his waist-band. One of Dodic's keys fit the lock. He cautiously opened the door, waiting for an alarm to sound. Hearing only the creak of the metal hinges, he puffed out a deep breath, and guided her out in front of him.

Fresh air, the first he'd breathed in what seemed like a lifetime, filled his lungs. In the immediate foreground, a thick stand of tall pines grew close to the building. A narrow dirt road cut through the trees, and beyond, a weed-covered field. No perimeter fence. No people.

The road continued around the prison building, encircling it. In the distance, beyond the field, he could see the outlines of a forested mountain. The scene appeared strangely familiar. Was it the "mystery" mountain from a different prospective?

He turned and gazed back on his prison: two stories of cement-block painted in camouflage green and black to blend in with the tall pines. Nearly windowless. From where he stood, he could see only one side of the building. Pushing the woman ahead of him, he took a few steps into the dirt road. Now he could make out another small cement-block camouflaged structure. Probably a barracks for the guards. The complex had undoubtedly been built with recon planes and earth-orbiting satellites in mind. Enough speculation. His immediate objective: get the hell out of here.

He spied a dust-covered sedan near the smaller building. He pointed to it. "Yours? *Dein?*"

She shook her head. "Dodic."

Something else he could thank Dodic for. He led her to the car while he brought out the keys, but could see that none were car keys. Inside the car, there was nothing in the ignition. He regretted not knowing how to cross ignition wires. With gestures he asked her about the key.

She shrugged and pointed to the prison building. "*Dodic hat der Schlüssel.*"

Dodic had the key? Where did he keep it? "*Wo?*"

She shook her head, said something he couldn't understand.

This was wasting valuable time. Over the mountains in the distance, the brighter clouds meant he was looking west toward a lowering sun. He had to leave before the others returned. "Damn it! *Wo?*"

That got her attention. She threw up her arms defensively, whimpered and pointed to the prison building. "*Innenseite.*"

He was tempted to take off on foot. But after a moment realized he'd be no match for pursuers. No, he needed the car. He guided her back inside the prison building.

She led him to the kitchen and pointed. Beyond the refrigerator were three metal locker cabinets.

"Which is Dodic's?"

She touched one of the end lockers.

He pulled on the door. Locked.

Gazing around for something with which to smash it open, he turned—in time to see her rushing at him with a long-bladed kitchen knife in her upraised hand. He sidestepped as she brought it down, felt a sting in his forearm, but grabbed her wrist, twisting the knife out of her grasp. Twisting her arm, he forced her to the floor, kicked the knife out of her reach and picked it up. A better weapon than the one he'd fashioned from the fan blade.

This woman could be dangerous. He'd been lucky this time. He hadn't noticed the rack of knives held to the side of the refrigerator by a magnetized plate. Turned his back on her for a moment, and almost paid the price for it. He was going to have to find a way to control her. She lay face down on the floor sobbing, while he scanned the room for something with which to bind her hands. On a shelf next to the stove he spied an electric mixer. The electric cord would have to do.

Once her wrists were bound behind her back, he went for the car key. On Dodic's key ring he found the key to open the locker. Hanging inside was a wool jacket, and in a pocket, car keys.

He threw Dodic's coat over the shoulders of her thin housedress and led her outside.

Dusk was rapidly setting in as they walked to the car. He placed her in the passenger's front seat, got in the driver's seat and prayed the old jalopy would start. He turned the key and after a few wheezes, when the motor coughed into life, he gazed upward. Someone up there had answered his prayers.

The gears ground noisily as he shifted. He was slowly releasing the clutch when, in the road that led to the prison, a dust cloud appeared. Damn!

☠ CHAPTER 29

O'Brien's mind was racing. Decision time. Now. Take off in the car, or stay here? There was only one road, so he'd have to head toward whatever vehicle was coming. And the road was only wide enough for one car.

He switched off the ignition, pushed the woman off the seat to the car floor, and put his finger to his lips. He held the point of the knife against her throat. "*Verstehen sie?*"

She nodded. Yes, she understood.

The sound of the approaching vehicle grew louder. He slid down in the driver's seat, peeking out of the windshield. A dark brown truck with a canvas top hooped over the back came into view. Troop carrier? Behind it, a jeep carried, besides the driver, two rifle-bearing men in camouflage fatigues. The truck and jeep stopped at the entrance door to the prison, about 50 yards from Dodic's car. A rifle-bearing guard jumped from the passenger side of the cab, and went to the back of the truck as the driver got out to unlock the prison gate. The two guards and driver piled out of the jeep, and with the truck driver, formed a cordon, rifles pointing toward the ground, as some 30 gaunt men, heads shaven, in loose gray trousers and shirts, stepped down from the back of the truck and filed through the prison door. Even at this distance he could see that they were shackled to each other by a chain or rope that ran around each at the waist. Thirty inside that truck! As the last prisoner shuffled inside, the guards and drivers followed. A prison work gang, now going back to their cells.

Wait a minute. Only 30? Inside the prison there was room for 80 to 100 men. Where were the…? The question died in his head. Two more identical trucks chugged up the road, each followed by a jeep carrying two guards, and one by one discharged their cargo.

He had counted about 90 prisoners and 12 guards. The three truck drivers probably doubled as guards bringing the total to 15.

All were now inside. How long would it take them to realize the cook was gone and Dodic was—wherever his sad soul rested? Rapidly falling darkness might make his departure easier.

He was about to start the car when he realized that much faster and more reliable transportation stood waiting 50 yards away.

He pulled Dodic's coat over the head of his lady prisoner to muffle her cries if she started to yell, and left her trembling on the floor of the car. After yanking the keys out of the ignition, he got out of the car and closed the door quietly behind him. Crouching, he ran down the line of vehicles, ripping keys out of their ignitions, and stuffing them in his pocket. When he reached the last jeep, he hopped in, tossed the knife under the dashboard, started the motor, and after wheeling the car around, roared off down the road.

The headlights, probably partially taped over to act as dimmers, gave some light, and he bounced along as fast as the rutted road would permit. Wind whistled past his eyes and ears in the open car. Any exhilaration he might have felt was tempered by his anxiety over Lesley. The thought gnawed at his gut. He *had* to get to a phone.

The bulk of all those car keys in his pocket dug uncomfortably into his side, so one set after another, he tossed them out into the weeds.

The road was little more than a narrow path through the thick forest. Judging the direction from which the setting sun brightened the overlying clouds, he must be headed west. East was Serbia and Montenegro. West was Croatia and the Dalmatian coast, friendly territory.

Driving slowly now that darkness was closing in, he picked his way along the lane, wondering how long it would take for an alarm to go out and a roadblock to form. Eventually he would have to ditch the car, but before he did he wanted to get as far from the prison as he could.

He looked for a cut-off, but the forest was so thick that even in daylight he would have easily missed a side road. Now, in complete darkness he could barely see the road ahead. And even dimmed, the headlights probably stood out like beacons in this dark, primeval thicket.

After about an hour, he felt it was safe to stop and stretch. He gazed up, but clouds obscured any stars he might use as guides. In the glove box he found a working flashlight, and on the back seat, a half-filled plastic bottle of water which he gulped down, and a wool jacket that he put it on.

Under the dashboard was a field radio with attached microphone. He switched on the receiver, and heard through the crackling static a voice speaking Serbian. He could imagine that the message was nothing favorable to his welfare. It prodded him to start moving.

Another drive of about half an hour brought him to the edge of the woods. Beyond was a large open plain. Far off in the distance, a light twinkled faintly. A farmhouse?

He stopped, doused the headlights and debated his next course of action. Stop here or go on? In the wooded area, he had felt some degree of security. So far, there were no car lights in the road behind him. If he waited here until daylight, he'd have a better idea of what lay ahead. Besides, after the physical and mental acrobatics of the past few hours, he could feel fatigue creeping into his body. He'd stay here.

The small, four-wheel drive vehicle was maneuverable enough to park between two thick bushes about 30 yards off the road. He crawled into the back seat, used the jacket as a blanket and closed his eyes.

Now, in the moments before sleep, thoughts of his family filled his consciousness. Lesley. Poor little Lesley. If there were only some way he could will her back to recovery. All he could do was hope. Peg. How does anyone deal with her child's serious injury and her husband's disappearance at the same time? If anyone could handle it, she could. Remarkable, capable, resourceful Peg. He pictured her dashing from Lesley's hospital bed to Pennsylvania Avenue, cursing out everyone from the President to the Director of the CIA for letting him out of his cage. Berating them for not mobilizing every branch of the military to find him. Then running back to Lesley's bedside.

The urgent need to communicate with someone who could assure them he was still alive had him biting his lip until he could taste blood. Maybe there were scouting parties hunting for him. But they'd have no way of knowing where to look. Even *he* didn't know where he was. Like *Alice in Wonderland.*

The chirping of birds brought him awake. In the half-light of early dawn he heard a cock crowing. A nearby farm?

He got up and stretched out the kinks. He heard running water and followed the sound about 50 yards to a creek where the water flowing down from the mountains appeared clear. Although the thought that it might be contaminated briefly crossed his mind, he dismissed it. He had little choice. He scooped up handfuls and drank. He stripped to the waist, knelt and ducked his head in the icy water, then raised up let it run down his chest. The first bath, such as it was, he'd had in so long he couldn't remember.

The edges of the wet adhesive tape strapped to his chest had begun to curl, and for the past few days his skin under the tape had itched. Probably time to remove it. Slowly, he peeled the tape off. His skin beneath was red and dotted with small pimples. A square of gauze caked with dry blood covered the actual wound. Gritting his teeth, he slowly pulled it off, surprised that the procedure was not painful. Now he had his first view of his wound: a thin gash, three inches long, between two ribs, crusted over with a scab in which were a dozen or so black sutures. He gently scratched at the scab and found it partly free from the underlying incision. When he touched the scab, he could see that it was ready to fall off. With a finger he nudged the crusted material. It came loose with the sutures embedded in it. Under the scab was a thin red scar, probably the incision made to extract the bullet—at least he assumed the bullet had been extracted.

He patted himself dry with the blood-free tail of Dodic's shirt, tossed it into the bushes, and put back on the shirt they'd given him for the video session.

When he returned to the jeep, he heard the tinkle of cowbells coming from the meadow beyond the woods. Cautiously, he crept to the forest edge. Ten yards from where he stood, three black-and-white cows munched on the overgrown weeds. He scanned the surrounding field for signs of a cow herder, but it appeared that they had been put to pasture unattended. Plump, bulging udders.

He returned to the car and retrieved the plastic water bottle, brought it back to the meadow. The only time he'd milked a cow was for the news cameras when he was on the campaign trail. Nothing to it. Back then, the cow stood patiently in a stall flicking flies with her tail, while he sat on a stool and yanked on the teats. He recalled the hiss as the milk spurted into the pail.

Now, plastic bottle in hand, he inched up to the nearest cow. He could almost taste the warm, sweet milk. "Nice Bossy." Spoken quietly, soothingly.

Bossy raised her head from her meal. Her large brown eyes viewed him with suspicion. He reached for the teat and she suddenly shied away, out of reach. She watched him for a few moments, then put her muzzle into the weeds but kept him in her sight with a sideways look.

Again he crept toward her. This time, he'd try foreplay, stroke her first. He had barely touched her flank when she shied, loping away, the other two cows following her. Briefly he gave chase, but he'd have to trail them back to the barn if he wanted to milk them. The hell with it. He wasn't that crazy about milk anyway. He returned to the creek and filled the bottle with water.

As he carried the bottle back to the jeep, he was startled to see a tall figure rise from the opposite side of the car. A man with a gray-flecked beard, fierce black eyes under a black beret, dressed in overalls and a checkered shirt. The man pointed a pitchfork at him and shouted something O'Brien did not understand.

O'Brien took a step backward. Would he be able to make a run for it?

The question proved academic. A hand firmly gripped his shoulder. He spun around and faced another black beard, this one even taller, standing at least a head above his. The arm that held him was as thick as a tree limb. He grabbed the back of O'Brien's shirt and held it wadded in his fist. His guttural command accompanied by a shove left no room for misinterpretation.

Obviously farmers. He was probably trespassing on their land. There was no other vehicle in sight, so they must have walked here from their farmhouse. Although both were well over six feet tall, the giant who held him appeared much the younger. Father and son? He had to convince them he meant them no harm. He smiled. "I'm an American. Do either of you speak English?"

Blank stares.

Damn. Why hadn't he learned to speak some Serb-Croatian in the weeks he'd been here.

"Sprechen sie Deutsch?"

If they understood, they ignored the question, held a brief conversation, undoubtedly trying to decide what to do about him. They nodded at each other and the one who'd held the pitchfork, probably the father, got into the driver's seat, tossed his pitchfork on the floor. The other man pushed him into the back seat and, keeping a lock on his arm, sat beside him. The driver started the motor, ground the gear, and after a series of jerks drove the jeep from the woods. When they reached the road, he steered the car right, back in the direction O'Brien had taken in his escape from the prison camp.

Until this point, O'Brien felt quite sure he could make them understand that he was lost, needed to make his way back to Sarajevo. Now, it appeared they were taking him back to prison.

He bolted upright. Although the chances of getting away from these two were slim, before he'd submit to being returned to the prison, he'd fight with every ounce of strength he had left. Mind racing, he rehearsed what he'd have to do: yank his arm out of the grip of the man who held him. Vault over the door of the jeep. Start running like hell.

The one holding O'Brien's arm seemed to feel his body stiffen and tightened his grip. There was no way he was going to be able to pull it out of his grasp. No, Plan A wasn't going to work. Somehow, he'd have to figure out something else.

They had gone about a quarter mile when the jeep slowed, and the driver turned left into a narrow path that ran between the trees. Last night in the dark, O'Brien had driven past it without noticing it. He sighed out a deep breath. Although he didn't know where he was being taken, at least they were no longer headed toward the prison. He sat back, relaxed and waited.

The jeep bumped along for another quarter of a mile, when directly ahead a two-story stone farmhouse and barn came into view. The path ended at the house, and they all got out of the car, the one man still holding on to O'Brien's arm.

The two men removed their Wellington boots just outside the front door and gestured for O'Brien to remove his boots. He was pushed into to a neat, simply furnished large room that occupied the entire lower floor. The odor of roasting meat hit his nostrils and he instinctively drew in a deep breath. At the far end of the room was a kitchen in which a middle-age plumpish woman, an apron tied around her middle, stood at a stove stirring something in a blackened pot. She glanced up when they trooped in. Fixed her eyes on O'Brien for a moment then turned back to her cooking.

The older man went upstairs while the other pointed to a straight-backed chair. O'Brien sat.

The woman stood at the entryway to the kitchen wiping her hands on a towel, gesturing with her head at O'Brien. Probably asking who the hell he'd brought in. His answer caused her to raise her eyebrows.

O'Brien scanned the room looking for a phone. He spotted it mounted to the wall at the kitchen entryway. He pointed. "Telephone?" Accompanied by appropriate gestures.

The woman looked inquiringly at the man. He shook his head emphatically. No interpretation needed. He was not going to let the son of a bitch sitting in that chair use the phone.

O'Brien mimed speaking into a phone. "American-consulate. Oo-Ess-Ayy." He'd have gotten to his knees to plead if he thought it would help.

They turned away. U.S.A. did not impress them.

The father came down the stairs, wearing a mackinaw and carrying another jacket that he handed to his son. *Looks like we're going somewhere.* His disappointment at not being able to use the phone was compounded by the realization that he was not even going to be fed.

The two men led him out the door where everyone re-booted. He assumed they'd be getting back in the jeep, but when the son grabbed his arm and they all headed for the barn, O'Brien's pulse sped. He could visualize being hanged from a rafter, but forced himself not to show his fear. With relief, he saw that inside the barn stood an ancient pickup truck. Along one side were three or four stalls. He allowed himself a grin. These guys didn't have to chase the cows to milk them.

Minutes later, his hands bound behind his back, O'Brien was seated alongside the older man in the pickup, chugging back along the road they had taken to the farmhouse. Behind them, driving the jeep was the son.

O'Brien had tensed his forearm muscles while he was being bound. Now relaxing them, the rope was looser so, if he worked his hands, he felt he might be able to slip out of the binding, open the truck door and jump out. They'd probably catch him, but if he saw they were on their way back to the prison, it was worth the chance. He waited to see where they were headed.

They reached the road he'd taken from the prison. Left went toward the prison. The truck stopped, then turned right. Although his destination was still a mystery, he felt as though a weight had been removed from his body. He stopped trying to work his hands loose.

He estimated they'd gone about ten miles along the dirt road, no other vehicles passing in either direction, when they reached a paved road. A signpost stood at the intersection. They turned onto the road before he could get a good look at the signs. The brief view he'd had did not turn up any familiar names.

Now a tractor and a few old vintage autos passed, signs of a populated area. Finally, they reached the crest of a hill, and he looked down on to a village. Civilization. *Phones.* He estimated they had traveled about 20 miles.

From his vantage point, the town consisted of a main street flanked by three or four lesser streets or alleys. At its center stood a small church. The bulb-shaped spire topped by a patriarchal, double-barred cross identified it as Orthodox. Serbian territory.

He searched the skyline for the dome of a mosque, but saw none and knew it was unlikely both Orthodox Christians and Muslims would be living together in such a small community. No, he was in Serbia.

The man drove slowly into the village that consisted of a dozen low buildings that housed shops and markets. A brick building stood separate from the others. A flag that he recognized as Serbian flew from a pole in front. *Milicijska Stanica* carved into the stone above the entrance meant nothing to him—until he saw two uniformed men lounging alongside a blue-and-white car. They had arrived at the police station.

Flanked by his two captors, his hands bound behind his back he shuffled to the entrance. Two men and a woman strolling by stopped and stared. He didn't need a mirror to know he looked like a homeless bum: unshaven, unwashed, grimy clothing hanging on his frame. Running through his brain were words from a song he recalled: "If they could see me now." And he was going to try to convince a cop, whose language he didn't speak or understand, that until a few months ago he was one of an elite 100 senior legislators of the world's most powerful country?

A uniformed policeman was seated behind a desk in the small room just inside the station entrance. He pointed to a wooden bench in front of his desk, O'Brien sat. The father and son remained standing. The policeman said something in a questioning tone and the older man started responding. O'Brien watched the expression of the policeman as the father gave a lengthy answer. The policeman listened, nodded gravely with his eyebrows drawn, glanced at O'Brien, then dropped his gaze to the desktop while he shook his head, his lips compressed. What in hell was he telling the cop?

O'Brien couldn't just sit in silence while he was being accused. "Pardon me," he interrupted. "Does anyone here speak English?"

The cop pointed at him and growled something. He didn't need a language course to interpret: shut the hell up.

He felt the blood rise to his face. He'd eaten all the shit he could take. Pointing to his chest, he shouted. "American. You-ess-ayy. Goddamit, get me an interpreter, a lawyer. An advocate."

"*Advokat? Advokat?*" The cop gave O'Brien an incredulous look.

Hooray! He'd said something the officer understood. He nodded. "That's right, an *advokat*."

The policeman slowly pulled himself up from his seat. Was everyone here over six feet tall? This one weighed close to 300 pounds, all of it muscle. He kicked his chair back and with menacing deliberateness walked around the desk to stand glowering inches in front of O'Brien.

His pulse beating at his temples, O'Brien peered up into the red face of the policeman. He stuck out his chin. If the son of a bitch was going to swing at him, defenseless, hands tied behind his back, let him. For five seconds they stood looking into each other's eyes. Suddenly, the policeman's face broke out into a grin, and he shoved him back onto the bench. He strode to the doorway, shouted to someone and went back to his seat behind the desk.

A moment later, a young police officer came to the doorway, spoke to the one behind the desk and after receiving what sounded like an order, took O'Brien by the arm and led him out of the room.

They went down a flight of stairs at the bottom of which was a steel gate. The policeman released his grip on O'Brien's arm while he fished out of his pocket a ring of keys. A minute later, the binding on his wrists removed, O'Brien was again ensconced in a jail cell. He plopped down on the single wooden stool, looked around briefly at the canvas cot, the seatless toilet bowl, the six-by-eight-foot space, wondering what crime he'd been accused of committing. Could word have reached them that he'd escaped from that prison? Or worse, that he'd murdered Dodic?

CHAPTER 30

Although the meat was overcooked and dry as toast, the carrots and peas soggy, the bread stale with edges that were green with mold, the tea more like warm water, O'Brien couldn't recall having eaten with more relish. He scraped the last morsel off the tin dish with the remaining crust of bread, and savored it in his mouth before permitting himself to swallow. His first meal in—he'd lost track of the number of days, or was it weeks?

After a few satisfying belches, he lay on the cot, his arms folded behind his head. This town—he hadn't discovered its name as yet—obviously was a low-crime area. He was the only prisoner in the block of three cells. Not a bad jail as jails went, and he was becoming a connoisseur.

More than half a day since he got here, and so far no one had come to drag him back to the prison camp. Nor did they seem to understand his request to make a phone call. He desperately needed someone who spoke a language he could understand.

With each passing hour, he was becoming more convinced that the people here had no connection with Dodic and the crowd that ran that prison. Didn't even know of its existence. Maybe, just maybe, the people running that prison were not even part of this government, but were members of a renegade or terrorist group. The Serbs, in spite of the bad press they'd gotten, were probably just another Balkan state whose nationalistic fever ran a few degrees higher than the others. Sure, they'd committed monstrous crimes against the Muslims, but the Muslims and the Croats had blood on their hands as well.

No, chances were that the gang operating the labor prison had an agenda of their own. He hadn't yet figured out what that was, but in his gut he didn't think it ran with government sanction.

So why was he here in the lockup? Trespassing? Come on.

The clank of the cellblock gate and the sound of voices stirred him to sit up, then jump to his feet. The young cop came into view, followed by a short dumpy man in a business suit, carrying a briefcase. The officer unlocked the cell door, directed the man inside and closed the door behind him.

The visitor, his head swiveling around to examine the cell, stammered, "You speak English, no?"

Thank God. "Yes. I'm an American."

"Ah, *Americki*." He pronounced it amereechkee. "Good, good. I am Jorno Kupreskic, *Advocat*. Or, as you say, lawyer, no?" Nervous little giggle.

O'Brien extended his hand and Kupreskic grabbed it, and held on shaking it for several seconds before he could extract it. "Glad to see you Mr. Kupreskic Before we do anything else, I'd like you to tell whoever is in charge here I need to make a phone call."

"Yes, yes. Of course."

Kupreskic did not move. Kept standing, shifting his weight from one foot to another.

"I mean now."

"Telephone?"

"Yes."

He shook his head. "It is not possible."

The rules here obviously did not include making a phone call. "Well, will you make one for me?"

"Yes, yes. Later. First we must talk."

O'Brien wanted to get this conversation over in a hurry. Get this weird character out to make a phone call for him. Although he would have preferred having him call Peg to reassure her, this guy did not inspire confidence. He'd better make the call simple. Have him phone Shaw at the U.S. Consulate in Sarajevo, ask him to come here. "What do you want to talk about?"

"Your charges."

"Okay."

He fumbled with the latches on his briefcase, finally opened it and withdrew a sheet of paper. "First, you are accused of attempting to steal a cow."

Steal a cow? O'Brien stared at the lawyer for a few seconds before breaking out in a loud guffaw.

Kupreskic's face turned beefy red. "The people here do not consider such—such crimes a joke."

Apparently he'd touched a nerve. Have to watch what he said. "Sorry. I didn't mean that stealing a cow was funny. It's just that I did *not* try to steal a cow." He wasn't about to go into a long spiel about his captivity, his escape and bungled try at milking the cow. "The simple truth is that I was lost, wandered into this man's field. I was hungry. I hadn't eaten anything for days. Saw the cow and tried to milk it." He added, "I didn't even get to milk it. The cow ran off."

Kupreskic nodded. "I see. We will try to make the magistrate understand when your trial comes up."

He would have to wait for a trial? "When will that be?"

"*Utorak.* Sorry, Tuesday. The magistrate holds court here on Tuesdays."

"What day is today?"

"Thursday."

Shit. Was he going to have to sit locked up for five days. He remembered the money he'd taken from Dodic's wallet. He took out the bills and offered them to Kupreskic. "How about having me released on bail."

Kupreskic smiled, pushed his hand away. "That money would not buy a package of cigarettes."

He was getting nowhere. His best bet was to get Shaw here and straighten things out. "All right, Mr. Kupreskic. Please do this for me and I will see that you are well compensated. Telephone the United States Consulate Office in Sarajevo. Ask for Mr. Shaw. S-H-A—don't you want to write this down?"

Kupreskic was closing his briefcase. What the hell was going on? Now he recalled Kupreskic had said "charges." Pleural.

When Kupreskic finally looked up, O'Brien could see the anxiety in his face. The lawyer swallowed, dipping his head. "I'm afraid this is more serious. You are charged with stealing automobile belonging to the Yugoslavian People's Army."

Of course, the jeep. "Look, I can explain that. Please make that call for me."

"I hope your explanation will satisfy the magistrate because a month ago when the automobile was stolen, along with several army trucks, the soldiers who had been driving them were found—" Long pause. "—by the roadside." Pause. "Murdered."

Jesus. This *was* more serious. No real surprise to learn that the bunch who ran that prison were killers. It explained where they'd gotten the jeeps and trucks, and confirmed his suspicion that they weren't part of the official government. Well, he could prove that he wasn't even in Europe a month ago. No, wait. He *had* been here more than a month.

Kupreskic coughed into his palm. "The soldier driving the jeep was stabbed to death with a knife—"

This guy was dragging out the bad news piece by piece.

"—like the knife found on the floor of the Army car you stol— were driving."

CHAPTER 31

O'Brien sat on the edge of the cot facing Kupreskic, who was seated on the wooden stool. It was Saturday, two days since Kupreskic had dropped the bombshell, informing O'Brien that he'd been accused of a series of crimes that made those of Bonnie and Clyde seem like dime-store shoplifting. Two days during which O'Brien had beaten his fists raw against the walls and steel bars, in his frustration over not being able to communicate with someone outside this hole.

Kupreskic said, "You must be honest with me, mister. It will make it much easier for me to defend you."

O'Brien suppressed the urge to punch his face. "The name is O'Brien. And I *have* told you the truth, every word of it. If you don't believe me, I'd better get another lawyer."

Kupreskic gazed at the ceiling. "Yes. Another lawyer." He rubbed his eyes. "Listen, I am court-appointed. You understand what that means?"

O'Brien resented the patronizing. "I'm a lawyer myself. I know what that means."

"You are not in Sarajevo or Belgrade or London. This village is Krjevak. It has two thousand inhabitants. There is beside myself one other *advokat.* He is seventy-nine years old and cannot always find his own house. Do you understand?"

O'Brien sighed. "I've got you or no one."

"I am afraid that is the case."

"Will you at least try again to contact the consulate? Ask Mr. Shaw to come here?"

"Mister. I have told you twice already. Mr. Shaw insists Matthew O'Brien is dead. This is confirmed. He doesn't know who you are, but says you are not who you say you are, and he refuses to make an unnecessary trip."

The story Kupreskic had relayed from the consulate was that Matt O'Brien had been a patient in a private hospital in Sarajevo after having been wounded by a sniper's bullet. He had been kidnapped from the hospital by terrorists and the consulate had arranged through an intermediary whom they trusted to pay a huge ransom for his release. The money had been delivered and the intermediary was given, in exchange, instructions to go to a house where O'Brien was waiting to be released. The house was empty, except for a videocassette. When the consulate played the tape, it showed O'Brien hanging from a makeshift scaffold.

"Dammit, I told you," O'Brien insisted. "The video was a phony. Trick photography. They stuck the picture of my head on someone else's body."

Apparently, the terrorists had used the real video, in which he had read the I-am-well bullshit, to convince the consulate to turn over the ransom money. They had had no intention of releasing him. He was sure they'd planned all along to kill him. It wasn't clear why they went to the trouble of making the doctored tape. Why didn't they wait to make another video after they had *really* hanged him? They could have just made the exchange with a blank tape, unless it was to rub shit in the faces of the arrogant Americans. *Thanks for the money, here's your man O'Brien back. Sorry if he's not in mint condition.* Then he screwed up their plans by taking off before they had the chance.

Kupreskic turned up his palms. "I can do nothing more to convince the consulate. But perhaps you will have the opportunity to prove you are Mr. O'Brien—if that is who you are."

O'Brien waited while Kupreskic cleared his throat. The man seemed to be anticipating a drum roll every time he had something to say. Finally—"Mr. Shaw informs me that Mrs. O'Brien insists her husband is alive. At her insistence they are arranging transportation for her to come to Sarajevo."

Peg coming! Of course he could depend on her persistence—and faith in his resourcefulness. What took this idiot so long to tell…? Never mind. The important thing was that she was coming. It also probably meant that she no longer had to remain with Lesley. His daughter was out of danger. He refused to allow himself to think of the alternative. He grabbed Kupreskic's hand in both of his. "Thank you. Thank you. That's marvelous news. When will she be here?"

"I am to telephone Mr. Shaw tomorrow to learn her schedule."

"Listen, you must make arrangements for her to come here as soon as she arrives in Sarajevo."

"Yes. I will try. Meanwhile, we must make preparations for your trial next Tuesday."

He droned on for what seemed an hour, explaining in detail how the trial system worked. O'Brien half-listened. He was already picturing Peg's arrival, their tearful reunion bringing him word of Lesley, and his release. If she got here before Tuesday there would be no trial. She'd figure a way to have these ridiculous charges dropped.

*   *   *

He awoke in his jail cell screaming. Sweat soaking the sheet covering him. That dream. Again. It had been years since the last time. Always the same dream. A small man dressed in fatigues is tearing off his scrotum.

It started during his recuperation period after he'd returned from Vietnam. A psychiatrist at Balboa Naval Hospital had warned him that it might recur. It did. At first at monthly intervals. Later, every year or two. But this was the first time in at least five years.

The psychiatrist had said, "It's understandable after…"

Two VC soldiers had dragged him out of the pit and shoved him into a hootch. They stood, one on each side of him, before an officer who asked him where Marine ammo was stored.

"Matthew O'Brien. Second lieutenant. Serial number 563473—"

He gave the same answer to all the questions. Finally, the officer ground out his cigarette and shouted an order to the soldiers. Moments later he found himself lying on his back on the straw-covered floor, his trousers pulled down to his ankles.

The officer glared down at him. "I want answer. Now."

"Matthew O'B—"

His testicles felt as though a vice gripped them.

When he had finished screaming, he gazed down and saw a wire leading from his scrotum to a box held by a soldier.

"Answer me!"

"Matth—" The shock that tore through his groin was beyond any pain he could imagine.

"We will fry your balls. Answer!"

"MATTHEW—"

A bomb went off somewhere between his legs, and he dimly recalled being thrown back into the rat-infested pit. Even after his rescue, for weeks the burning pain in his genitals was so severe, he was sure when he looked down he'd find them ablaze.

At Balboa, after his operation, the urologist told him he might eventually be able to produce viable sperm. The prognosis left him wondering and worrying. And when, one morning he awoke with an erection, he planted a kiss on the bald head of the male nurse who'd brought him breakfast.

He could never bring himself to tell Peg—or anyone except the psychiatrist. He even pushed the memory back so far in his own brain, that it surfaced only during sleep, when he had no conscious control.

*   *   *

O'Brien rubbed his smooth cheeks. It was Sunday, two days before his trial, if it ever came to that. His first shave in a week or more. He handed the razor to the policeman who had stood by watching. They didn't trust him with anything sharp. The haircut he'd given himself with the dull scissors at best kept the hair out of his eyes. Would get a good laugh out of Peg—if she could still laugh after all she'd gone through.

He sat back on the cot while his jailer relocked the cell door behind him. *Let's see, she arrives in Sarajevo late Monday. Probably wouldn't be able to get here until Tuesday morning.* He got up and paced the small cell. He could think of nothing else since Kupreskic told him Peg was on her way—well almost. He wondered who would stay with the girls. Maybe she'd have her mother come from Dayton to stay with Lesley until she'd fully recovered. Brooke was really able to take care of herself. She'd be out of high school in less than a year. Just thinking about them misted his eyes, tightened his throat. God, he couldn't wait to hold them again.

Clanking of the cellblock door brought him to his feet and to the bars of his cell. He was again their only guest, since the drunk they brought in to the adjacent cell last night was released this morning. Had to make sure he made six o'clock Sunday Mass.

He stared at the smiling man who stood before his cell door. Could it be? Jasajovic? Jasajovic, the Serb who'd served with him on the Missing Persons Committee, the replacement for the guy Zee had recognized as a former interrogator at the Omarska prison camp? "My God. What are you doing here?"

"I might ask the same of you, Mr. O'Brien. And I might add how relieved I am to find that you are alive. Maybe you are not aware, you were reported to be dead."

"Yes, I know. Christ, I'm glad to see you." He reached through the bars and grasped Jasajovic's hand.

Jasajovic laughed. "Well, I'm flattered that you call me The Savior. Perhaps I can fulfill that role. I understand you have had some—uh, difficulties since I last saw you."

Difficulties. What an understatement! "Listen, Mr. Jasajovic, there's so much to tell you, I don't know where to begin. But why are we holding this conversation through bars? I assume you can explain to these people who I am and get me out of here."

"All in good time. But first there are some legal technicalities to get out of the way."

Jasajovic's words suddenly caused a chill to run down his spine. "All in good time." Where had he heard that expression? Stilted, but probably common phrasing used by people to whom English was an adopted tongue. He shook it off.

Jasajovic peered at him inquisitively. "Does it come as a surprise that I can't just wave a hand and have the authorities release you? It *is* Sunday, you know, and—"

"Of course. No, I realize there are official channels. It's just that I'm impatient. Can't wait to breathe fresh air again."

"Yes. Of course you are anxious, as am I. Well, let me go back upstairs now that I know you are safe. That is the main thing. I will try to expedite matters. Just try to be patient for a short while longer. Eh?" Jasajovic emphasized his words with a wink.

After Jasajovic left, O'Brien sat on his cot but less than a minute later was back up pacing. Soon he'd be out. Freedom at last. *Real* freedom this time. Not like the escape from that stone prison. He didn't know yet how Jasajovic had learned he was here, but would forever be grateful that he took the time and trouble to make the trip to see him. Not like that asshole Shaw. If he still any influence at State, he'd see that the officious bastard was reprimanded.

Half an hour later, the policeman who guarded the cellblock was back. He unlocked the cell door and beckoned O'Brien to follow. No handcuffs? Apparently Jasajovic had pulled it off.

He followed the policeman to an office on the main floor. A slender man with a thin black moustache and wearing a white bud rose in the lapel of his neatly pressed blue suit, sat at a desk reading a sheet of paper. In a chair opposite sat Jasajovic, smiling. He got up when O'Brien entered. "Ah, there you are. Please, meet Mr. Brlisic, he is head of the police department. Also he is mayor of Krjevak."

O'Brien extended his hand, and Brlisic glanced up from the paper, took it unsmiling in a limp palm and went back to reading.

Jasajovic continued. "Mr. Brlisic was kind enough to leave church services at my request."

"Thank you."

A slight nod.

"Mr. Brlisic does not speak English. But I think he understands a little."

Brlisic looked up from the paper and spoke to Jasajovic.

Jasajovic interpreted. "He says that normally you would be held until you had been found not guilty in the court of law. But for me they will make an exception. You must sign a release form and post a bond."

"How much of a bond? I have no money, of course."

"Naturally. The bond is sixty thousand dinar. But, of course, I will advance the money."

Jasajovic was willing to lay out about $10,000 for him? He was even *more* impressed with the guy. "I'll see that you're repaid as soon as my wife gets here tomorrow or the next day."

Jasajovic waved. "Please. Do not concern yourself. I am only happy I can be of service."

"I can't begin to thank you." Would Shaw have been as gracious? "I wish my own countrymen were as thoughtful."

Brlisic pushed a sheet of paper across his desk and handed a pen to O'Brien.

After briefly glancing at the typed Slavic words, O'Brien said, "I suppose as a lawyer I should ask what I'm signing, but—"

Jasajovic shook his head. "A mere formality. You are signing away your life." He sat back and guffawed. "A small joke, of course. It states that you will appear for trial at the scheduled time and place, et cetera, et cetera, or forfeit the bond, be held in contempt of court, and serve a sentence to be determined by the court as well as pay a fine that comes to the amount of the bond, et cetera, et cetera. But, of course, we will straighten these matters out." He pointed to a line at the bottom. "Here is where you sign."

While Jasajovic wrote out a check for the bond, O'Brien scratched his signature on the paper, and handed it to Brlisic. "I'd like to use your phone." Maybe he could still reach Peg before she took off for Sarajevo. Even if she'd already left, he could speak to the girls. Assure them he was alive.

Jasajovic said something to Brlisic, listened to his response, then turned to O'Brien. "International call?"

"Yes. My wife."

Jasajovic shook his head. "I'm afraid international calls cannot be made from this phone."

"There must be *some* phone in this village I can use."

"You must realize that the war has torn up much of what you people call infrastructure. Telephone lines are one of the casualties. Today you cannot even be connected to Sarajevo."

O'Brien found it hard to believe. Serbia had not suffered from war damage like Bosnia-Herzegovina and Croatia. Besides, Kupreskic had phoned the U.S. Consulate in Sarajevo. Someone was lying, but arguing would get him nowhere. "Is there a means of radio communication I can use?"

"Another time I might be able to find a radio operator, but—" Jasajovic turned up his palms and shook his head. "Today is Sunday."

That was that. He'd have to wait. "How do I get back to Sarajevo?"

Jasajovic smiled. "Of course. I will take you."

CHAPTER 32

Jasajovic led the way to the shiny black Mercedes parked at the entrance of the police station. A muscle man, mid-forties, with misshapen nose and thick scar tissue over his eyes, was leaning against the car fender smoking a cigarette. When they approached, he sucked a last draw into his lungs, flicked the butt away and got into the driver's seat. Jasajovic opened the back door, gestured for O'Brien to get in, then settled himself beside him. O'Brien reminded himself that this was still a communist country; chauffeurs and their employers were on an equal footing.

O'Brien said, "How long will it take?"

"We have to make a stop first, so I can't tell you."

They left the outskirts of Krjevak and were speeding past fields of freshly tilled soil. Jasajovic made no attempt at conversation, but a question nagged at O'Brien's brain: How did Jasajovic know he was in the Krjevak jail? According to that bumbling public defender Kupreskic, even Shaw, his own consulate, was convinced he was dead. He started to ask Jasajovic, but when he glanced over, he saw that his eyes were closed, his head thrown back, mouth agape. Well, he'd wait until he awoke.

For a while, O'Brien watched out the window, gazing at long stretches of farmland, pine forests, occasional small herds of dairy cattle and sheep. They passed through villages where the only people he saw were through the open doors of Orthodox churches.

He kept his mind occupied with thoughts of Peg and what he'd planned to say. For 20 years she'd let him play his little game of self-indulgence. And it was finally wearing her down. Tearing apart their marriage. Funny thing, she was smart enough to have figured out that's what he'd been doing, even if she didn't know why he had to. Thrill-seeking. That's really what it boiled down to. Isn't that what he'd been doing since he returned from the war? Those political offices. His speeches rang with patriotic platitudes. Wasn't he willing to sacrifice his financial security so he could do good for all the people in his district, then his state? Bullshit. Now Bosnia. He'd been able to convinced himself that he was here on a humanitarian mission. Come on. This was another contest. Another challenge. Another way to prove he had the balls for it—*literally.* Well, he was through trying to prove his manhood. Somehow he'd have to convince Peg he'd hung up his Super Nintendo joystick, and was ready to be a dutiful husband and father.

He was jarred from his daydreaming by the bumping of the car. They had left the macadam-paved highway and were now on a rutted dirt road that ran through a meadow. Ahead were woods, the road narrowing but continuing through the forest of tall pines. His ears felt as though they were plugged with cotton. So, they had been climbing an elevation while he dozed. He popped his ears to clear them. The sun was directly above them, noon. He estimated they had started at around 10:30. They had been driving about an hour and a half.

Jasajovic had said they had to make a stop. That's where they seemed headed now. O'Brien peered through the side windows. Before he'd dozed off, they'd been passing through villages, past farmhouses, populated areas. Now there was no sign of a dwelling. Jasajovic was awake now but silent and gazing straight ahead.

O'Brien said, "How did you know—what made you suspect it was me back there in the jail?"

The words barely out of his mouth, O'Brien felt the hairs back of his neck prickle. Trouble.

Jasajovic didn't answer, didn't turn his head.

While the car bounced along for another half mile, O'Brien's thoughts were racing. They had reached the woods. *Get out of the car. Now.*

He slowly reached for the door handle. He felt Jasajovic's hand on his other shoulder. Heard his sharp command. "No!"

Jasajovic said something to the driver in his own language. The car braked to a stop. The driver turned around, brought a hand up pointing over the back of the front seat, and O'Brien was looking into the barrel of a gun.

Jasajovic said something to the driver, then turned to O'Brien. "This, my friend, is the end of the line."

O'Brien waited for the explosion of the gun.

Jasajovic's voice rasped in his ear. "Get out."

For a fleeting moment he thought, *He's letting me go.* He saw the driver start to slide out of the car and realized, *He just doesn't want to get my blood all over the inside of his car.*

O'Brien had been sitting in the left back seat, behind the driver who was already out and pointing the gun at him. He flung open his door, and shielded from the driver, ducked, hit the ground running and raced into the woods. He felt the whistle of the bullet past his ear before he heard the shot. Then a sting along his cheek as a second bullet grazed him. He kept running, dodging side to side. Another bullet pinged into a tree to his right. His surging adrenaline pumped into his legs. The farther he got from the shooter, the poorer a target he became. He raced on, changing course every third step, dodging around and between trees. He heard no more shots, so the driver must be reloading, chasing after him, or both. He slipped on pine needles underfoot, but caught himself before he fell. Glanced back for an instant and saw the driver lumbering through the woods about 50 yards behind. He forced his legs to go faster. Heard another shot and at the same moment a thud as the bullet hit a tree to his left. If he was shooting, he must have stopped running. O'Brien puffed up an incline. His lungs were afire, his legs now lead weights. Sweat poured down from his forehead, stinging his eyes. He reached the crest of the hill and let his weight carry him flying down the other side. He flicked another glance behind. The driver was no longer in sight. But suddenly the trees ahead vanished into clear blue sky. A few paces later he was at the edge of a sheer cliff, peering down into a canyon and a river that looked miles below him. He was at the summit of a mountain. In the distance were other peaks, some snow-capped. He ran left along the edge of the cliff, the loose earth crumbling underfoot, but after 50 feet the rim ended, dropped into nothing.

O'Brien stopped and looked back into the trees. The driver had not yet come into view. He had two ways to go—one, take a dive. The second choice was just as unacceptable since it brought him back to his pursuer. Below him, the cliff dropped off sharply. The only object between where he stood and the floor of the abyss was a foot-wide rocky ledge, about five feet below the edge of the cliff.

The sound of crashing through the woods behind prodded him into a decision. He dropped to the ground and eased himself off the cliff edge directly above the ledge. His fingers dug into the earth until his feet touched the ledge. The dirt began to crumble under his fingertips. In seconds either the shelf would support his weight or it would give way and he'd plunge into the gorge. It held. He drew in a deep breath.

Above his head he heard the footfalls of the driver. Crouching, he pressed himself into the face of the cliff. Bits of dirt and rock in the air from above and to his left told him the guy was close to the rim, coming toward the ledge on which he stood. He held his breath, willing his body to become invisible. The footfalls came closer. A rock fragment dropped inches from his face. It was now or never.

He rose suddenly from a crouch, his shoulders level with the rim of the cliff. The driver was peering into the woods, pointing his gun toward the trees. The backs of the driver's legs were inches from his eyes. He was vaguely aware of a gunshot as he reached up, grabbed the driver's belt with both hands and yanked. It took all his strength to pull the man back over his head, his own skull serving as a fulcrum. The driver's back brushed his neck as he plunged screaming, flailing into the gorge. But the action had thrown O'Brien off balance. Now he felt himself teetering backwards, his feet slipping off the ledge. With one hand he grabbed a thin shoot growing out of a crevice in the rock face. A second later, it pulled loose and he felt himself falling. His windmilling hands caught the edge of the ledge. He dangled in midair. He couldn't hold on for more than a few more seconds. With his feet, he frantically scrabbled at the cliff face, until one boot found a spike of rock that jutted out. For the moment, some of the strain was off his hands. Now his other boot found a crevice. He pushed himself up so that his elbows and forearms rested on the ledge. The muscles of his shoulders and neck cried out with pain, screamed for rest. He ignored them and dug his boots into the cliff face, pushing with his legs and pulling with his arms until he got one knee on the shelf. Straining until he thought his lungs would burst, he boosted himself to get his other knee on the ledge. Sucking air, he rested on his hands and knees until some of his strength returned.

He looked down, saw the driver's body sprawled on the rocky river bank below. One down.

He flexed and extended his elbows and wrists to relieve the dead feeling and then reached up to grasp the rim of the cliff. It took three unsuccessful tries to find toeholds for his boots, and with the help of his fingers digging into the ground above him, he crawled back to the top. Eyes closed, he lay prone for a full minute, unable to move.

The sound of a voice calling out echoed through the woods. Somewhere out there was Jasajovic. He raised his head and peered through the trees. It seemed unlikely that Jasajovic was armed, since the driver had probably been his bodyguard.

Again he heard Jasajovic calling. The sound louder, he was coming closer. O'Brien quickly looked for a place from which to ambush Jasajovic. The tree line ended about ten feet from the edge of the cliff—a ten-foot clearing consisting of earth covered by clumps of grass. He scrambled to his feet and, crouching, withdrew to a few yards inside the woods. Flattening himself on the ground, he was partly hidden behind the trunk of a pine tree. He now could hear Jasajovic's footfalls in the distance as he came crashing through the woods, calling out as he approached. He couldn't make out what Jasajovic was shouting, probably the name of the driver.

Through the trees, O'Brien could see Jasajovic's stocky form. He still had on the suit and tie he'd worn to the jail in Krjevak. He watched while Jasajovic hurried to the clearing beyond the trees. Now he stopped, peered out over the cliff, then into the woods. Gazing down into the abyss, he started walking away from where O'Brien lay. Then he stopped, took a handkerchief from his pocket and wiped his brow. He turned around. Began walking slowly along the cliff edge, toward O'Brien's lair. Turning his head quickly from side to side and behind him, he appeared to sense danger. Now he was walking along the rim of the cliff. Jasajovic was only about 20 feet away, so close he could hear the man's breathing. He thought about leaping forward, pushing him off the edge of the cliff. But lying prone, he'd have to get to his feet first. No good. Pulse hammering, he lay and watched while Jasajovic stopped, peered into the trees, head inclined forward. He seemed to be gazing at the place where O'Brien lay. Had he been spotted? O'Brien's body tensed until it felt like a giant rubber band stretched to the breaking point. But Jasajovic slowly looked away, then resumed his slow pace while peering down into the gorge. Suddenly he stopped. His hand flew to his face. He had spotted the driver's body. He spun around, looking into the trees. O'Brien could see the bewilderment in his eyes. Jasajovic's hoarse, rapid breathing cut through the stillness of the forest. Suddenly, Jasajovic began to run toward the woods, back to the car, his path on a line five feet from where O'Brien lay, knees pumping in short, rapid strides. Now!

O'Brien leaped up and threw his arms around Jasajovic's legs, a tackle that would have made his old high-school coach proud.

Jasajovic crashed to the ground with a grunt. In a moment he was thrashing, flailing with both arms and legs. A vicious kick caught O'Brien flush in the face, snapping back his neck. Lights flashed in his head. The guy was a tiger—and strong. Jasajovic started to crawl up on hands and knees. O'Brien tried to pin his arms in a hammer hold, but Jasajovic squirmed loose, swung a fist that whistled by O'Brien's head. O'Brien ducked away. The lessons he'd learned so well at Quantico were not forgotten. Jasajovic was on him, sitting on his chest, pounding his face. Now flat on his back with his arms outstretched, O'Brien was beyond the point where he could feel pain. One of his hands touched a smooth round rock. He grasped it. With the last ounce of effort left in his body, he swung his hand up, the rock thudding into Jasajovic's temple. In slow motion, Jasajovic's body sagged into O'Brien's chest.

O'Brien could smell his sweat. He pushed the man's bulky form, rolling him off his own body. Jasajovic twitched, slightly at first, then jerked with violent spasms and finally lay still. Not breathing. O'Brien put his ear to Jasajovic's chest, heard his rapid heart beat. He was not dead.

O'Brien patted Jasajovic's pockets, assuring himself that he was not carrying a gun. He removed the man's suit jacket, lay it open on the ground, then rolled Jasajovic face down into it, tied the sleeves tightly together behind his back, fashioning a crude strait-jacket. He secured it by removing Jasajovic's belt and buckling it snugly around his chest to further pin his arms. He took off Jasajovic's shoes and socks, tossed them into the canyon—another tactic for which he could thank his OTS drill instructor. If Jasajovic was able to free himself, he wasn't going to do any running on the pine needles and branches that littered the ground.

Jasajovic began to groan. Although his eyes remained unfocussed, he was regaining consciousness. In one of his trouser pockets, O'Brien found the car keys. He debated whether to take off, leave Jasajovic trussed up here in the woods. Eventually he would free himself and crawl to the road. But before he did, there were questions to be answered.

Jasajovic was barely stirring. Incoherent sounds came from his lips. O'Brien grabbed him by the ankles and dragged him, his limp body bumping over the ground.

☠ CHAPTER 33

He watched Jasajovic open an eye, squint into the overhead sunlight.

"Good afternoon," O'Brien said. He had dragged Jasajovic, trussed and half-conscious, to the clearing between the tree line and the cliff. They sat six feet from the edge.

Jasajovic's lips moved but the sound that emerged was gibberish. A lump the size of a golf ball had come up on the side of his head where O'Brien had clobbered him with the rock. He cleared his throat, blinked rapidly, glanced at O'Brien, then tried to move his arms.

O'Brien said, "Remember me?"

A nod.

"What's my name?"

"Brn."

"Know where you are?"

Jasajovic raised his head as far as his bonds would allow. Turned his head from side to side, squinting through half-opened eyes at his surroundings. His brow creased. He shook his head. Spittles of saliva ran from the corners of his mouth. "W-Water."

"Water?"

A vigorous nod.

"All in good time." Give the bastard back his phrase. O'Brien would have liked a drink himself, but until he found a stream, it would have to wait.

"Mmmmk?"

"Your driver?"

A nod.

"He's gone."

"Gone?"

Jasajovic seemed to be awake enough to comprehend. No more small talk. "All right, Jasajovic. I'm going to ask you some questions, and I want straight answers. *Versteh?*"

O'Brien waited a moment. Jasajovic had not responded, but he went on. "Where is Wilson?"

Jasajovic's brows drew together. "Vilsn?"

"Hank Wilson. The radar engineer who was here to locate mine fields."

He shook his head. "I do not know this Wilson." His speech now more coherent.

"Let me refresh your memory. Wilson was taken by your people from his garage, along with his truck and equipment."

O'Brien watched his face closely. Jasajovic had been looking directly at him, now for the briefest moment, glanced away.

"I tell you, sir. I do not know this—"

"Okay, you flunked question one. What's inside that cavern?"

"Cavern?"

"The one in the mountain. The one trucks go in and out of. The one that has anti-aircraft weapons."

"I know of no such—"

"You fail another one. Question three: Who planted the bug in my hotel room?"

"Bug?"

"Electronic listening device."

"In your hotel room?"

"There seems to be an echo from these hills."

"Sir, if there was a listening device in your room, it was probably left over from the previous administration. Planting such devices was common practice, but now—"

"Who shot me?"

"You were shot?"

This bastard was not going to give any straight answers. O'Brien got to his feet. "Okay, Jasajovic, so far you haven't gotten one answer right. Here's one question you should ace: Who's going to shove you and your lying ass off the edge of this cliff in ten seconds?"

He grabbed Jasajovic by the shoulders and sat him up so that he faced the cliff. Jasajovic jerked his body back. "Take a good look, Jasajovic. See if that jogs your memory."

"I swear to you—"

O'Brien pushed him toward the cliff edge. Jasajovic tried to brake by digging his bare heels into the ground, but O'Brien kept pushing until his feet were off the edge.

Jasajovic cried out, "For God sake, I don't know. I swear it."

O'Brien bent over so that his nose was inches from Jasajovic's. "Now listen, you prick. Tell me you didn't order your bodyguard to kill me just half an hour ago. I don't believe a word out of your fucking mouth." He pointed to the canyon floor. "Take a good look down there. There's your killer. In five seconds you're going to join him."

O'Brien moved behind Jasajovic and placed his hands on the small of his back. Would he have the guts to push the man off the cliff? Killing the prison guard Dodic, and Jasajovic's driver had been acts of self-defense. This would be murder. Maybe the son of a bitch *really* didn't know where Wilson was. On the other hand, didn't he order the driver to kill him? He started to shove.

Jasajovic's legs were now over the edge. The dirt under his buttocks began to give way. He screamed. "Wait!"

O'Brien threw his arm around Jasajovic's throat in a chokehold to keep him from sliding into the gorge. "Ready to talk?"

He felt Jasajovic's head bob under his grip.

O'Brien pulled him back until he was securely on firm ground. For the moment glad to be relieved of his role as executioner.

Jasajovic's voice was a hoarse whisper. "Wilson is..." The last unintelligible.

"Where is that?"

Jasajovic shook his head slowly. "I will have to show you. You could not find it on a map. I have heard rumors that he is in a detention camp there."

Rumors. He was lying, of course. He knew goddam well where Wilson was. Just as he knew that he, O'Brien, had escaped from that prison camp in a jeep he'd "borrowed" after someone had prematurely declared him dead. Jasajovic probably had ordered his execution, but the bumbling guards at the prison camp had screwed up. "What other rumors have you heard?"

"I am telling the truth, so help me God."

"How did you know where to find me?"

"Again, rumors. This is a small country."

This answer probably had a grain of truth. The lawyer, Kupreskic, had phoned the U.S. Consulate at O'Brien's request. Obviously, when Jasajovic heard that some American who claimed to be O'Brien was in jail, he knew where to find him.

O'Brien bent and picked up a large rock and held it in front of Jasajovic's face. "If this is a trick—if you're not telling me the truth, I swear I'll beat you to death with this stone."

Jasajovic's head was bowed. "No, it is no trick. I promise you."

No point in wasting any more time with questions Jasajovic wasn't going to answer. At least he got him to admit he knew about Wilson's abduction. But he couldn't bring himself to shove him over the cliff. Take his car and leave him here? He wasn't sure whether or not he'd have further need for him. He helped Jasajovic to his feet and walked behind him as he stumbled barefooted through the woods back to the car.

He sat Jasajovic on the ground next to the car while he rummaged through the glove box. "Do you have a touring map in the car?"

Jasajovic watched, shook his head. "In this country such things are not readily available."

In the trunk he found the tire lug wrench and tossed it on the front seat. This would make a better weapon than the rock. In a corner of the trunk he found a five-gallon drum filled with gasoline and a coil of rope. He wrapped the rope around Jasajovic's waist and tied it snugly to ensure that his arms were pinned securely to his sides. Jasajovic winced, complaining that it was too tight.

"Good. Now tell me, where are we going?"

"I shall have to point it out as we go. I can't describe it."

"Try."

"It is 40 kilometers at least."

"Which way?"

He inclined his head. From the position of the sun now starting to descend toward the mountaintops, he judged the direction toward which Jasajovic pointed to be north. "We go back to the main paved road?"

"Yes."

"Are we in Serbia?"

"Here?"

"Yes, here."

Jasajovic shrugged. "I don't know for sure the boundaries. Maybe northern Montenegro. For us it is the same as Serbia."

So far, it fit. Northern Montenegro's mountains were among the highest in the Balkans and were divided by deep canyons and gorges. O'Brien recalled that Montenegro was still considered by the Serbs to be part of Yugoslavia, although they had recently voted to become an independent republic, to the displeasure of the ruling Serbian government.

O'Brien said, "Where Wilson is, is that Bosnia?"

Jasajovic hesitated. "I am not sure. Again, the boundaries are unclear."

"What is the name of the village or town?"

"It is not a village or town."

"The closest one. Wait. Is it near that village where I was jailed, where you picked me up. What was it called, Krjevak?"

The slightest hesitation. "Well, not very far."

Could it be the prison from which he'd escaped? Was Wilson one of the chain-gang laborers? Was Jasajovic leading him back to the prison camp? He had no doubt Jasajovic would try pulling a fast one. If he'd been the one tied up, he'd have done the same.

Time to move on. Thankful for the extra fuel, he removed the drum of gasoline from the trunk and placed it on the floor in front of the back seat. He pointed to the open trunk. "Get in."

"The boot?"

"Whatever."

"I'll suffocate."

"No you won't. Get in before I throw your ass in."

Awkwardly, Jasajovic got into the trunk and O'Brien slammed it shut. Now he wouldn't have to worry if the son of a bitch worked himself loose. Also, if they came to a road checkpoint he wouldn't have a trussed-up passenger sitting alongside him yelling for help. Of course, if they checked the trunk…

Dusk settled quickly, and once the sun disappeared behind the mountains the temperature nose-dived. He wasn't dressed for the cold, but fortunately, the car had a good heater. For an instant, he felt a pang of sympathy for Jasajovic, whom he pictured shivering back in the trunk. But when he recalled how he'd ordered his execution, all sympathetic thoughts vanished. Let the bastard freeze.

He drove slowly down the dirt road, stopping only when he came to a small wooden bridge that crossed a narrow stream, and just beyond, a waterfall. He'd had nothing to eat or drink since early morning, and the sound of the running water intensified his thirst. He found an empty wine bottle rolling around on the floor of the car, probably a leftover of the driver's lunch, and he lay prone on the bank filling it from the waterfall. After he slaked his thirst, he refilled the bottle, retrieved the lug wrench and cautiously opened the trunk. Jasajovic lay on his side blinking, his bonds in place. He held the bottle to Jasajovic's lips and poured water into his mouth until he turned his head away to signal he'd had enough.

"Very kind of you."

He wasn't sure if the remark was sincere or sarcastic, but wondered if their roles had been reversed whether Jasajovic would have been as considerate.

By the time he'd relocked the trunk and started driving, all reflected sunlight had disappeared. The road, bordering on a deep canyon, ran steeply downhill without guardrails, causing him to drive at little more than a walker's pace. Finally, it leveled off, and in the distance he made out winking lights, probably a village. Twenty minutes later he arrived at its intersection with a macadam-paved road. Recalling approximately the direction in which the sun had set, he turned north onto the paved road.

Half an hour later, he passed through a village consisting of an Orthodox church, some stone houses, three shops and a bar-restaurant, all dark.

Except for the occasional reflection from pairs of animal eyes that quickly skittered out of his path, he had the road to himself. The monotony lulled him into drowsiness, when suddenly the car engine began to sputter. He had a moment of fright until he thought to look at the fuel gauge. Empty.

After fumbling in the dark, he found the fuel tank opening in the fender and emptied into it the spare drum of gasoline.

A few minutes later he momentarily dozed off at the wheel. He had to get some rest.

He pulled off through a shallow ditch and into woods that bordered the road. He stretched out on the back seat, ignoring the thumps and muffled cries of his prisoner in the trunk, and drifted off.

He awoke to the gray light of a misty dawn. The musty odor of the damp woods surrounding him brought back memories of camping with his friends as a teen-aged boy in southern Ohio, and of bacon frying over a campfire. For a few moments he lay trying to remember how long it had been since he slept in a real bed with his clothes off. Peg must have already arrived in Sarajevo. Somehow he had to get word to her that he was alive and not far away.

The noise of Jasajovic's kicking prompted him to get up and open the trunk. He had already decided he had no further use for Jasajovic. He had gotten from him all the information he was going to get. Jasajovic had hinted that Wilson was in or close to that prison camp near Krjevak. Whether or not he was telling the truth, even whether Wilson was still alive, remained to be seen. In any case, the prison camp was a starting place to investigate. He had no intention of going there alone. Once he got back to Sarajevo, he'd organize a search team.

Jasajovic said, "I've got to pee."

O'Brien had the lug wrench in his hand. He removed the rope from around Jasajovic's waist. "Sit down."

"On the ground?"

"Unless you can find a chair around."

Jasajovic stared at the lug wrench. "Are you going to kill me?"

"It's a tempting thought."

After Jasajovic was seated, O'Brien bound his feet and legs with the rope, pulling the knots as tight as he could. Jasajovic would be able to free himself, but it would take time. Enough time for him to be on his way—without Jasajovic.

Fifteen minutes after he drove the car back on the road, a pickup truck traveling in the opposite direction passed. Shortly thereafter, a tractor followed by several dusty cars passing the opposite way, warned him that he was approaching a populated area. Ahead the road divided. At the fork, a direction sign told him the left branch led to Sarajevo. He pumped his fist in the air. He'd made it—almost.

Then he spotted, about a quarter mile ahead, a short line of cars and what appeared to be a sentry post. He was approaching a checkpoint, possibly a border. While driving last night, he had anticipated facing this situation and had weighed the options: One, drive to the checkpoint and if he was lucky through it. Two, turn around, drive back a mile, abandon the car and try to walk through the checkpoint. Three, try to circle on foot around the checkpoint.

A glance along the side of the road was enough to rule out Option Three. Signs at 50-foot intervals bore huge red letters in Cyrillic and Romanic: "Warning. Danger. Minefields."

If he was going to be held at the checkpoint, it wouldn't matter whether he was driving or afoot. That settled it. He gunned the car forward and braked behind the last vehicle in line, a beat-up farm truck bearing a load of cabbages.

He fidgeted for five minutes, examining his stubble-faced, unwashed reflection in the rearview mirror. The clothes he wore were still the same ones he'd been given for the video shot in the prison camp. How long ago? Weeks? A month? He'd lost track of the days. He must smell to the heavens. Driving a Mercedes? A raw rookie police officer who hadn't advanced beyond ticketing parked cars would know it had to be stolen.

Rummaging through the glove box for registration papers or an ID, he found only the vehicle's manual.

He watched while a soldier leaned into the window of the truck ahead of him, spoke briefly, then nodded. Another soldier raised the black-and-white striped barrier and waved the truck on.

The first soldier motioned for him to move up. He drew in a deep breath.

☠ CHAPTER 34

The soldier gazed at the license plate. He walked slowly around the car, then leaned into the window and said something. O'Brien smiled, turned up his palms and shrugged. Maybe the Mercedes' license plates indicated that it was an official car. The soldier pointed and gestured for O'Brien to pull the car up next to a wooden hut. A jeep and two motorcycles were parked at the place he designated. For an instant he thought about driving the car through the barrier and taking off. However, a glance at the assault rifles slung over the shoulders of the two soldiers was enough to change his mind.

He parked and sat in the car until the soldier opened the door and beckoned him out. He slid out of the seat and stood alongside the car. The soldier said something, his tone implying that it was an order. O'Brien again turned palms up. The soldier roughly shoved him face forward against the Mercedes, kicked his legs apart and patted him down. No, the car or its license plates didn't impress him. Apparently satisfied that he was unarmed, the soldier grasped the back of his shirt and pushed him into the hut.

The room was small and musty with a rough wood floor. A husky, uniformed man sat behind a desk. Pinned to his epaulets were silvered pips. Probably an officer. He pointed to the only other furniture in the room, a straight-backed wooden chair. O'Brien sat down.

"*Englez?*"

"No, I'm American. *Americki.*" One of the few Serbo-Croatian words he'd learned, this one from his lawyer, Kupreskic, about the only thing he'd done for him.

The officer nodded, "Ah." He shuffled through a pile of papers on his desk, withdrew one and waved it at O'Brien. "*Gdje* Jasajovic?"

Where was Jasajovic? The car, of course, was a giveaway. Inwardly O'Brien prayed that they hadn't heard about himself. He smiled trying to project confidence he didn't really feel. "Back in Krjevak. Official business." He wondered if his nose had grown longer.

The officer peered at him quizzically.

"Official business," he repeated. "He sent me back for some papers. In Sarajevo."

The officer kept gazing at O'Brien. He could hear the wheels in the guy's head meshing; debating whether to labor through the paper work necessary to detain him, check on his story. An eternity later, the officer nodded. "You come back for him later?"

He was buying it! "Yes, later."

The officer rose and extended his hand. O'Brien shook it. "Thank you. Goodbye." He wasn't going to take a chance asking if he was free to go. He headed for the door, restraining himself from running.

The officer walked out with him, shouted something to the soldier at the barrier, then turned smiled and gave O'Brien a palsy-walsy slap on the shoulder.

He strode to the car feeling as though his feet hovered above the ground. At the open barrier he leaned out of the car, pointed down the road and said, "Sarajevo?"

The soldier nodded.

Fifty yards ahead was another barrier he hadn't noticed. A soldier wearing the white leggings and blue helmet of the United Nations guarded this one. As he approached, the gate was lifted and he was waved through. The roadside sign read, "*Dobrodosli U Bosnia-Herzegovina.*" If it had been Washington, D.C., he couldn't have felt more relieved.

Thirty minutes later, he sped through the outskirts of Sarajevo. He bypassed the hotel at which he'd been staying, certain he no longer had a room there.

At the gate to the U.S. Consulate, a Marine guard carrying a clipboard stopped him. He leaned into the car. "Your name, sir?"

"O'Brien." He was tempted to add "Senator," but decided his appearance and odor defiled the office.

The Marine consulted his clipboard. "I don't see your name on the visitor's list, sir."

"I'm here to see Mr. Shaw."

"One moment, sir." He retreated to the sentry box and picked up a phone.

O'Brien watched, fidgeting. The conversation seemed to go on endlessly. Anxious to find Peg, he inwardly screamed: *Get on with it!*

Finally the Marine hung up and approached the car. Pointing to a parking area, he said, "Pull in there and get out of the car, sir."

Silently, he stood guard alongside O'Brien. Five minutes later, Shaw appeared on the top step of the consulate building. He spied O'Brien, and although he was 50 feet away, O'Brien heard him shout, "My God, it *is* you."

Shaw raced down the path and embraced O'Brien. A moment later, he withdrew, held him at arm's length and turned his head away to take a deep breath.

O'Brien said, "Where's Peg?"

"Mrs. O'Brien may still be at the Hotel Strand." He glanced at his watch. "She was due to leave for home today. Come on. Maybe we can still catch her." He grabbed O'Brien's arm and pulled him along.

O'Brien paced Shaw's office, gazing mindlessly at the photographs on the wall while listening to Shaw's end of the phone conversation. Peg had left the hotel for the airport, now Shaw was trying to contact airport operations. He put his hand over the mouthpiece and addressed O'Brien. "The Vice-President offered to send Air Force Two to pick her up, but she didn't want to wait. Decided to take commercial—" He turned back to the phone. "Yes? They're on the tarmac? Stop the plane, get Mrs. O'Brien off. O-B-R-I-E-N. Do it now." He slammed the receiver down. "They were just cleared for take-off. We'll soon know if they were able to abort."

"If they don't?"

"Next stop is Vienna. Worst case, she'll get off there."

The phone rang. Shaw picked it up listened for a moment, then handed it to O'Brien.

His hand trembled as he put the phone to his ear. The room blurred through the mist that filled his eyes, and the golf ball in his throat made it hard for him to get the word out. "Peg?"

CHAPTER 35

Peg ran her fingers down O'Brien's rib cage. "God, Matt. You must have lost at least twenty pounds."

"A little home cooking will take care of that."

They were lying in bed in their room at the Sarajevo Holiday Inn. It was the morning after O'Brien's return.

She caressed the scar over his chest. "Did they get the bullet out?"

"If I ever locate the doctor who took care of me, I'll ask."

Peg was not amused. "When we get back to the states, we're going to have you x-rayed."

He stroked her hair. "Peg, tell me again. Lesley is all right?"

She rolled her eyes. "For the fifth time, Matt. Lesley's fine. She regained consciousness a few minutes after I spoke to you on the phone. The doctor sent her home two days later."

"They did all the necessary tests?"

"Of course. MRI, neurological studies, the works." She smiled. "The day she got home, she insisted on getting back on Taffy."

"My God! You let her?"

"Walking, of course. And I walked alongside."

O'Brien shook his head. "Take a spill. Get right back in the saddle. She's her mother, all right. Fearless."

"Look who's talking."

O'Brien stretched his arms. "Much as I hate to leave, I'm going to have to get out of bed pretty soon. I'm scheduled for a debriefing at the U.N. Headquarters."

"I'm coming with you. I'm not letting you out of my sight."

"Forever?"

"Forever."

"Promise?"

She tickled him.

He lay silently gazing at the ceiling.

She said, "You're thinking about Hank Wilson, aren't you?"

"Uh-huh."

"You're *not* thinking of going after him, are you?"

"'Course not."

She raised herself on her side, resting on her elbow, cupping her cheek in her hand. "Because if you have any thought of going back out there to hunt for Hank, I'm getting right back on that plane and flying out of your life. Forever."

He looked into her blazing green eyes. Still the redheaded fireball. After 20 years she still looked her most appealing when she had her ire up. Still his child bride, barely five feet tall, except for the two times she was pregnant, she never weighed more than 100 pounds. Yet she could make all six feet of him cower when she was mad. A gutsy lady, his Peg. Grew up an army brat. Her Dad, a regular army colonel now retired, had dragged his family all over the world. Matt always felt a little guilty that he'd misled her. Convinced her that as a lawyer's wife, she'd be able to settle into a housewife's role. Then came politics and with it the moves. He had the feeling that she was secretly relieved when he lost the election, and the family would grow roots somewhere.

Peg's eyes became moist. "I mean it, Matt. You won't sweet-talk me out of it this time. I swore I'd never again go through the misery, the chest-beating anguish I felt after Larry Jackson came to the house to tell me you were…" Her voice choked.

"The Vice-President himself came to tell you?"

She nodded. After a moment she regained her composure. "I didn't believe you were dead. He said someone had driven by the consulate building here, and thrown out a bundle of your clothing, all covered with blood." She shivered. "And that video. They didn't want to show it to me, but I insisted. I *had* to see for myself." She shook her head slowly. "Whoever prepared the fake did a professional job of it. Almost convinced me."

"Almost?"

"I guess my faith in your ability to survive blinded me to what everybody else saw as real."

He was still awed that she'd hopped on a plane and flown almost halfway around the world to look for him when she was officially a widow. He drew her into his arms, muzzled his face into her hair, breathed in the fragrance. He raised her chin and kissed her hungrily. She inclined her head back, raised her eyebrows archly. "Again?"

He said, "Remember, I've been starved."

She murmured, "Likewise, I'm sure."

*   *   *

He sat on the bed waiting for Peg to finish putting on her makeup. He felt his chest tighten at the joy of watching her now. Could he conceive of leaving her again to go on the hunt for Wilson? Sadly, he confessed to himself he was wondering how he could do just that. What was wrong with him? Hadn't he taken a pledge? Okay, he was addicted. But, by Christ, this time...

Peg stood, smoothed her slacks while gazing at her reflection in the mirror. "I'm ready. Shall we go?"

*   *   *

The driver let them off in front of the building under the huge blue banner of the United Nations. The clerk at the information desk smiled and said in accented English, "They are waiting for you in the Operations Room. That is up in SFOR."

Peg whispered, "Is that the door after S Three?"

O'Brien whispered back, "SFOR—the NATO Stabilization Force."

A long mahogany conference table surrounded by leather-upholstered chairs occupied almost the entire room. An easel at the far end held a large white pad. On a side wall hung a map of the Balkan republics.

The chairs scraped back and the five people who had been seated at the table stood as Peg and O'Brien entered. Two wore uniforms. Maxmillian Van der Velde sidestepped the chairs in his path and hurried toward them, his pink face wreathed in a broad smile, his arms widely spread. "Ah! Mr. O'Brien. I can't tell you how relieved—" He spied Peg. "Mrs. O'Brien! So good to see you again, and under such pleasant circumstances. A little different from last week, no?"

O'Brien glanced from Van der Velde to Peg. "You've met?"

Peg said, "Mr. Van der Velde and all the U.N. people were very solicitous. I can't tell you how comforting you were, Mr. Van der Velde."

He gave a slight bow then turned to the others. "Allow me to introduce Colonel Clarence McLanahan. Colonel McLanahan is commander of our Special Forces Unit in Sarajevo."

A tall, redheaded, man, mid-fifties, with china-blue eyes peering from a weathered face, inclined his head slightly. Probably British, O'Brien thought.

Van der Velde gestured to the man seated across the table. "Major Jeffrey Forrest is Colonel McLanahan's next in command."

Forrest was in his early thirties, lean, had a thin mustache. He smiled and jauntily touched his fingers to his forehead. "Howjado."

The other two were a man in a dark business suit and a petite Japanese woman. Van der Velde introduced the man as a "staff member of UNMIBH." The woman, Norika Hanaoka, was Deputy UNHCR.

Peg's laugh brought raised brows to the staid gathering. She shook her head, an embarrassed smile on her face. "I'm sorry, I didn't mean that as ridicule. It's just that I thought Washington had canned all the alphabet soup."

O'Brien felt his cheeks heat up. He patted her shoulder. "Peg means that she's impressed by the U.N.'s use of acronyms."

Van der Velde smiled. "Of course. It *is* confusing. UNMIBH—United Nations Mission In Bosnia and Herzegovina. Ms. Hanaoka's department is United Nations High Commission for Refugees."

"See, Peg, nothing to it."

They waited until Peg had taken a seat before they all sat.

Van der Velde said, "Well, Mrs. O'Brien, now you will have a chance to enjoy the sights of Sarajevo before you return home, no?"

Peg flicked a glance at O'Brien seated next to her. "I'm sure there is a lot to see, but I don't think we'll be spending much time here after Matt finishes his business."

"Of course. You are anxious to return to your family. Two girls, is that right?"

She nodded.

Van der Velde slapped his hands on the table. "Well. Shall we get down to business?"

O'Brien took from his pocket the outline he'd scribbled on hotel stationery. "I'll describe my experiences in three parts." He went on to tell how he and Wilson and later Powell searched for gravesites. He told them about Wilson's excited phone call and his subsequent abduction. When he and Powell had returned to the area to resurrect the data that had been stolen, the surveillance craft was apparently shot down.

Colonel McLanahan had been sitting quietly taking notes. Now, he sat up. "Did I hear you correctly? It was *shot down*?"

"That's right."

"Why wasn't I notified of this?"

"I *did* notify the U.N. Is there a Barton on your staff? He's the person I spoke to."

Colonel McLanahan shook his head. "Not on *my* staff."

The civilian staff man coughed into his hand. His face turned red. "Barton is one our junior people." He emphasized "junior." He began writing, his pen pressing deeply into his pad. "I will speak with Barton. Find out why Mr. O'Brien's call was not passed on to you."

O'Brien said, "Shall I go on?"

Van der Velde nodded. "Please."

O'Brien told of his excursion into the area where the helicopter had been shot down, and of observing trucks go into an opening in the side of a mountain. "They went into what I surmise was the cavern Wilson and Powell had picked up from their ground-penetrating radar reflections."

McLanahan said, "This was where the anti-aircraft fire came from?"

"It was the same area. I can't be sure if the AA came from the cavern. I saw no gun emplacements."

"Did you report this?"

"I'm doing that now. I never had a chance to make a report." He related being shot while standing at the window of his hotel room less than two hours after his return to Sarajevo. "You all probably know as much as I do about my being abducted from some hospital here. My first recollection of the entire affair is waking up in a prison camp. It was only later that I learned I had been reported dead."

He described the videotaping and his escape.

Peg sat, her hand to her cheek, her mouth agape. When he finished telling how he had overpowered Dodic, she cried out, "Oh, Matt. How awful."

McLanahan said, "Is this the first you've heard about this, Mrs. O'Brien?"

"I haven't had a chance to go over the details with Peg. Don't forget, I just got back yesterday." O'Brien grinned. "We had more important things to catch up on."

"Of course."

Major Forrest said, "Sounds like you've been trained in survival methods."

"I've had some training, yes."

Peg said, "He's too modest to tell you. He was taken prisoner in Vietnam and escaped."

"Come on, Peg. If I start telling war stories, we'll be here forever."

Van der Velde turned to Ms. Hanaoka, "Norika, what about the prison camp Mr. O'Brien told us about?"

"We have been assured by the Bosnian and Serbian governments that all detainees have been repatriated. If there are any prison camps remaining, they are not authorized."

Detainees. O'Brien smiled at the euphemism.

"Norika and her co-workers have had a challenging job," said Van der Velde. "They've repatriated and resettled more than two million war refugees and prisoners." He addressed O'Brien. "Please continue."

"The final chapter in this saga concerns my next imprisonment."

He told of his capture by the farmers, of being jailed in Krjevak, and of his being bailed out by Jasajovic.

Van der Velde rose in his chair. "Is that *our* Jasajovic?"

The faces of the others took on quizzical expressions. O'Brien explained that Jasajovic had been a member of their committee.

"Well," said Van der Velde. "*That* was kind of him, no?"

"Jasajovic had other plans for me." He told of his being driven up to the mountain in or near Montenegro. "There *our* Mr. Jasajovic ordered me out of the car and told his driver to shoot me."

Van der Velde put his hand over his mouth. "*God in de Hemel!*"

"Yes, I'm sure *someone* was looking over me." He described his escape into the woods and his overpowering Jasajovic's bodyguard/driver.

"And Jasajovic—did you throw him over the cliff too?"

"No, but I thought about it."

He concluded with the account of his drive back to Sarajevo in Jasajovic's car.

Van der Velde sat back, removed a handkerchief from his back pocket and mopped his face. "I feel as though I have just finished seeing a cinema with the American actor Harrison Ford."

Forrest said, "More like James Bond."

McLanahan stood and went up to the easel at the front of the room. "We have some work to do."

☠ CHAPTER 36

With a grease pencil, McLanahan marked a place on the map. "You think this is about where the prison camp is located?"

O'Brien said, "As well as I can judge."

McLanahan turned to Forrest. "What do you think, Jeff? The Rambler?"

Forrest nodded. "Yes, should be just the thing."

O'Brien said, "Mind if I ask what The Rambler is?"

"We're planning a fly-by. Surveillance. We'd rather not risk loss of personnel or a conventional plane. Don't need the speed and altitude— or expense—of a UAV such as Predator or Firebee II. We have in our arsenal a drone that should be just right for this."

"The Rambler?"

"Our code name. Developed by a man named Michelson at Georgia Tech Research Institute."

O'Brien snickered. "Ramblin' Wreck from Georgia Tech."

"It was designed for urban traffic surveillance. Flies at low altitudes. Small enough to make a difficult target. Yes, should be just the thing." He turned to O'Brien. "I'm sure you'd like to come along when we're set up. See how it operates."

Peg shook her head fiercely. "No you don't, Matt."

O'Brien turned his palms up. "You heard the lady. No, I've had enough excitement for a while. But—" He spoke to Peg, eyes pleading. "I'd like to hang around here, see the results."

Peg's lips compressed. "When do you expect to do this by-fly thing?"

"Fly-by. Within a day or two."

She sighed. "Well, I guess we can wait another day or two before we start back home."

He leaned over and kissed her cheek. "Thanks, Mom."

She shoved his shoulder. "My hero."

*   *   *

Two days later, Peg and O'Brien had just returned from a drive to Mt. Jahorina. Peg was still ecstatic about the scenery.

"You can imagine how spectacular it is when it's snow-covered," said O'Brien.

"I wish I could have gone skiing with you. And wouldn't the girls have loved it?"

O'Brien said, "You go on up to the room. I'll stop at the desk to see if there are any messages."

The clerk handed him an envelope. It bore the NATO seal. His pulse sped as he tore it open. The message read: "Photo recon completed. Stop by. McLanahan"

Up in his room, he showed it to Peg. "I'm going to grab a taxi, run over and see those photos. Want to come?"

"No, you go along. I'm going to rest a bit. Where shall we go for dinner?"

"There's a good restaurant about two blocks from here. *Plav Kamenica.* Means blue oyster, only they don't have oysters. But the veal is excellent."

*   *   *

McLanahan and Forrest were bent over a table examining a dozen or more photos with hand lenses. Forrest glanced up.

"Ah. There you are." He handed O'Brien the lens. "Have a look. Is this the place?"

The photos were still damp, the edges curled, but he flattened one out and peered through the glass. The image was grainy, but after studying it for a half minute he could make out the cement-block building with camouflage-painted sides. He recognized the door through which he had left and the small window at the kitchen. There were no cars or trucks present. "Did you get these from your Rambler?"

Forrest nodded.

"The detail is remarkable. You'd never pick it up from a satellite photo if you didn't know where to look or know what you're looking for."

McLanahan said, "Nobody seems to be around the building."

"No, all the action is inside. When I was there, everyone was gone all day except for a guard and a woman who does the cooking. The woman told me the prisoners are out somewhere working. I never asked her where. I assume in the fields."

"Fields? What fields? We did a fly-by recon in all directions around the building. There's no cultivation anywhere for miles in our photos."

O'Brien shrugged. "Then I have no idea where they go. But they return in trucks just before dusk."

"Odd," said McLanahan.

"What's that?"

He went to a corkboard mounted to the wall. Pinned to it was an aerial photo. He pointed. "We parked the drone in the woods here, engines shut down. Had our video camera trained on the building from dusk to dawn. None of the frames show any activity whatsoever."

"You can do that? Park it and re-start it from a control station?"

Forrest said, "That's only one of its capabilities. The drone we used has a 20-millimeter gun on a swivel-mount. It's coupled with a Doppler radar. If anybody came within 20 yards of the drone to, say, damage it, they'd end up Swiss cheese."

"Was the drone shot at?"

"No. That's another thing," Forrest said. "If it *were* shot at and if the engines were to be knocked out, it can glide for a short time. Then a ballistic parachute in the tail cone is deployed. We'd get our Rambler back home."

O'Brien shook his head. "I was awed by the technology of Wilson's camcopter. This one is right out of Star Trek. Where did you launch the drone from?"

"There's a burned-out prison camp about 20 klicks away. A dirt road runs into it off the main road from Sarajevo."

O'Brien said, "That's probably the place we parked and—wait. That's where we launched our UAV for recon. Where our bird was shot down."

The place from which Wilson, and later Powell, had launched their UAV, and had discovered the mountain containing the cavern was the same site from which Forrest had launched The Rambler for reconnaissance of the prison camp. This wasn't coincidence. The open field adjacent to the burned-out prison was one of the few places for miles not covered by dense forest, making it a natural launch site.

It was coming together. *The mountain with the cavern was close to the prison camp.* The prisoners weren't cultivating fields. They were trucked each day to the nearby mountain. *Their work was in the cavern.*

Forrest said, "How many guards did you say there were?"

"I judged there were about fifteen."

McLanahan nodded. "That would fit. There seems to be a small barracks behind the prison building. It probably would accommodate about that number, more or less." He turned to Forrest. "How soon do you think we could assemble a commando team, Jeff?"

Forrest drummed the table, then re-examined three of the photos. "Flat roof. Probably could fast rope an eight-man team. Good chance to use ROCKING HORSE. Give me forty-eight hours."

"Let's do it."

"ROCKING HORSE?" O'Brien said. "Mind clueing me in?"

"Jeff's developed a technique for rescuing hostages. He's got a team that has been training for a situation like this for—what is it, Jeff? A month?"

"Six weeks."

McLanahan nodded. "Why don't you describe it?"

"Yes, sir. We want the fastest insertion possible. Maximize surprise. Briefly, our squad flies to the area in a Sikorsky UH-60 Blackhawk helicopter and hovers while an escorting Apache AH-64 gunship does a thirty-second sweep to take out roof sentries or periphery guards, then—"

"Hold it, Major. Isn't this a night operation?"

"Yes sir. Midnight, or a bit after. Pilots and most of our squad use night-vision goggles."

O'Brien said, "Okay, they should be able to see the prison roof. But trees surround the building. If there are guards outside they'll be shielded by foliage."

"No problem, sir. Apache's 30-millimeter chain gun is equipped with automatic thermal tracking and firing. Trees can't hide body heat." He glanced up, added, "In case we have to call in additional fire after we're down, we all wear IFF markers."

"Identifies friendlies. That answers my next question. Awesome. Please go on."

"Apache zaps the barracks with a laser-directed Hellfire II missile. That should take care of any guards who aren't already in the main prison. Blackhawk hovers, lowers a 90-foot line to the roof of the prison building. Our squad can rappel down in under 20 seconds. They don't brake with their feet. Use their hands. At the bottom their gloves are smoking." He picked up one of the photos, pointed. "Two men with H&K MP5K-PDWs equipped with Starlite sights move along the back and sides of the roof. Take out any of the guards that may be left standing. Four others drop ropes and rappel down the side of the building to the ground. They cover each side of the front gate. The last two men lay a light demolition charge up here, on what appears to be a roof access door. We're in contact with each other by small FM radio headsets in our helmets. At a signal, we simultaneously blast open the front gate and roof access. Move in from top and bottom. In training, we've made it from helicopter to inside a building in less than three minutes. If our estimate of the total number of guards is right, there should be no more than three or four on duty in the main building at that time of night. We should be able to take them without harming any of the prisoners. Once in we—," He hesitated. "—do whatever's necessary."

There was little question what Forrest meant. "Take no prisoners" applied only to the guards. "How do you propose to evacuate your men and the prisoners?"

Forrest grinned. "Till now we've never planned for one hundred hostages. They've got trucks, right? No reason we can't borrow them, is there? To be honest, once the operation is secured we'll just wing it."

O'Brien's imagination was jump-started. Going along on a raid, even as an observer was out of the question. But maybe he could talk Peg into staying here to see the result of the raid. There was the slim chance that Hank Wilson was alive and would turn up among the prisoners. On the other hand, he couldn't wait to see his girls and hold them.

A young woman was at his elbow. "Mr. O'Brien? Phone for you. Take it in my office."

Peg was on the line. "Are you almost finished?"

"Uh-huh, we're done. I'll call a taxi, be there in ten minutes. Get ready."

"I *am* ready. The restaurant's just two blocks from here. The doorman showed me the direction. Blue Oyster, right? It's a lovely evening. I'll meet you there. I need the walk."

It took a moment for Peg's words to register.

"Wait! Peg." No response. Shit. Goddam unstable Sarajevo phone lines. He couldn't count the number of times he'd been cut off in mid-conversation. He banged the phone back in its cradle. Doubted Peg'd call back; figured she'd already said her piece. Damn. He didn't want her wandering around Sarajevo by herself even though it was early evening. Maybe the doorman could catch her before…He punched in "O." The operator came on after ten rings. Couldn't understand his request for the phone number of Holiday Inn. No phone book around, either. The young woman who'd called him to the phone had gone somewhere back in the building. Damn. Damn. Too late now anyway, Peg'd be halfway there.

☠ CHAPTER 37

To call for a taxi now and wait for one to take him to the restaurant, forget it. He raced back to the office where McLanahan and Forrest sat on either side of the table. The photos were piled in the middle. Forrest was scribbling on a yellow pad.

O'Brien was breathless. "Could I ask one of you gentlemen to run me over to *Klav Kamenica?*"

Forrest looked up. "Glad to. Jolly good food. Needn't be in such a rush. They're open till midnight."

"Sorry to hurry you, but I'm meeting Peg there. She just called. Said she's walking over from the Holiday Inn."

McLanahan and Forrest exchanged glances. Forrest dropped the pad on the table, grabbed his uniform jacket from where it hung on the back of a chair, and slipped it on while he was halfway through the door. "Let's go."

The white van with U.N. markings stood in the small fence-enclosed parking lot next to the building. Forrest jumped into the driver's side and unlocked the passenger's door for him. Yelling for O'Brien to buckle up, he gunned the van out of the lot. "Shouldn't take over ten minutes," he said. His eyes were on the road ahead. "Her idea, walking to the restaurant?"

"Yes. Probably not a good one, right?" He hoped for a contradiction, some encouragement.

Forrest kept silent for a few moments. Then. "We'll soon see, won't we."

O'Brien tried to will the car to go faster with his body. At an intersection they ran into a traffic snarl.

Forrest muttered, "Damned evening rush." He spun the wheel to the left, bypassing the line of cars in his path, crossing into the lane of cars coming toward them, narrowly missing a head-on collision with a pickup truck. He darted back to the right through a small space in the line of cars going in his direction, ran one wheel up on the sidewalk and raced on, the van tilting to the left, until a parked car at the curb loomed into their path. He slammed on the brake, throwing them into their seat belts. Blocked.

Hand on the horn, he swung back out into the line of cars but they were forced to inch along until they arrived at an intersection. He cut the wheel to the right, turning into the side street. There was less traffic here. "We'll bypass that mess. Little farther this way, but…"

O'Brien had his foot pressed to the floorboard. Forrest's estimate was off. It was already 15 minutes since they'd left the U.N. building. Four more minutes until he finally spotted the blue neon restaurant sign half a block away. A line of trucks and cars, barely moving, stood between them and the restaurant. "I can make it faster on foot." Without waiting for an answer, he opened the door, was partway out when he was choked by the seat belt. After releasing it, he leaped to the pavement and raced down the sidewalk.

Be there, Peg. Be there, Peg. The plea kept cadence with his feet pounding the pavement.

He flung open the door. Soft music and a smiling, tuxedo-clad headwaiter greeted him. He scanned the small room. Half a dozen tables. White tablecloths, white napkins ballooning out of wine glasses. Two couples seated at separate tables, eating. Peg nowhere in sight. The floor sagged under his feet.

"Is she here? My wife?"

The headwaiter had a blank stare on his face.

"My wife, damn it. Has she arrived?"

The headwaiter gestured toward the dining room. "Not one of these people?"

O'Brien hurried back out of the restaurant, peered both directions down the street. As far as he could see there were no pedestrians. He took a few steps in the direction of the hotel, hoping, hoping to find her. A bleating horn at the curb stopped him. Forrest had pulled up, leaned his head out of the van window. "Not there?"

O'Brien shook his head.

"Get in. We'll cruise on down."

He drove slowly, while O'Brien peered out the window into door-ways of shops along the way, all shuttered closed. They came to a nar-row intersection. Fifty yards down the alley, he spotted outdoor tables and chairs of a small restaurant. Maybe…O'Brien jumped out of the van. Over his shoulder, he shouted, "Going for a look. Be right back."

He sped to the restaurant. A man in a white apron, a white towel over an arm, leaned against the doorframe. He swept an arm to the inside. "*Vecera?* Dinner, sir?"

In the restaurant, tables were covered with red-checkered cloths. A gray-haired man was seated at one, his face bent over a plate.

O'Brien turned and ran back down the street, hopped into to the van. The Holiday Inn entrance was a block away. "Let's go to the hotel."

The traffic had thinned. At the hotel, O'Brien jumped out, heard Forrest call, "I'll wait here."

In the lobby, O'Brien found the doorman leaning against the bell captain's desk. He rushed up. "Did you see my wife leave?"

The doorman stared, uncomprehending.

"American woman. Asked directions to the Blue—*Klav Kamenica.*"

"Ah. Yes."

"Did you see her go?"

He gazed at the carpet for a moment. Then looked up. "No. I was busy. No, I did not see her leaving. But she could find it easily. It is just down—"

O'Brien dashed to the house phones, punched the "O" and asked for his room. After six rings he slammed the phone down. His own fault. His own fucking fault. Why didn't he leave this place when she wanted to go?

He dashed back to the street where Forrest sat in the parked van. He leaned into the window. "She's not there. Something's happened to her. Major, it can't be more than half an hour since she left the hotel. If—." He couldn't bring himself to say the unthinkable.

Forrest said, "We'll have to get the city police on this. Wish we had a phone in this van. Have to use the hotel phones." He bounded out of the van.

"I'll come with you." O'Brien hurried alongside Forrest, heading for the phones in the lobby. His anger at himself was mixed with frustration. The Sarajevo police. They hadn't been any help when Wilson had been snatched. He didn't expect them to be any more efficient now. "Aren't you part of the police force?"

"We're military police, but we can help. If someone's carried her off, they can't have gotten very far. I'll contact our communications center. Set up roadblocks around the periphery of the city. We may be able prevent anyone from leaving Sarajevo with her."

While Forrest spoke on the phone to someone at SFOR, O'Brien hurried to the front desk. It would take him too long to explain the problem to the police on the phone; better let the desk clerk do it. "Something's happened to my wife," he told the clerk. "Call the police."

When the clerk hesitated, he growled, "Do it now." No mistaking the desperation in this voice.

"Yes sir."

He stood at the desk while the clerk spoke rapidly into the phone. After he hung up, he said, "Police will be here in a few minutes. Is your wife injured?"

"Don't know." He wasn't going to start a lengthy explanation.

Forrest had finished his call, and walked over to stand next to O'Brien. "I'll instruct the police to start their search from here."

There was some relief in having someone who could take charge, someone who appeared to know how to handle the situation.

CHAPTER 38

O'Brien spent the night speeding around the city with Forrest, going from one roadblock to another on the outskirts of Sarajevo, responding to reports of cars carrying foreigners being stopped. All were false alarms. By morning, Forrest, obviously weary after the long night, left him off at the hotel and went home to bed.

O'Brien paced his room, kept busy phoning. He called Brooke and Lesley. After telling them of their mother's disappearance, he tried to sound encouraging. But judging by their choked voices, knew he'd failed.

He spoke to his brothers. Mark in Minneapolis offered to come to Sarajevo, but he convinced him there was nothing he could do. Luke, who lived in Reston, said he and Shaina would make sure the girls were all right, stay with them if the woman who was house-sitting with them had to leave for any reason.

As he expected, all Shaw at the U.S. Consulate could offer were platitudes.

At ten in the morning a man on the phone identified himself as Detective Elkasovic of the Sarajevo Detective Bureau, and a chill shook his body.

"We may have in the case of your wife, a very small break," the detective said. "A woman living near the hotel claims she saw a lady being forced into a car. This happened yesterday evening. My superiors instructed me to call you and inform you of our progress." He was leaving his office to question her now.

Thank God. At last a chink in the void. "Can I come with you?"

"I cannot promise anything will come of it, but certainly you are welcome to join me."

Forty-five minutes later, O'Brien was seated on a worn couch in the tiny living room of a two-story apartment building above a row of stores, a block from the Holiday Inn and on the opposite side of the street. Alongside him sat Detective Elkasovic, portly, about 50, with a waxed moustache. In a rocking chair opposite them was a thin elderly woman dressed in a black chador, her dark-complexioned face creased by wrinkles.

The detective nodded while she described what she had seen, then translated for O'Brien in his thickly accented English. "Yesterday evening she was looking out of the window. A woman was walking across the street. A black car drove slowly alongside her, then stopped. Two men got out. They held the woman by the arms and put her in the car."

O'Brien said. "Did she describe the men?"

Elkasovic spoke to the woman and relayed her reply. "It was too dark. She did not see their faces clearly."

O'Brien had watched Peg unpack, knew she had brought only one "dressy" outfit, a deep purple pants suit. No doubt that's what she'd have worn. "Could she tell how the woman was dressed?"

Her response to Elkasovic's question was, "*Tamno plav.*"

"She thinks it was dark blue."

"A dress?"

"*Ne. Pantalone.*"

The description fit. "That's Peg!"

The lady tried to resist being pulled into the car. But with two men...?

"Why didn't this woman call someone to help, phone the police?" O'Brien had a hard time hiding his annoyance.

The detective swept an arm around the tiny room. "These people have no telephones. And to go out on the street, even if she called the man living next door to help, most of these men have used up all their heroic acts in the—troubles."

He finished questioning the woman, made notes in a pad and thanked her.

Back at his hotel, O'Brien paced the room, pounding his fist into his other palm. Even when he was held prisoner, he had never felt so lonely and helpless. As a captive, he had kept his mind occupied planning ways to escape. This was different. Peg was part of him, an extension of himself, out somewhere beyond his reach. He had to be actively doing something. Anything.

He left the hotel and walked the route Peg must have taken toward the restaurant. At the spot where, according to the old woman's description, she had been taken, he examined every inch of the sidewalk and gutter and the street, looking for clues the police may have missed. Nothing.

O'Brien knew that the chances of finding Peg alive and in reasonably good shape diminished with each passing hour.

Forrest called late in the day. After inquiring about Peg said, "Don't know if you have any further interest in that prison camp you told us about, but SFOR is going ahead with preparations. The commando raid is on for tonight."

"Good." Two days ago he'd have given a month of his senate pension for the chance to go along. Now they couldn't pay him to leave.

"I'll keep you informed."

At the coffee shop counter he pushed food around on his plate, leaving most of it uneaten.

For hours he lay fully clothed on his bed, dozing spasmodically, seeing Peg's face in shadows on the ceiling. Shortly after two in the morning, unable to keep his eyes shut, he went down to the lobby. As he walked to the door the bell captain on duty called to him. "Sir, perhaps you should not walk out on the street. It is dangerous at night."

"I know." He kept on walking.

He wandered aimlessly along the deserted street leading from the hotel to the restaurant. The police were treating this as a random abduction. Even a foreigner, especially a woman, Detective Elkasovic had said, should know better than to be walking alone in the city. *Any* city. O'Brien wasn't convinced. No, Peg had been a target. They had probably expected him to be with her, and had planned to take him as well. Jasajovic and his gang had a hand in this. But how did they know where to stalk their prey? Who would have known that she would be going to the—. Jesus. Of course, the bell captain. The hotel had no concierge at the moment. On his way out of the hotel to see the SFOR surveillance photos, O'Brien had told the bell captain to make dinner reservations for seven o'clock at *Klav Kamenica*.

He raced back to the hotel. The lobby was deserted except for a reservation clerk and the bell captain. He rushed up to the bell captain's desk. This wasn't the same guy. "Where is the bell man on evening duty?"

"Sir?"

He spoke slowly. "I want to speak to the bell captain who was here day before yesterday, at around six in the evening."

"He is off duty, sir. Can I help?"

He started to explain but stopped. Trying to get anything accomplished in a country where he didn't speak the language made him want to tear his hair out.

O'Brien hurried to the reservation desk. He asked the clerk to place a call for Elkasovic at police headquarters. Waiting while the clerk placed the call, he heard an annoying tapping, looked down for the source found it was his own foot on the floor.

The clerk placed his hand over the mouthpiece and addressed him. "Detective Elkasovic is off duty."

"I want to speak to whoever is taking his calls."

The clerk relayed the message, listened, then turned back to him. "It is a detective called Icic."

"Good." He reached for the phone.

"But he does not speak or understand English."

Shit. "When does Elkasovic come on duty?"

The message was conveyed and the answer came back. "He will be off for the next two days."

Everybody in this goddam country was off duty. "Is there anyone there who can—never mind. I have to have the name and address of the bell captain who is on duty evenings."

Hesitation. Then, "Sir?"

He repeated through clenched teeth.

"I am very sorry, sir. I am not permitted to give out such information."

Of course. "Who is?"

"Perhaps the manager."

"Good. Let me speak to him."

"He will be in after nine in the morning."

He debated having the clerk phone the manager at his home for the information he wanted. But decided he would need someone who could go with him to the bell captain's home. Someone with expertise at interrogation.

Forrest. He had to reach Forrest.

He apologized to the woman who answered in a sleepy British accent, for calling at this hour. "My name is O'Brien. Are you Mrs. Forrest?"

"Yes. Oh, of course. Mr. O'Brien. Jeff has told me about the dreadful thing that happened to your wife. How awful. You'll want to speak to Jeff, I'm sure. But, he's not at home. He's—he's out on NATO business, I'm afraid."

Of course. He'd forgotten about the commando raid. Forrest had gone along. It was ten minutes till three. He had no idea how long it would be before he returned.

Mrs. Forrest was still talking. "He called an hour ago to tell me—reassure me he was all right."

"Yes, I know he went along on a commando mission."

"Oh, you do know about that. Well, they're back safely. Actually, they're at the office now. Writing up their report."

Thank God. "Thank you so much, Mrs. Forrest."

"It's Keri. And I do pray with all my heart for the safety of your wife."

*   *   *

He handed a five-mark note to the hotel bellman who drove him to the U.N. building, thankful for the transportation at this time of the night when it would be impossible to get a taxi.

Keri Forrest had given him the number of the direct phone line to SFOR. He had called before leaving the hotel, and a night watchman admitted him and directed him to the SFOR offices.

The group seated around the long conference table looked like a conclave of weary Martians. Their faces were still painted in green and black camouflage colors. They wore fatigues and boots and holstered side arms.

Colonel McLanahan stood at the head of the table next to a large pad on an easel. Forrest was seated alongside the head end of the table. He raised his hand in greeting when O'Brien walked into the room.

McLanahan said, "Ah, Mr. O'Brien. Please have a seat. We're just now reviewing the expedition."

Although he was anxious to get Forrest aside, he'd have to wait until this session was over.

When he was seated, McLanahan said, "This proved to be a valuable exercise."

Exercise? "You *did* find the prison I described, didn't you?"

"Oh, yes. Your description was most accurate. Our team went in by helicopter. We hoped to take them by surprise." He smiled wryly. "Unfortunately, *we* were the ones that were surprised. The place was deserted—empty as a tomb. Everything had been cleared out."

CHAPTER 39

O'Brien shook his head. "I'm sorry if you were misled. I can assure you when I was there—"

McLanahan raised a hand. "Oh, I don't doubt your word. There was sufficient evidence that the evacuation had been recent. Even though ours turned out to be a dry run, it gave us an opportunity to hone our skills. I repeat what I said before, it was a valuable experience. How many prisoners did you estimate had been there, Mr. O'Brien?"

"Ninety more or less, judging by the number I saw returning in trucks."

Forrest said, "That fits. We counted the cells and assumed there had been two or three to a cell. Our problem now is, where could they hide that many men?"

"Perhaps 'dispose' might be a more accurate term," said McLanahan.

O'Brien said, "Are you suggesting they may have all been killed?"

"It wouldn't be the first time that has happened in this war."

No, McLanahan was right. O'Brien recalled the horror stories he'd heard from the lips of survivors. "I have another thought. Maybe I'm over-optimistic, but I've theorized that these prisoners were slave laborers. That they were doing some type of work inside that cavern I told you about. Maybe they're being kept inside the cavern."

McLanahan nodded. "It's a thought. There's one way to find out." He glanced at the wall clock. "But, it's been a long night. Let's adjourn and get some sleep. We'll discuss our options after we've given them further thought."

Chairs scraped back as they all stood. O'Brien worked his way around the table to Forrest. Although he would have liked to suggest that they go now to the bell captain's house, a closer look at Forrest's red-rimmed eyes, his sagging shoulders, convinced him it would have to wait.

Forrest watched as O'Brien approached. "Did you want to ask me something, Mr. O'Brien?"

"It's Matt. Yes, I am quite anxious to talk to you."

"I assume there's no word about your wife?"

"I'm afraid not. But—"

Forrest said, "They're locking up this room. Why don't you come along with me? We can talk on the way to my car. By the way, can I drive you back to your hotel?"

"I'd appreciate that."

"Not at all."

While Forrest drove, O'Brien told of his suspicion that the bell captain may have divulged to someone where they had planned to go for dinner. "I'd like to question that bell man, find out who he may have given that information to."

"I assume he's not on duty now."

"He works evenings."

"Would you like me to go with you to his home and try to get him to talk?"

"Jeff, you're a mind reader."

Forrest grinned. "I knew you didn't come to our office in the middle of the night just to hear about our little raid. Can the interrogation of the bell man wait till I've washed the paint off my face and changed into some clean clothes?"

"By all means. Meanwhile, I'll speak to the manager when he comes in. Find out where the bell man lives."

*   *   *

Josip Sahbaz, manager of the Holiday Inn, looked up from the notation on his desk. "I would like to accommodate you, but may I ask your reason for requesting this information, Mr. O'Brien?"

After O'Brien explained, Sahbaz said, "Isn't this a matter for the police to investigate?"

"The Sarajevo police detective in charge of the investigation is off for two days. His replacement has no knowledge of the case, and if he has to be briefed, it will just waste more time."

"What makes you think my bellman knows anything about your wife's disappearance?"

"Look, I'm not accusing your man of doing anything illegal, but the officer of SFOR with whom I am working might be able to get a lead from him." He'd tried to plead his case without being confrontational. But this guy was putting up hurdles. He leaned over the desk and glared. "I don't know how to make this any clearer, Sahbaz. We're not talking about fixing a stopped up toilet in my room. We're talking about my missing wife. Every minute that goes by is another minute during which her life is in jeopardy. Do you understand?"

Sahbaz drew back. He flicked a glance at the door, then at the phone on his desk.

O'Brien sat back down. Maybe he'd been coming on too strong. He didn't want to scare the guy into calling security. "Look, Mr. Sahbaz. I'm tired. And I'm worried. Worried sick. I need help—your help."

Sahbaz gazed at his desktop for a few moments, deep in thought, then scribbled a notation on a piece of paper and handed it to O'Brien. It read: "Salih Gutic." Following the name was an address.

O'Brien folded the paper and put it in his pocket. "Thank you, Mr. Sahbaz. And I'm sorry if I lost my cool." He got up to leave; his hand was on the doorknob. He turned. "One other thing. I'd appreciate it if you don't alert Gutic that we're coming."

Sahbaz was silent for two beats. Then, "I think I owe that much to my employee. Why would you object?"

"If he's done nothing wrong, neither you nor he have anything to worry about. If he *has*, I'm sure you wouldn't want to protect him or do anything to impede our search for my wife."

"Such as?"

O'Brien shrugged. "Give him time to concoct a lie. Warn those who have taken my wife. Run off and hide. I don't know, but anything that might make it more difficult to find my wife."

Sahbaz nodded. "I see your point. I will consent to your wishes. And, Mr. O'Brien, I pray to God that you find your wife and that she is well."

Forrest's call came at 9:15 a.m. A few minutes later he pulled up at the hotel, and O'Brien got in the van.

Gutic's apartment was in a multi-storied building. Half a dozen people who had been walking by, stopped and stared when the white van with U.N. markings parked in front. O'Brien heard murmurs as Forrest, wearing his uniform with holstered sidearm, got out. The outer door of the building was locked, but a man who was leaving held the door for them. Forrest asked him which apartment Gutic lived in.

They walked up two floors, pressed the bell button outside the door. A blonde woman about 35 peered around the partly open the door. At the sight of the uniformed man her eyes and mouth opened. When Forrest asked for Gutic, she stammered an answer.

Forrest said, "She says he's still asleep." He turned back to her. "Do you speak English?"

"A little."

"Would you mind waking him? We would like to speak with him?"

She hurried to the back of the apartment.

Two minutes later, she reappeared followed by a pajama-clad man in his late thirties or early forties. His tousled black hair, half-open eyes and stubble-bearded face attested to the hotel manager's promise that he would not alert Gutic to their visit. Although he looked quite different out of uniform, O'Brien recognized him as the man who he had asked to make reservations for Peg and himself at the restaurant.

Forrest said, "Mr. Gutic, I'm Major Forrest of the United Nations International Police Task Force. This is Mr. O'Brien. Perhaps you remember him. He is a guest at the Holiday Inn."

Gutic swallowed and nodded. No smile.

"We would like to ask you some questions."

"Wh-what questions?"

"May we come in?"

He stepped aside and led them to a tiny but neat living room furnished with a sofa, two easy chairs and a coffee table. On the floor was an ornate oriental rug. The wall behind the sofa was occupied by a large painting on black velvet of the Dome on the Rock in Jerusalem.

Gutic gestured to the easy chairs. His wife sat on the sofa and he sat next to her. From a back room came an infant's cry. Gutic's wife glanced briefly in the direction of the crying child, but she remained seated and reached for her husband's hand. Her knuckles, O'Brien saw, were white.

Forrest said, "Do you recall making reservations for Mr. O'Brien at *Plav Kamenica?*"

No small talk. No beating around the bush.

Gutic shifted his gaze to O'Brien, held it for a moment as though trying to recall, then made a small nod.

"Do you remember, after you had made the reservations at the restaurant, a man asking you where the O'Briens were having dinner?"

Forrest was obviously a skilled interrogator. Even O'Brien was taken by surprise at the question.

Gutic's dark complexion suddenly turned gray. "The man who said he had an anniversary surprise for them?"

Bingo!

"Yes. Do you know the man?"

"No. I thought most probably he was, like Mr. O'Brien, a guest at the hotel. Probably a friend of his. Yes. I remember he called him by his first name. I don't remember what that was."

"Do you remember what he looked like?"

Gutic looked at his wife, then gazed at the carpet. He looked up at O'Brien. "A man maybe about fifty or sixty. Serbian, I think. Quite pleasant. Heavier than either of you. His hair on the top was gone. How do you say? Bald?"

Could it be the man who had given him the script to read for the video recording at the prison camp? The one O'Brien thought of as Baldy?

Gutic's glance went back and forth from Forrest to O'Brien. "Is something wrong?"

O'Brien said, "My wife has been abducted. Kidnapped. Stolen."

Gutic sat bolt upright as though he had been knocked back in his seat. Mrs. Gutic's hand flew to her cheek. She drew in a sharp breath. "No, no. Salih did not do this."

O'Brien held up a hand. "We know he did not. But we believe that the man who asked your husband where we were going had something to do with it. That is why we want to get as accurate a description of him as we can."

Gutic pressed his hands together. "Oh, *now* I make the connection. I had heard of a hotel guest—. This was your *wife?* I am so sorry, sir. I will help in any way that I can."

Mrs. Gutic leaned over and gently placed her hand on O'Brien's forearm. "Oh, sir, I am so sorry for your wife—and for you."

These were honest people. O'Brien felt guilty for having suspected Gutic of collaboration.

Forrest stood. He removed a card from his pocket. "Well, thank you for your cooperation. We won't keep you any longer. If you can think of anything else about the man, you can phone me at the number on the card or let Mr. O'Brien know."

Seated in the van, O'Brien told Forrest about Baldy. "I wonder if it's the same guy Gutic described."

Forrest raised an eyebrow. "Know how many bald Serbian men there are in this city?"

O'Brien sighed. "Yeah. I guess it's back to square one." He had a fair idea where square one led.

*   *   *

Forrest dropped him off at the hotel. A message from Shaw informed him that, "We are distributing circulars offering a generous reward for information concerning your wife."

O'Brien wasn't impressed. He wondered how much success they'd had here with such offers. They hadn't done anything to bring Wilson back.

At noon, Zee called from the lobby offering his sympathy and help. O'Brien invited him up.

Seated in the room, Zee said, "I have in Sarajevo many friends. I have alerted them. Our community is closely knit. If your wife is somewhere in the city, sooner or later they will hear about it."

It had better be sooner. Later may be too late. "Thank you, Zee. We can use all the help we can get."

"You have had such bad experiences here," Zee gazed at the floor. "Most of our people are good, honest and work hard. I am sad because there are a few…"

"You don't have to apologize for your people, Zee. I've met the good ones. The other kind are all over. I know."

Shortly after Zee left, the phone rang and he snatched it up, eager for any news. Van der Velde was calling from his office at the U.N. "Good afternoon, Mr. O'Brien. I'm still in shock about Mrs. O'Brien. I just wanted you to know that our resources are at your disposal."

"Thank you. As a matter of fact I thought about calling you to ask for your help. I can't help but wonder if Jasajovic, or those with whom he is associated, is behind this. You are in the best position to find out where he is."

"Yes. That thought had occurred to me also, and I have already started making inquiries. After you told us how Jasajovic had tried to have you killed, I had our representatives in Belgrade learn more about the man. So far, I found out that he had been in the Srpska government. As you know, they control the parts of Bosnia populated largely by Serbs. He represented the Srpska interests on our Missing Persons Committee.

"He no longer has any official role in the government. Even President Milosevic tries to disassociate himself from him. But Jasajovic is a member, perhaps the leader, of a small group, many are former Chetnicks. Ultranationalists, militants who have assembled what in your country are known as paramilitary extremists.

"Recently they have found strong financial backing which they are using to quietly buy arms, perhaps even nuclear devices."

Great, all we need is another nuclear power, particularly one run by kooks. He should have killed the son of a bitch when he had the chance. "Are you implying that he is obtaining financial support from some other country?"

"That is the mystery. Our sources, which I believe are reliable, have found no other country that would deal with them, except to sell them arms for cash. And suddenly they are rich in cash."

Although he was quite sure Jasajovic was behind Peg's abduction, at the moment he had no interest in the man's political ambitions. "If you learn where Jasajovic is, please keep me informed."

"Certainly. And remember, we are all working toward getting your wife back."

He still had his hand on the phone when it rang. Colonel McLanahan was on the line. "Wonder if you'd mind sitting down with us for an hour or so. We're trying to figure out where this magic mountain of yours is. I'll send a car over for you if you can come."

It was an opportunity to keep occupied. Here, he was just sitting around waiting for word from the police who reported that they were scouring the city. "Gladly. But you should try to get the computerized reconstructions that were made by Sam Powell. He's a radar tech—"

McLanahan broke in. "We're already on that. We're in the network with NATO and USAF at Aviano. Powell's back there, you know. He e-mailed us all his material."

Fifteen minutes later, O'Brien was standing alongside the doorman in front of the hotel, waiting to be picked up. He was peering down the street in the direction from which the car would be coming, when a strong shove sent him sprawling to the sidewalk. A heavy body fell on top of him, knocking the wind out of his lungs. He struggled, trying to push the person off. A voice screamed in his ear, "Down!" The doorman lay on top of him, his hand pressing O'Brien's head to the sidewalk. A moment later he heard the roar of an accelerating car motor and the tinkle of breaking glass.

The doorman rolled off him, scrambled to his feet and helped him up. He brushed dirt off O'Brien's suit. Breathing heavily he said, "I see gun point out of car. Sorry if I hurt you."

O'Brien pulse was racing. He hadn't heard the shot, but glancing behind him saw that the plate-glass door of the hotel was shattered. A moment later, a van screeched to a stop at the curb and a man in a U.N uniform leaped out. "What's happened?"

O'Brien was still too dazed to answer. The doorman said, "Someone shoot him."

Not satisfied that they'd snatched Peg from him, bastards were determined to kill him. Now recovered, O'Brien said, "He pushed me down. Saved my life."

*   *   *

O'Brien was unable to understand what the doorman told the police when they arrived, but the U.N. soldier interpreted. A black sedan had been parked in front of the hotel when he came on duty about half an hour ago. Two men were in the car—Serbian, he thought. They told him they were waiting for one of the guests. He paid no further attention until he saw the barrel of a gun poke out of a side window. He pushed O'Brien down.

After the police indicated O'Brien was free to go, the U.N. soldier said, "Feel well enough to come along?"

He shrugged. "Sure. Better than staying here and providing someone with a target."

At the U.N. building, McLanahan expressed shock at O'Brien's narrow escape. "Buggers seem intent on getting you one way or another, don't they?" He gave a small headshake. "Shall we get on with it, or would you rather—?"

"No, no. I'm fine."

McLanahan laid out on the table a large aerial photo and secured the ends to keep it from curling.

"This looks familiar," said O'Brien.

"It's satellite-generated. Powell sent it over. You say you had made several GPS fixes on your position?"

"Yes. Unfortunately, I lost the list of coordinates somewhere in the woods when I was chased. But, maybe I can find it from the photos." He started from the ruins of the old prison camp where they had launched the drones. The photos were remarkably detailed, but the truck trail had been so cleverly hidden that only because he knew its approximate location, could he find a few visible segments of it. After studying several photo enlargements, he finally traced his route through the wooded area, across the valley, back into the forest at the base of the mountain, then up the trail to where he had seen the opening into which trucks drove in and out. He put his finger on the spot. "You can probably walk right by it without knowing there's an entry here. But this is where it is."

McLanahan said, "It would be helpful to have you along to show us. Would you care to come? You can remain in the background so you won't get into the actual fighting, if it comes to that."

"Thank you. I'd like nothing better. The prospect of a fight doesn't bother me. But while the hunt for Peg is on, I want to stay around here."

"Of course. I understand."

"When do you expect to go?"

McLanahan shrugged. "We have to assemble a force. Normally we'd train for an operation like this. Take a few weeks in rehearsal. We don't know what we'll be facing, so we have to be prepared for any contingency. Plans and alternate plans." He smiled. "For all we know, it may be another dry run."

O'Brien gazed at the ceiling and slowly shook his head. "Colonel, I'm not sure you have the luxury—maybe not the right word—of a long training period. If the men who ran that prison have already evacuated, they know we're getting close. I have a hunch those prisoners are dispensable. And soon."

McLanahan nodded. "We've been thinking along those lines. And, no, we won't be spending as much time on preparation as we'd like."

"Well, good luck, Colonel."

"Same to you, Matt."

*   *   *

The phone was ringing when he walked into his room. The voice on the other end said, "You can have your wife back." Male. Heavy accent. "We're finished with her now. Blekic farm. Ugorsko." Click.

☠ CHAPTER 40

Bastards.

We're finished with her now. The words indelibly inscribed in his brain.

Thank God Forrest was at the NATO/SFOR office. "Ugorsko? Sure, I know where it is. Three or four kilometers outside Sarajevo. Lots of deserted farms there. We'll find the Blekic place. Give me fifteen. Pick you up."

The white van squealed to a stop and the door flew open. "Hop in."

O'Brien buckled in and the van careened on to the road. He glanced around. Two uniformed men were seated in the back, along with several strange pieces of equipment.

Forrest's eyes were on the road as he wove around cars. "Brought reinforcements. Could be a trap, you know."

O'Brien hadn't even thought of a trap.

"Back there's Fred Singleton, our demolition expert. Borrowed Fred from MAC—Mine Action Centre. Down the hall from our office. If there's a booby trap, he'll ferret it out."

Singleton touched his cap. The stone-faced blond man sitting next to him had an AK-47 across his lap.

"Other bloke's Gunner Bargar. Gunner's his real name. Also what he does best. His mother knew what she was doing when she named him."

O'Brien said, "How'd you get this team together so quickly?"

"We got lucky. We were all in operations when you phoned. Making preparations for MAGIC MOUNTAIN."

"MAGIC MOUNTAIN?"

Forrest grinned. "Code name for the assault on your mystery mountain. It'll be going down soon. Don't suppose you're interested, though." He flicked a glance at O'Brien.

O'Brien shook his head. "Peg's on my mind."

"Of course."

The conversation ended. His thoughts were on Peg. Almost dreading how he'd find her. *We're finished with her.* Was it a voice he recognized? No one came to mind.

They'd left the city. The sunlight had faded and dusk was settling in. Forrest nodded toward lights in the roadway ahead. "Ugorsko."

The village consisted of little more than a main street and several houses surrounding it. Forrest pulled up to a red brick building with a flag flying from a pole in front of it. "Police headquarters. Be right out." He jumped down from the van, raced into the building and a few moments later appeared in the doorway with a policeman who was pointing toward the south.

Forrest returned to the van and gunned the engine back on to the road. "Blekic farm's off a dirt road, two klicks from here. Policeman says it's been deserted for a couple of years. He's following us."

Questions swirled around in his head as the van bumped over the dirt road. Would he find Peg alive? Injured? Would he find her at all, or was this a hoax? Ahead he could now see the outline of a stone structure he assumed was the farmhouse. They drew closer. No glass in the windows. A door hung crookedly on one hinge. Tall weeds surrounded the house.

Forrest braked a few feet from the door and grabbed a flashlight from the dashboard.

O'Brien drew a deep breath, flung open the car door and leaped to the ground. The others were already out of the car.

"Wait!"

An arm reached out and grabbed him by his jacket. He spun around, saw it was Bargar, and tried to pull himself free.

"Let me go."

"Not yet. Not until we've made sure—"

If it was a booby trap, let it blow up in his face. "I don't give a shit about security. Goddamit, let me go in."

Bargar shook his head, held firm. Meanwhile, Singleton had begun sweeping the gravel walk leading to the doorway with a long-handled metal detector. When he disappeared into the house, Bargar released his hold and O'Brien raced into the doorway. "Peg." His voice echoed in the empty space, the dark room. The only sound was the wood floor creaking under his weight.

Forrest was behind him now lighting the room with his flashlight. Singleton pushed him aside while he continued to sweep the room.

The light beam hit the far corner of the room. Peg lay naked, sprawled on her back, arms and legs spread-eagled.

He ran to her side. Spikes had been driven through her palms and feet. Nailed to the floor.

He heard his sobbing voice. "Oh, Peg." He dropped to his knees beside her. Put his cheek to her mouth. Felt her warm breath. Thank God. She was breathing. Peg was alive. He kissed her lips, felt their warmth. "I'm here, sweetheart. It's going to be all right." His throat so tight he could hardly breathe.

☠ CHAPTER 41

Her skin felt cold and he stripped off his jacket and threw it over her. "Get these nails out," he yelled while he gently rubbed her legs and arms, trying to stir warmth into her body. Peg had not made a sound.

A moment later someone threw a blanket down, and he unfolded it over her, adding another layer of covering.

Forrest knelt at his side with a pair of pliers and started working loose the spike holding one of her feet. Singleton yelled, "Wait." He knelt beside Forrest, played the beam of a lantern around her feet then nodded. "Okay."

Singleton moved to her head and inspected her hands, while Forrest twisted the spikes holding her feet to work them loose. O'Brien bent over Peg, held her upper body close to his chest, to shut her ears to the squealing as the spikes twisted in the wood floor. He could feel Peg's pain, the indescribable suffering the extraction must be causing; yet she lay immobile, as silent as if she'd been anesthetized. As much as he wanted to hear her, he took some comfort in her unresponsiveness. Maybe it was better this way.

Forrest tossed aside the five-inch spikes he had removed, and maneuvered around O'Brien to get to those holding her hands. He was about to grasp the head of the spike protruding from the back of her left hand when Singleton grabbed his shoulder, pointed to her right hand and shouted, "This one's wired."

O'Brien couldn't see the wire, but Singleton appeared to be tracing it, careful to avoid disturbing it, playing the light beam as he slowly crawled away from her. Reaching the other side of the room, he stopped, leaned close to the wall. "Got it," he shouted. He dug something from a pocket of his jacket. Singleton's back screened whatever he was working on, but after what seemed like minutes, O'Brien heard a click and Singleton straightened up holding a small package. "This little bundle could have blown us all sky high." He nodded to Forrest. "Okay, it's defused. You can pull out those other nails."

Forrest quickly removed the spikes holding her hands, and O'Brien scooped Peg and her coverings in his arms, and carried her to the van. Peg did not utter a sound. Her silence was chilling.

A police car was parked alongside the van, a policeman stood next to it. He said something O'Brien couldn't understand, but Forrest spoke briefly to him, then opened the van door and helped O'Brien ease Peg in. Together they laid her across the rear seat. O'Brien tucked the blanket around her, and sitting sideways next to her, leaned forward, trying to warm her with his own body heat. Peg stared unblinking at the ceiling.

Forrest drove rapidly back to Sarajevo with Singleton and Bargar crammed next to him in the front of the van. He spoke over his shoulder to O'Brien. "Heading directly to our small military hospital, infirmary really, but staff's top notch."

O'Brien, recalling his abduction from the hospital in Sarajevo, said, "I'm sure it's foolish to ask, but I assume she'll be well protected there."

"No one unauthorized can get in. Guaranteed."

*   *   *

Two hours later in the U.N. infirmary, O'Brien paced outside the operating theater. Every minute or two he stopped to peer through the small windows in the paired swinging doors, giving him a view of a corridor, empty except for a nurse in a green scrub suit who periodically scurried in and out of a treatment room into which they'd taken Peg. He could only wonder and worry about what was going on.

He phoned to tell Brooke and Lesley in a carefully edited version that their mother was safe. They shouted with joy and asked to speak to her.

"She's being examined by a doctor to be sure she's all right," he said. "But as soon as she's able, she'll want to talk to you."

He instructed them to pass the news on to the rest of the family, then returned to his vigil, awaiting word from the tall Swedish surgeon who was attending her.

A question kept running through his head. Why Peg? Surely the booby trap was aimed at him, but he could have been targeted just as he was that day he stood at the hotel window, or today in front of the hotel. It *had* to be Jasajovic getting back at him. The evil son of a bitch knew hurting Peg would cause him more pain than if they'd pulled out his own fingernails.

An hour after she had been admitted, Dr. Johan Engelberg emerged from the operating theatre. He pulled down the mask that covered his nose and mouth and removed the cap from his blond hair. Unsmiling, he said, "Please sit down." O'Brien felt as though a rope suddenly tightened across his chest.

"Your wife will recover."

The rope loosened.

"But there are problems that will take time to resolve. She suffers from hypothermia—prolonged exposure. The puncture wounds in her hands and feet fortunately did only minor damage—an extensor tendon in her hand we repaired. Infection, of course, could be a problem. Tetanus in that setting, you know. But we've given her antitoxin in case she hasn't had a recent booster. She'll be getting intravenous antibiotics. They should also control the pneumonia from which she also suffers."

"But she *will* recover, won't she?" He needed the reaffirmation.

"From her physical injuries, I can confidently say yes. From the emotional trauma, I cannot speak with authority since I am not a psychiatrist."

"You mean the abduction? Peg is a very strong person."

"She will need all the emotional strength she has—and you as well. I will speak frankly. She has sustained multiple internal and external vaginal lacerations, evidence that these beasts repeatedly raped her. Perhaps even violated her with foreign objects." He shook his head. "They are not fit to be members of the human race."

O'Brien shut his eyes, clenched his fists. They will pay. The bastards will pay.

*   *   *

He sat at her bedside caressing her forearm above the dressing. He wanted her to know he was there. He got up only to allow the nurses and doctor to change her dressings or replace bags of I.V. solutions. These moments he used to tend to his own needs. The nurse brought food to the bedside for him, but he could only toy with it, sending most of it back. At times he found his head resting at Peg's side on the bed, realized that he had dozed off.

On the second day, she opened her eyes. She lay staring at the ceiling, not responding to his voice telling her that she was safe, that he loved her, that Brooke and Lesley sent their love, that she would go home soon and see her family.

That afternoon, the doctor came in, clamped the intravenous tube but left the needle in place, its end sealed with a plug which could be removed to administer her intravenous antibiotics.

"We must get her out of bed," he said. "It is not good for her to remain lying down constantly."

O'Brien moved out of the way to allow the nurse help Peg to a sitting position and then to stand. When Peg's heavily bandaged feet touched the floor, a whimper came from her lips, the first sound she'd uttered.

He heard himself wince. He reached out to touch her. He wanted her to know he was there, that he felt her pain.

The nurse draped Peg's arm around her neck and moved slowly along the side of the bed while Peg tried to shuffle along beside her. "That is fine. Enough for now," the nurse said after five or six steps.

With O'Brien helping, they sat Peg in a wheelchair, elevating her feet on the raised leg rests. He wheeled her down the corridor, pointing out the sights: "This is the operating theater. British influence, 'theater.' In America it's called operating room. And there's the kitchen. Food's pretty good, as you'll see when you try it this evening."

If Peg heard, she showed no sign of comprehending. The doctor had said there would be an emotional reaction to the torture, but could there be brain damage? The thought caused his gut to knot.

That evening he spoon-fed her, the first solid food she'd had. It was like feeding an infant. She opened her mouth in response to the spoon at her lips, and when she'd had her fill, she turned her head away.

O'Brien questioned the doctor about her infantile behavior.

Engelberg said, "Yes, acute stress response. I've already called for a psychiatrist."

"Good. Do you have someone you feel is capable? Experienced?"

"Dr. Zoltan Ascher. He's an Israeli on the U.N. staff." He smiled. "Experienced? He cut his teeth, so to speak, treating his own people after each of the Arab-Israeli wars. Since the war here, about a quarter of the population suffers or has suffered from stress in one form or another. Dr. Ascher probably has more experience than anyone in the world today. He has a staff of therapists and his success rate is exceptionally high."

"When will he see her?"

He shrugged. "I have put in an urgent call for him. He has always responded in a day or two at most. Meantime, we will be treating her physical ailments."

All of Peg's wounds were healing with only superficial infection, and her pneumonia had cleared. Engelberg was pleased with her progress. Now that she was out of danger, O'Brien decided to go back to the hotel to sleep in his own bed. He said, "Goodnight, Peg."

No response.

He leaned over to kiss her, but she turned her head and raised her arm shielding her face. He tried to rationalize: *She's not ready for contact with another person.* But her muteness, her refusal to allow even him to touch her, was agonizing.

Early the following morning, refreshed by the first shower he'd had in three days, he dressed in fresh khaki trousers and shirt. He'd bought them with the rest of the wardrobe he replaced the day after his return to Sarajevo. All his other belongings had been sent back to Washington after he had been prematurely declared dead.

He entered the infirmary to find Peg already out of bed, walking unassisted in the corridor with the nurse by her side. Thrilled by her progress, he watched her from behind. When she stopped and turned around, she spotted him. He beamed. "Great, Peg. You're doing beautifully."

She shrieked. "Get him away from me! No. I won't. I won't."

"Oh God, Peg. It's me, Matt."

He ran to her, tried to put his arms around her. Her screams intensified. She beat at his face with her fists.

The nurse nudged him away. "Leave her, please. Go into the waiting room where she can't see you."

Dr. Engelberg came into the waiting room half an hour later and sat beside him. "The nurse told me what happened this morning." He took a deep breath. "Your wife sees you as one of her attackers. It is probably the clothing you're wearing. To her, it is a soldier's uniform."

In a few minutes, the nurse helped him into a long white laboratory coat, and he inched into Peg's room.

She was sitting up in bed, her hair neatly combed and tied in back with a small velvet bow. When she saw him she smiled.

He came to her bed, kneeled next to it, his eyes misting. "Oh, Peg. You're back."

"Matt," she said quietly.

He leaned forward to kiss her, but she quickly withdrew, her smile suddenly vanished. He moved back. He wanted so to hold her, she wasn't ready to be embraced.

He spent the rest of the morning sitting at her bedside, telling her anything that came into his head. He told her he'd spoken to the girls. Brooke was going to the Senior Prom with Tom Nelson. Lesley had fully recovered from her fall. She had written a play for her class in school. And on and on. She listened, offering no comments, but occasionally nodding as though she approved. He told her that as soon as she was able to travel, they would leave for home. She smiled.

Thank God, she was finally returning to a semblance of normal. Her conversation was still limited to one- or two-word responses to his questions and comments, but at least she was making sense, understanding him. He began to wonder if psychiatric treatment would really be necessary. Once she got out of this country and was back to familiar surroundings, he was sure she'd make a rapid recovery. He'd ask the doctor about taking her out of the hospital as soon as the intravenous medication was discontinued.

At lunchtime the nurse brought a tray with food for both of them, and placed it on a small table in the room. With the nurse, he helped Peg out of bed and they sat side by side, eating a grilled fish. He chattered away, all the while watching Peg. She took small bites, but ate most of the food in front of her, then drained her glass of water.

She sat back, patted her lips with a napkin. "Could you get me a glass of milk?"

Finally. A complete sentence.

He laughed. "Must be the country air. I can't remember the last time I saw you drink a glass of milk."

He walked back to the kitchen, where the cook filled a glass with milk, and he carried it back to her room. Peg was seated, her back to him, working at something he couldn't see until he came around the table.

She was sawing away at one of her wrists with the table knife.

☠ CHAPTER 42

"Classical PTSD—Post-traumatic Stress Disorder." Dr. Zoltan Ascher stroked his pointed goatee. "It's as though she read the textbook. Incidentally, I wrote the chapter."

O'Brien wasn't interested how he labeled it. "Will she recover?"

They were seated in a small office behind the nurses' desk. Ascher was short, rotund, accompanied everything he said with wide gestures of his soft hands. He had spent an hour with Peg, but O'Brien wondered if she'd responded to any of his questions.

"Will she recover?" Ascher repeated O'Brien's question, raised his eyebrows and shrugged. "I can give you a qualified yes, if that is helpful. You tell me that she has never had previous emotional problems. That is good. The prognosis for someone with a history of emotional instability is not as good."

"I can't believe she tried to kill herself."

"Suicidal ideation. Not unusual. She was treated like dirt. Can you imagine what that did to her self-esteem? Fortunately, the knife was dull. The laceration is superficial. It won't even leave a scar."

"She won't let me touch her, even get near her. God, if I could only get through to her, tell her she's safe, protected."

"Look, Mr. O'Brien, it isn't *you* she's rejecting. It's the uniform you're wearing—or what she perceives as a uniform. And the fact that you are a male figure. We call it intrusion. The traumatic event is a flashback that intrudes on her thinking. You can't get through to her—we call it an avoidance phenomenon. She is avoiding any close emotional ties. She screamed and beat at you when you tried to touch her? Typical hyperarousal."

Avoidance, hyperarousal, psychobabble bullshit. "Did she tell you what happened to her?"

Ascher pursed his lips, lowered his head. "You don't want to know."

"Tell me."

"Why? So you can torture yourself?"

"Tell me."

Ascher drew a deep breath. "Two of them pushed her into a car. An older man was in the car. When they got to where they were going, they pushed into a house and locked her in a room. It must have been out in the country, because sometime later she heard a cock crowing."

Perceptive Peg.

Ascher continued. "The older man came in the next day and told her—are you sure you want to hear all this?"

"I'm sure."

"The older man said something about evening a score with you."

"With me?"

"Yes."

Jasajovic. It had to be him. He should never have let him live. "Go on."

"Next day this man came back with some soldiers."

"Soldiers?"

"Men in uniform. Four, maybe more. The old man laughed. Told her to have a good time. He left them alone in the room with her. I will not describe for you what happened."

O'Brien couldn't bear to hear more. Put his hand up, then buried his face in his hands. This man—Jasajovic—must die. He would see to it.

"I warned you. It would not be a pretty story."

The following day the psychiatrist returned with a woman he introduced as Ruth, a psychotherapist. O'Brien left them with Peg while he waited in an adjacent lounge.

A knock on the doorframe caused him to look up. A young, attractive blonde woman wearing an emerald-green sweater and slacks, said, "May I come in?" English accent.

"Sure, come on in."

"Thank you." She extended her hand. "I'm Keri Forrest. The receptionist told me I'd find you here."

"Jeff's wife! It was good of you to come. Your husband has been a godsend. Please, have a seat."

She sat on the chair he held for her. "I came down straightaway to see if there was something you or your wife needed."

"How thoughtful. At the moment I can't think of a thing. But, if you can stay, I'd like you to meet Peg. The doctors are in with her now."

"I'll wait. I'd love to meet her."

For 20 minutes they chatted. She'd been horrified to learn of Peg's ordeal. She asked about their home, their children. She and Jeff had none of their own—yet. "Gives both of us freedom, but I think we're ready."

Ascher and the therapist emerged from Peg's room, told him he could go back in. Ascher said, "Your wife is a remarkable woman. Such resilience."

He already knew that, but the confirmation was encouraging. "Any idea when she'll be ready to go back home?"

Ascher turned to the therapist. "What do you think, Ruth. A week maybe?"

Ruth nodded. "I should think so." She turned to O'Brien, "Of course, she'll need further therapy. I can help you find someone in Washington who can continue her treatment."

Peg was sitting in a chair. She greeted him with a smile and brightened even more when he introduced Keri. For the first time since her rescue, she spoke with animation. She was the Peg of old—almost.

By early evening it was obvious that the day's activities had exhausted her, and after she was tucked away for the night, he returned to the hotel. He tried to read, but couldn't keep his mind on the printed page. Knowing that Jasajovic had directed Peg's gang rape as an act of retribution made him hunger to tear the man's heart out. If he knew where he could find Jasajovic at this moment, he'd charge out of this room, go any distance, break through any barriers to get to him, and strangle him with his bare hands. Could he leave Peg long enough to do it? It was a question he couldn't answer until he located Jasajovic. But his torment wouldn't end until he'd put the man in his grave.

He phoned Van der Velde, still at the U.N. office in Sarajevo, to find out if he had learned where Jasajovic was.

"There is no trace of him. Incidentally, I was so pleased to hear that Mrs. O'Brien has been found. I trust she is recovering."

"Thank you. She is getting better. We hope to leave for home soon. But please keep trying to find Jasajovic. You have resources here few people have."

"Of course." He paused. "It sounds as though you have plans for him."

"I'd rather not discuss that."

"Naturally."

After he hung up, the phone rang. Colonel McLanahan was on the line. "Could I have a word with you? I'd like to come to your hotel, if you can spare the time."

"Now?"

"If it isn't inconvenient."

He had envisioned getting to bed early, wondered why it couldn't be discussed on the phone. "Certainly. Can you tell me what it's about?"

"Too sensitive for the phone lines."

He'd learned about that.

Half an hour later, McLanahan phoned from the lobby. "If it isn't too much to ask, would you to meet me down here?"

O'Brien, tingling with curiosity, found McLanahan pacing in the lobby. Spying O'Brien, he inclined his head toward the door to the street. "My car is out front. Would you mind?"

More intrigue.

When they were seated in the Chevy van, McLanahan said, "The walls have ears you know."

"How well I *do* know."

"We need your help."

O'Brien was silent.

"We're just about ready to move. MAGIC MOUNTAIN. We have to assume we'll meet armed resistance. Unfortunately, the terrain doesn't lend itself to surprise."

"Can you clarify that?"

McLanahan snapped on the car's map light. He pulled out of his pocket a paper. Unfolded, it was a small aerial photo showing the mountain and its surroundings. "We insert by helicopter. Land in this open field at the base of the mountain. We have to make our way by foot about two klicks up the trail." He traced the course O'Brien had earlier pointed out, leading to the approximate location of the cavern entrance.

O'Brien said, "Concerned about surveillance?"

"Right on. Little question the opposing force will be mobilized and ready for us. We can live with that, but we have to be certain exactly where the hidden entry is."

O'Brien thought for a moment. "Rather than use helicopters, why not truck your troops along the trail I took? Trucks would make less noise."

McLanahan shook his head. "That trail is sure to be under visual or electronic surveillance. They'd spot trucks long before they got to where a helicopter would land. If we knew exactly where the entry was, we'd insert using somewhat the same technique we did for our commando raid on the prison—fast rope our squad in from a hovering helicopter. But…" He shrugged.

"Okay, where do I fit in?"

"You're the only one who knows the exact location of the entry. Unfortunately, you don't fast rope. Our drone surveillance has given us detailed photos of the place you've pointed out on the map, but damned if we can see where the opening is. They've got it well camouflaged."

"Can't you blast a hole anywhere in the mountain from the air?"

"And risk collapsing the cavern, burying all the prisoners we're trying to save?"

"You still have to blast your way through the entry."

"True, but we can use a limited explosive."

O'Brien could see where this conversation was going. "You want me to go in with your troops, right?"

"Not exactly. We propose to fly you in, and lead us up the trail to point out the entry. Then your job's done. Back down the trail you go to the LZ where the chopper picks you up and flies you out directly. You would not be involved in any of the—uh, activity, assuming there is activity." He held up a hand. "I don't mean to minimize the danger: mines, exposure to sniper fire on the way up the trail, other circumstances I can't even anticipate. Hell, the helicopter could be shot down. But knowing exactly where we make our penetration is critical."

O'Brien gazed out at the darkened street. It wasn't the danger that concerned him. He'd survived risky missions before. But was it worth leaving Peg's side, particularly now when she seemed to be making a recovery? Unequivocally yes, if it led him to Jasajovic. Peg would recover, he was convinced of it.

McLanahan saw his hesitation. "You're concerned about your wife, right? If our plan goes as expected, your involvement would not take more than a few hours. Night operation, of course. After she'd be asleep."

O'Brien had made up his mind before McLanahan started speaking. There was little doubt that Jasajovic had a vital interest in whatever was taking place inside that cavern. His attempts to get O'Brien out of the way—permanently—along with the fact that he damn well knew about Wilson's abduction, made that deduction a safe bet. Wilson. He hadn't forgotten him, nor the possibility that he might be one of the prisoners. "When does this operation go down?"

"Tomorrow night."

*   *   *

O'Brien sneaked a peek at his reflection in a window in the airfield shed. Green and black face like the 21 others in the assault team as they waited to board the helicopter. The medium body armor was light enough, but wearing it he looked as though he'd put on ten pounds. A helmet sat on his head, and under it a metal band that terminated in an earpiece that fit into his left ear. A filament microphone, sensitive enough to transmit whispers, projected just under his lower lip. The apparatus was connected by a wire that ran under his shirt to a low voltage FM radio the size of a cigarette pack strapped to his waist. A button activated his mike, the receiver stayed on so he could hear incoming signals.

The night-vision goggles he'd been issued were attached to a face-plate. "They'll amplify the ambient light about 5,000 times," the equip-ment sergeant told him while helping him adjust the straps and lens focus. They were lighter and brighter than the NVGs he'd grabbed from the perimeter patrol soldier he'd run into on his solo excursion to the mountain a few weeks before.

Two UH-60 Blackhawk helicopters would carry the team to the field at the base of the mountain. From there they'd hike up the trail to the entry point. Two Apaches would escort them.

At the final briefing half an hour earlier, one of the SFOR troops, the NATO Stabilization Force, had asked about using tanks or armored troop carriers. McLanahan said, "There's no way we can get tanks on the narrow trail. Armored troop carriers, maybe. But we'd have to drive them in over about ten klicks of dirt road. We've got to assume the road is mined. No, we'll do without them. Anything further?" He glanced around the room for a moment. "That's it, then. We go wheels up at 2330."

The others carried H&K MP5K-PDWs, a compact assault weapon that would support both single and full automatic fire. O'Brien had only a holstered 9mm Heckler & Koch automatic pistol, and he had even protested carrying that. McLanahan insisted he take it, "Just in case."

"'Just in case' of what?" He had reassured O'Brien that he would not be around for the shooting.

"You've been in combat, Matt. I don't have to tell you there are contingencies no one can predict."

In the end he strapped on the H&K.

At 11:10 p.m., a sergeant called into his earpiece, "Board."

His pulse quickened.

The flight took only 20 minutes. O'Brien sat buckled in between two grim-faced soldiers. Neither was a youngster. No one attempted conversation, probably, he thought, going over in their minds the details of the assault.

He gazed into the blackness outside the small port behind his seat. In his ear he heard, "This is it. LZ." The landing zone. A winking red light from below caught his attention. At first he thought it was on the body of the chopper, but soon realized it was on the ground. McLanahan had told him that an advance two-man squad had trekked in by foot in daylight hours to mark the site for landing with a chem light.

He felt the craft's forward progress stopping, it hovered and now started its descent. Less than a minute later he felt the wheels thump down. The cabin door slid open. A voice in his earpiece said, "NVGs on." A moment later, "Go." He followed the others hopping down from the craft. As he hit the ground, the helicopter motor roared for lift-off, picking up a whirlwind of debris. He crouched and instinctively protected his eyes and mouth until the helicopter left the ground.

Moments later, the second helicopter set down and discharged its troops. The helicopters would hover in the vicinity until the squad was ready to be evacuated.

Guided by the advance team on the ground, the helicopters had set them down on the same narrow dirt trail he'd taken a few weeks before.

Directly ahead through the gloom, he could make out their objective rising about 2,000 feet above the valley in which they now stood. It resembled a huge Egyptian pyramid—no, a dunce cap. And maybe he should be wearing one for agreeing to go on this mission. Although his depth perception was distorted by the NVGs, he estimated that the mountain's base was about a quarter of a mile distant. He recalled how the trail spiraled once it began its ascent; how the upper branches of the tall pines covering the mountain formed a canopy over the trail. About a third of the way up from the mountain's base was the entry he was leading them to.

Someone touched his shoulder. "Follow me."

They walked in two single-file columns, one on either side of the trail. He was directly behind the point man. The rest followed.

For 20 minutes they slogged through the valley's thick, knee-high weeds. In their briefing McLanahan had cautioned them about the possibility of buried electronic sensors.

Intent on keeping his footing over the uneven ground, he suddenly realized that the trail had become steeper and the weeds had disappeared, replaced by the forest that clothed the mountain up to its peaked summit. Still no sign of the perimeter patrol he'd met last time. So far, so good.

The climb was steep enough to make O'Brien wheeze with the effort. He pitied the troops, each of whom carried a 20-pound ruckpack in addition to a heavy assault rifle. He had only the responsibility of finding what they'd come here for, as well as the concern that he might not be able to identify the camouflaged entry in the dark.

"Rest stop." The sudden whispered command hissing in his ear startled him. The troops sat on the ground or on their ruckpacks. He heard labored breathing in his earpiece. His own. He clicked off his mike. Then, under his seat he felt the throb through the ground. They were getting close. The man next to him noticed it too.

O'Brien nodded, activated his mike and whispered, "Generator motor."

McLanahan's voice hissed in his earpiece. "Copy that."

O'Brien peered left, through the trees, toward the upslope of the mountain. In the eerie blue-green light imparted by his night-vision goggles, the gently swaying tree branches were hairs on the head of a Gorgon-like monster. Deep in its bosom throbbed its heart. He shook his head to drive the image from his mind.

Without landmarks, he could only estimate they had about 300 yards before they reached the entry. He softly passed the information into his mike. Heard McLanahan acknowledge. A moment later, "Go." The men quietly rose, shouldering their packs.

McLanahan: "Safeties off." He heard soft clicks. Cracking of twigs underfoot. Odor of pine.

There. He saw it. Just to the right of the trail, on the downslope, the depression where he'd temporarily stashed his backpack the last time. He whispered into his mike, "About fifty meters to go."

"Copy, fifty."

Hairs on his neck tingling, he walked faster until he trampled on the heels of the soldier in front of him. Suddenly, there was a flash of light so bright he felt as though salt had been thrown into his eyes. Searchlights. "Dive!" The order boomed through his earpiece. He hit the deck face down. A hammer pounded in his head. A shot rang from somewhere on the hillside. He clamped his eyes shut. A moment later the ground under him lifted into his chest. A blast filled his ears. He was pelted with dirt and small stones that rained on him, pinged on his steel helmet. Someone shouted, "Rifle grenades!" Then silence.

He opened his eyes, but was enveloped in thick fog. He stripped off the NVGs, alarmed when he couldn't see his hand in front of his face. It took a moment to realize that the goggles had amplified the searchlights several thousand-fold. The white light burning into his retinas had blinded him. A moment later a voice cried out in his earpiece, "Christ, I can't see."

They were a small army of bats in bright sunlight. Helpless. His throat constricted with fear he hadn't known since his own war 30 years ago. He pounded the ground with his fist. Why in God's name had he let himself be talked into this?

McLanahan's voice crackled in his ear. "Stay down. It's the goddam NVGs. It'll wear off in a few minutes."

Another blast ripped the air; the shock wave thudded into his body. He felt his heart pounding his chest. Good sign. He was still alive. Moans now broke the silence around him. Others hadn't been as lucky. So much for surprise. So much for no resistance. He was about to look up when the order, "Stay down," growled in his ear.

A staccato of shots kicked up dirt to his right. The shooting stopped. He raised his head and peered into the milky world around him. Suddenly, the flames of tracers coming from some point above him on the mountainside cut through the fog. He could see! Okay, they were targets, but he could see again. He wiggled his fingers, could make out their movement. He drew in a deep breath. They might make it yet.

McLanahan: "Get those lights."

A fusillade from the assault team, and the searchlights blinked out. His world went from white to black. He wondered if the phosphor in his NVGs had been damaged by the bright light, patted the ground until he located his goggles and put them on. The forest turned blue-green. Thank you, God. He lay prone for what he estimated was five minutes. The firing had stopped.

McLanahan's voice in his earpiece, whispered four names.

Four voices. "Here, sir."

"See where those tracers came from?"

Four replies "Roger."

"You know the drill, right?"

"Harris here. I copy."

"Roberts. Copy."

The other two acknowledged as well.

McLanahan: "We'll cover. Go."

O'Brien heard rustling, saw crouching figures slinking toward the mountainside. They separated and he watched as they slowly made their way up, until the trees obscured them. He lay prone in the silent forest waiting, hardly breathing.

A voice in his ear: "Roberts to Colonel. Nothing here, sir."

"Simpson here, sir. I'm certain I'm above where we spotted the tracers. Nothing here."

"Harris reporting, sir. I've found some sort of hole. May be from a burrowing animal or…No, wait, I can smell cordite. It's a gun port."

McLanahan: "Watch yourself!"

"Harris. No gun in here now."

"Atwood here. I've found one, too. Empty shell casings on the ground. No question. They've been firing through ports from inside this mountain."

"All right. All of you, back down here."

"Copy."

Two minutes later, O'Brien could make out the four men scrambling down the mountainside.

McLanahan: "Move out but stay low and in the tree line."

O'Brien got to his feet. He didn't know how many wounded or dead they were leaving behind. Heard movement of the others around him.

Snaking between trees, O'Brien kept his eyes on the mountainside. Then he spotted it. The vertical rock face. The only part of the slope devoid of trees. In its center was the entry. "Got it."

Someone touched his arm. McLanahan. O'Brien pointed. "That's it. On the other side of the trail."

McLanahan spoke into his mike. "Fitzpatrick. Bring your charge." He flicked on a red light for a second.

From the gloom, a crouching figure appeared. "At your side, sir."

"Fitz is our explosives expert, Matt. Point out the entry. He'll lay a C4 charge down." He turned to Fitzpatrick. "Remember. We don't want to blow up the cavern, just the entry."

"Got it, sir."

O'Brien inched slowly from the protection of the trees toward the edge of the trail. McLanahan had assured him he was not going to be placed in danger? Any minute he expected to be peppered with gunfire, but now the only sound was the snapping of twigs as he made his way. In that rock wall devoid of trees was the entry to the cavern. Fitzpatrick was at his side. The short, bow-legged figure creeping in a crouch with a backpack slung over his shoulders looked like a small ape.

O'Brien pointed. "Entry is in the center of that rock face."

"Okay, sir. I'll take it from here. Go on back inside the tree line."

O'Brien turned and hurried back to where McLanahan and the other men in the assault force stood waiting.

McLanahan said, "We'll cover, Fitz. Go." He turned to O'Brien. "You've done your part." He pointed down the trail. "A jeep's coming up to take three men who were hit. They'll be evacuated by helicopter. You go back with them."

"A jeep?"

"Another chopper flew it in a few minutes ago. It's on its way up from the LZ."

They'd thought of everything. Great job of organization.

O'Brien took a few steps, then stopped. He damned well was not leaving now. Peg would be asleep. He'd get back before she awakened. No, he'd wait; watch as the operation went down.

Fitzpatrick had finished placing the charge, scurried back across the trail to join them inside the tree line. In his earpiece, O'Brien heard, "Stand clear. Okay, Fitz, on three. One, two, three."

The explosion was much quieter than O'Brien had expected. Little more than a dull thud. A puff of smoke erupted from the hillside. When it cleared, the entry was wide open. A black hole in the gray rock. They waited for gunfire from inside. Ten seconds. Thirty seconds. A full minute. Then he heard the sound of a car motor. It seemed to be coming from somewhere off to his right, on the backside of the mountain.

McLanahan's voice screeched in his earpiece. "They've got a back way out. Let's move."

Good news, bad news. The dangerous part was gone, but so was Jasajovic—if he'd been there in the first place. He'd have to wait and see.

O'Brien stepped aside as the troops behind him hurried into position alongside McLanahan in the tree line facing the opening.

A few moments later, McLanahan again: "Go."

Two of the troops, crouching, moved rapidly across the trail and took positions on either side of the opening, their weapons at the ready. McLanahan's voice whispered hoarsely into his earpiece. "Flashbangs."

The two men at the entry made under hand tosses into the opening. A moment later two bright flashes of light accompanied by a pair of dull thuds filled the gaping hole of the entryway. Dust and smoke poured out.

Now they waited half a minute until the smoke cleared. When there was no sign of movement from inside the cavern, they pointed their muzzles into the opening and peeked around.

He heard, "All clear."

The other men formed two columns and slowly moved across the trail, stepping over rocky chunks that had been the doorway, and into the mouth of the cavern. Two remained outside, one on either side of the entry. O'Brien watched until McLanahan and the others disappeared into the black hole. Then he moved across the trail to the entry. One of the stationed guards blocked his way. "No, sir. You wait."

There was no way he was going to stay out of that cavern. He activated his mike. "Colonel McLanahan, it's Matt O'Brien. I'm coming in."

The guard shook his head. "Sorry, sir. Orders."

A moment later, McLanahan's voice chirped in his earpiece. "We're secured here. All right, Matt. Come on in."

Secured? He turned to the guard. "You heard him."

The man shrugged and let him pass.

He walked into the entry, his breath hissing into his microphone in short, rapid bursts until he turned it off. Ever since he had seen the radar reflections of a large void in the mountain, his mind had formed pictures of what it looked like. Carlsbad Cavern of New Mexico? The Blue Grotto in Capri? Or a man-made mineshaft? He hadn't felt a tingle in his gut like this since he was a kid on Christmas morning. Hurrying, he stumbled on the rock fragments, but braced himself on the tunnel wall and regained balance.

About 30 yards ahead, the steeply sloping ramp curved to the left. At the bend, a faint light was reflected from farther down. The walls and roof of the tunnel were solid rock. Underfoot, dirt. Reaching the bend, he stripped off the facemask and goggles—and sucked in his breath. Before his eyes, a cavern that even in the dim illumination provided by the half dozen powerful hand-held torches, was at least the size of a football field. An irregular dome-shaped roof towered high above the floor. He felt as though he were on the set of a James Bond movie.

Along a far wall, two cylindrical vats, light reflecting off their metallic sides, each at least eight feet in diameter, about ten feet in height. Next to them, several pieces of machinery he couldn't identify. Ten feet above the vats, a narrow grated catwalk. At one end, a metal access ladder. A pair of narrow-gauge railroad tracks along the cavern floor ran from the vats to a darkened extension. A tunnel? Another room?

McLanahan and his troops had spread out from the center, and were probing into corners and crevices with gun muzzles.

A voice in O'Brien's earpiece called, "Over here, Colonel. Far end." Then, "Oh, my God."

O'Brien's blood chilled.

CHAPTER 43

Still at the bottom of the ramp, he watched McLanahan race to the far end of the cavern, and disappear into the darkness. He hurried across the cavern floor, following McLanahan into a tunnel that ran about 20 yards, and opened into a second room about half the size of the one he had just left, illuminated by powerful flashlight beams held aloft by three of the troops.

Bodies. Strewn on the floor. Lying in pools of blood. Bodies of gaunt men, hair and beards matted, dressed in wrinkled gray pants and shirts. Shackled in groups of four by rope around their waists. The prisoners. Probably all one hundred. Dead.

The fetid fecal odor along with the sight was more than his stomach could take. He ran to a corner and vomited. Bracing himself on the wall, he sucked in deep breaths for a few moments until the heaving quieted. Wiping his mouth, he returned to stand alongside several of the troops who, with McLanahan, handkerchiefs over their noses and mouths, had been staring down at the bodies. McLanahan looked up. Lips compressed, he shook his head. "If only we could have gotten here sooner."

A third eye gaping from mid-forehead of many told how their sentences had been carried out. O'Brien said, "How long do you think they've been dead?"

McLanahan turned to one of his men who'd been inspecting the corpses. "What do you think, Myerson?"

"Probably less than three hours, sir. Rigor mortis hasn't set in."

O'Brien said, "The guards are gone?"

McLanahan nodded. "Seems that way. Must be a back way out. We haven't explored the place yet, but there are tread marks of trucks or cars or both in the main room. They lead to another tunnel and probably a backside portal."

Jasajovic. O'Brien would have given odds that he was part of this operation—whatever it was. Gone. He felt his jaw clench until he thought his teeth would break under their force. His fists tighten until his nails dug into his palm. He wanted to strike out and hit something, anything.

A dozen troops poured into the room. Several, sickened at the sight and smell, turned away and vomited. Others, probably inured to massacres after months of duty, began cutting the rope that linked the corpses, arranging the bodies in rows, no doubt to facilitate a body count.

Hank Wilson. Was he among the dead? For a brief moment, O'Brien thought about looking into the tortured faces. A glance around the room, and he rejected the idea. The guy at one time had been as close to him as a brother. He didn't want Hank to live in his memory as an emaciated corpse. Let someone else make the identification. He'd seen enough, just wanted to get the hell out of here. He removed the radio communication equipment, and handed them along with the facemask and goggles, to McLanahan. "Here, I won't need these anymore." As an afterthought, he removed the holstered H&K. "This, too."

McLanahan said, "Sure you don't want to keep the pistol?"

He shook his head.

He walked back toward the main room, and in the darkened tunnel stumbled over a rail, landing on his outstretched hands. He got up, brushed gravel off his palms. Stupid not to have used the penlight he'd been issued. He dug it out of his jacket pocket and trained its beam along the ground. For a moment he was disoriented. Wait, the rails must run into the main gallery. All he had to do was follow them. He'd taken a dozen steps when he realized they led along a curved path to his left. By now he should be seeing light from the main gallery at the end of the tunnel. This wasn't right. Must have wandered into a branch. He was about to turn back when he saw 30 yards away, two small open-topped ore carriers resting in tandem on the tracks. Beyond them was a solid wall of rock. End of the line.

He was about to turn and walk back when a rustling sound caught his attention. It seemed to come from the tram closest to him. Rats? A debate went on in his head: look into the tram or go back. Curiosity won out. Cautiously, he crept up to the side of the carrier and shone the beam into its depths. Jesus! A pair of eyes in a gaunt face stared back at him. For a moment he thought he was gazing at another dead man— then the eyes blinked. The lips moved. A hoarse whisper. His heart hammering in his chest, he moved the light beam and saw a jumble of bare legs and arms. Another face. A third. A hand reached up and grasped the rim of the carrier, and slowly a figure pulled itself up. A stubble-bearded man clad only in a ragged loincloth stood, supporting himself unsteadily by holding the rim. His ribs stood out, barely covered by the skin over his chest. His neck pencil-thin. He spoke in rasping tones, the words unintelligible. The man bent, reached down and helped up from the bottom of the cart another skeletal figure, then a third.

O'Brien stood transfixed. *My God! How many of these poor creatures were in the carrier?* He edged closer to the men, his stomach churning from the putrid odor that wafted into his nostrils. Training his light into the car, he could make out another body lying on its floor. He looked up at the man who had been the first to stand. The man shook his head, and with his foot nudged the inert figure. Dead.

He heard sounds from the other carrier and watched as hands gripped the rim, and one by one four emaciated men slowly rose from its depths.

"Matt." He heard it as a whisper echoing off the walls of the tunnel in which he stood.

He turned around trying to find the source. Swept the light beam around the tunnel. Was he mistaken or did he hear someone calling him?

"Matt." This time clearly. A hand in the second carrier rose in a wave.

He squeezed into the narrow space between the first carrier and the tunnel wall until he stood alongside the other car. Peered into the bearded face of the man who had waved. Into eyes sunken into their sockets. Matted hair to his shoulders. The man stuck out his tongue, parched white. Pointed to his mouth. His voice, coarse as sandpaper rubbing on stone. "Water, for Christ sake."

O'Brien threw his arms around him. "Hank! Thank God."

*   *   *

O'Brien helped the men out of the trams, led them to the large room in the cavern, then ran back to get help and canteens of water the men poured into their mouths. Someone had found a switch at the generator and the room was now illuminated by a series of low-wattage bulbs strung at head level around the periphery.

Squatting alongside Hank Wilson, who sat on the dirt floor of the main gallery, O'Brien listened, trying to understand his labored phrases. Explaining how these few men had managed to remain alive.

Wilson's words came out in short spurts. "Lined us up on floor…room where you found the others…not so lucky…they didn't make it…" He stopped and sucked in gulps of air. "Me and three others roped to me…along with these other four guys…we were in last row. Others screaming, beating at guards…confusion like you wouldn't believe…we crawled out on our bellies…into tunnel…hid in ore cars."

Wilson stopped, wheezed another breath. He grinned, yellow teeth flashing through the grimy, matted beard. "What the fuck took you so long to get here." Same old Hank.

Now they waited for a jeep to take the men, too weak to walk, to the LZ. From there they'd be flown back to Sarajevo. The jeep had already made one trip into the cavern, and had taken the three weakest men. One could only lie, taking up most of the back seat. They were waiting for the jeep to return.

He was anxious to learn more from Wilson. Find out about his capture, where Jasajovic fit into this picture, what work he'd been put to. Ore cars? He was obviously talking about the mine carriers he'd found the men in. But all that would have to wait. Wilson was too exhausted from the brief narration to go on.

At the sound of the approaching motor, O'Brien stood up. A jeep rolled alongside. Along with two of the NATO troops, they crowded the remaining four rescued prisoners in. Although O'Brien would have liked to ride along with Wilson, there just wasn't room. He'd see him back in Sarajevo in a few hours. Give him a chance to recoup some of his strength.

Through eyes misted with tears of joy, he watched the overloaded jeep climb up the ramp toward the opening. Seeing Wilson alive, even though weak and starved, for the moment drove from his mind the horrors he'd witnessed in the cavern.

O'Brien heard a shout from a darkened corner. Although still preoccupied with Hank, he was curious to know the cause for the excitement. He hurried toward the sound of voices that led him through another tunnel. At its end, four of the troops stood before a gated doorway, shining a flashlight beam through the steel bars of the gate.

One of the men pointed. "Look in here, sir."

Beyond the gate, O'Brien could see in the light beam a room about ten by 12 feet and ten feet high. Through the bars of the gate, he could make out what appeared to be two waist-high stacks of small light-colored bricks, stacks that extended the length of the room. A narrow aisle separated the two stacks. The bricks gleamed in the lantern light. Metal?

He turned to one of the troops. "What is it?"

The man shrugged. "Don't know, sir. The gate's locked. If you'll stand back, I'm about to shoot the lock off."

O'Brien and three of the men retreated into the tunnel while the fourth aimed his MP-5K at the lock and shattered it with a single blast.

The door swung open and O'Brien followed the other three into the room. They crowded into the aisle between the stacks. He could now see that what he thought were bricks were actually dull, gray metallic rectangular bars each about the size of a cake of soap. O'Brien reached out and touched a bar on the top of the stack to his right. Smooth. Silver?

One of the men picked a bar off its stack. He handed it to O'Brien, gesturing for him to feel its weight.

O'Brien hefted it. It *was* heavy.

The soldier said, "Looks like silver, don't it?"

The same thought had occurred to him, yet this didn't quite have the shiny appearance of silver. He shrugged. "I'm not sure." Letters and numbers were stamped onto the surface of the bar. He examined them closely. "Pt" followed by "99.5" Under it another number followed by "g." Pt, was it an abbreviation for "point?" For a moment he was puzzled. Suddenly it struck him. Jesus in heaven. *Pt, the symbol for the element platinum.* Solid bars of platinum. Ninety-nine point five referred to its percent purity. The letter "g" probably was its weight in grams. Either this cavern was a storage place for the platinum, or a huge mineshaft.

The bars in the stack on the other side of the aisle were also silvery in color, but had a slightly duller sheen. He lifted one from the left stack. It was about the same size but slightly lighter in weight than those on the other side of the aisle. Stamped on its surface was, "Pd" followed by a number. Pd meant nothing to him. Had he misread the letters? He removed another bar and examined its stamping. No, Pd was correct. He culled his memory bank. Didn't the ore that contained platinum contain several other metals as well? Palladium. Pd was the symbol for palladium. Christ. Platinum, palladium. Higher-priced metals than gold. He gazed around the room. A fortune in precious metals. No wonder the place was so heavily guarded. And the machinery—the vats and other machines, they were probably used in processing the ore.

He heard one of the men speaking into his mike, calling McLanahan.

Moments later, McLanahan appeared at the entrance. O'Brien squeezed out of the crowded room. Let the others do the briefing. He started back toward the large gallery.

McLanahan called after him. "If you're ready to go back, the jeep will be returning shortly. Have the driver take you to the LZ."

At the main gallery, he waited at the bottom of the ramp leading to the surface. The troops had all left the large room; some to assist with the bodies of the prisoners, others probably exploring side tunnels that led from the main arena.

Alongside him were the machines. One was obviously the generator that fed power to the place. Another, a screw-driven ore crusher. Attached to the side of each vat, a traveling belt conveyer extended from the ore crusher to the top of each vat. A series of rectangular buckets on each conveyer loaded with crushed ore, would be carried on an endless chain to the top of the vat and dumped.

O'Brien walked up to one of the vats. Whatever was in it had an acrid odor. He'd see from the catwalk what the vats contained.

All of the lighting in the cavern came from low-wattage bulbs strung along the walls at a level with his head. The grated catwalk received only reflected light from below, and was in partial darkness so that he could barely make out the far end. Reaching the top of the ladder, he pulled himself on to the catwalk by grabbing the hip-high guardrails that ran along either side of its length. He walked to the center, leaned over the guardrail, peered six feet below into one of the vats. An amber liquid filled it to within a foot of the top. He could feel heat rising from it, burning his cheeks. The glass lining was an indication that the liquid was corrosive to the metal. The pungent odor that drifted up stinging his nostrils and causing his eyes to tear, was additional proof.

He took out a handkerchief and was wiping his eyes when he became aware of vibration underfoot, experienced slight swaying of the catwalk. Someone climbing up? He peered to his right, but saw no one on the ladder. He turned the other way and saw through his teary eyes a bundle lying on the far end of the catwalk. He started toward it, digging the penlight out of his jacket pocket. Suddenly, the "bundle" stood. He never heard the shot; only a ping. A bullet ricocheting off the top of his helmet. Son of a bitch! Two, three shots pinged off the metal catwalk, now swinging side-to-side. Another shot and something kicked him in the ribs. Thank God for the Kevlar jacket. He dropped to the grating of the catwalk. Heart pounding at his chest wall. *Lie flat.* Shots rang over his head. He lost count. Then quiet. Gun empty? Felt and heard clanging of footsteps. Closer. *Now.* He leaped up and charged at the shooter head down. A shot knocked his helmet off as he dove headlong into the shooter's belly. A grunt. The gun flew in the air, clanked against the catwalk then was gone. The guy was still on his feet, but O'Brien was face down on the grating. A moment later a boot was shoving him under the handrail toward the vat. His legs now hanging off the edge of the catwalk, he threw his arms out—grabbed a leg and held on. With his free leg, his assailant kicked O'Brien's face. Fingernails dug into his hands, trying to force him to let go. O'Brien held on fiercely with one arm, with the other, grabbed one of his assailant's fingers, bent it back, snapped it. A scream, and O'Brien saw the guy straighten up. Instantly, he pulled himself back on to the catwalk. Felt the grating under his body and got to his knees. He had his arms wrapped around his opponent's thighs. The guy was beating him on his head with his fists, but he struggled up off his knees, and got his feet under him until he was in a squat, his arms gripping the guy around his waist. He frog-kicked. Shot straight up. Felt the top of his head crush his assailant's lower jaw. A man about his own height, head thrown back, stunned by his skull-butt. He shot his fist up into the guy's throat. A sharp jab to the upper belly, air whooshed out of the man's lungs. He grabbed him by the throat. Looked into his face. Jasajovic.

He saw Peg's naked, violated, crucified body. *This man must die.* O'Brien's arms trembled, steel poured into his muscles, his fingers squeezed with all the force he could gather. Gripping his throat, he swiveled around forcing Jasajovic's back against the guardrail, and pushed. Jasajovic struggled to keep from going back over the rail, tried to pull O'Brien's fingers from his throat. The guy was strong, fighting for his life. But nothing, *nothing* was going to make O'Brien loosen his death grip. Jasajovic's back was now arched backwards over the rail, saliva foaming at the corners of his lips. Croaking sounds from his throat. His face beet red, then mottled purple. Eyes bulged from their sockets. Tongue protruded. Gradually, Jasajovic's fingers fell away from O'Brien's hands, his arms swung like rags from his body. With his last ounce of strength, O'Brien shoved. Jasajovic's trunk teetered for a moment, balanced on the rail, then slowly somersaulted over. His body splashed into the vat, then disappeared below the surface.

O'Brien, spent, exhausted, leaned with both hands on the guardrail, panting, sweat pouring down his face. He'd been lucky—again. For a moment, Jasajovic's head appeared at the surface of the liquid, his hands clawed at air, a hissing cloud of steam surrounded his face, his mouth opened but no sound issued. His arms lowered, disappeared into the liquid, his head melted like butter in a hot frying pan. For a few seconds there were ripples on the surface and steam rose, then bubbles, and finally the surface was smooth.

☠ CHAPTER 44

Peg's eyes opened. She smiled, stretched. "How long have you been sitting here?"

O'Brien said, "About half an hour."

She wrinkled her brow. "You look awful. Have you been up all night? And what kind of clothes are those?"

"Thanks. Yes. Dirty."

O'Brien had gone directly to the infirmary when he returned from MAGIC MOUNTAIN. He hadn't decided what to tell her if she asked where he'd been all night.

Peg reached up. "Come here. I need a hug."

His heart swelled. She was back. Peg was *really back*. "I'm a little ripe."

She sniffed. "Good male smell."

He leaned over and embraced her. Kissed her lips.

She pushed him away. "Go clean up. I'm going to get dressed after breakfast. Tell the doctor I'm over whatever they had me in here for. I want to get out of here and go home." Suddenly, tears flooded her eyes and she was sobbing uncontrollably.

One moment she seemed happy, the next back in the depths of depression. His elation at her progress was tempered by the knowledge that she'd need months of treatment even after they returned home.

*   *   *

Two days following MAGIC MOUNTAIN O'Brien was seated in McLanahan's office, Peg at his side. "Thanks, Colonel, for arranging Hank Wilson's transportation to Germany."

McLanahan nodded slightly. "Our medical facilities here are somewhat overcrowded, as you can imagine. The U.S. Base Hospital in Frankfort is better able to take care of him till he's well enough to travel back to the States."

"I'm amazed they kept him alive."

"Yes. Probably thought at some point they might use his radar expertise. Meantime, they put him to work."

O'Brien mulled over McLanahan's comment. Knowing Hank, he'd *never* have cooperated with those guys. "I have to make a report when I get back home. What can you tell me about the operation that went on inside that mountain?"

"What time's your plane?"

"Four-thirty."

"I'll tell you as much as I know at the moment. First, we did capture one jeep load of the terrorist gang."

"How."

"One of our helicopters caught up with them in a clearing near the forest. They ran out of ammo and surrendered to our men. I won't go into a great deal of detail, since you're pressed for time. The short story is: there were five of them. They'd grabbed as many of the ingots as they could carry and took off.

"This Jasajovic fellow, along with a younger brother, ran the operation. The younger brother was in charge of the prison camp—the one they took you to. "

The brother would, no doubt, be the one he thought of as Baldy.

"The older Jasajovic mucked about in the cavern trying to find some way to hide the booty, perhaps try to take it out later. The others took off without him." McLanahan smiled. "I guess you surprised him, climbing up on the catwalk."

O'Brien shrugged. "*I* was the one who was surprised. I'm just lucky he wasn't a good shot. The swinging catwalk didn't help his aim either."

"Well, you seem to be able to hold your own in a brawl, don't you?"

O'Brien laughed. "Grew up in a tough neighborhood." He turned serious. "That was an amazing stash, back there in the cavern."

"Yes. The mountain turns out to have one of the richest deposits of platinum and palladium outside the old Soviet Union.

"Since the end of the war, in 1995, they've been selecting 'detainees' from various camps, transferring them to the prison where they held you, and trucked them in to the cavern every day, digging out the ore and processing it. Do you know anything about how it's refined?"

O'Brien shook his head.

"Platinum and palladium are usually found together in the same deposit. They're resistant to single acids but dissolve in an acid combination, aqua regia."

O'Brien raised his hand. "Wait a minute, aqua regia. Isn't that a mixture of hydrochloric and nitric acids?"

McLanahan nodded.

"My God. That's what was in those vats, wasn't it?"

Another nod.

"If I remember my chemistry 101, aqua regia will dissolve almost anything." He shook his head. "Lord. Jasajovic's head just disappeared."

Peg said, "Please. This is making me sick to my stomach."

McLanahan continued. "I'll make this as palatable as possible. You know about platinum in the manufacture of jewelry, of course. Well, these chaps weren't interested in making pretty little bracelets. They could get richer selling it to the people who use it to coat missile cones and jet-engine fuel nozzles."

O'Brien said, "Do I smell an Iraq connection?"

McLanahan chuckled. "You're a quick read, Matt. Quite correct. But there's even a bigger market for both platinum and palladium as catalysts, mostly in the petrochemical industry and in catalytic converters as anti-pollution devices for automobiles."

O'Brien said, "Pollution control is something I know about from my work in the senate. And I follow the financial markets enough to know that right now platinum and palladium bring higher prices than gold."

"Yes. The Russians had been the largest supplier, but their sources have dried up. Jasajovic has already taken advantage of the fact. His people have sold tons of it to automobile manufacturing countries, principally Japan, through third parties, of course. Left a tortuous paper trail to try to follow."

O'Brien said, "Who does all this platinum and palladium belong to, Bosnia? Serbia?"

"Curiously, the mountain lies on the border between the two, so technically they both share the wealth. No matter, neither government knew of the find. How Jasajovic discovered it we haven't yet found out. He operated outside his official government."

O'Brien wondered what he planned to do with the money he was making.

McLanahan said, "Ambitious bugger, Jasajovic. Dreamed of building a bigger army than Milosevic's. He'd already been negotiating with arms merchants for guns, tanks, planes perhaps even nuclear devices. They had planned to take over the Yugoslavian government, for starters."

O'Brien knew how power-hungry Milosevic was. Had they done him a favor getting rid of Jasajovic? Where were the *good* guys in this country? "Now that the secret is out, who's going to decide who catches the brass ring—or in this case, platinum?"

McLanahan shrugged. "I'm a military man, Matt. That decision is a matter for you political types."

O'Brien rubbed his chin. "In this part of the world, history teaches us, they settle their differences on the battlefield."

McLanahan in mock seriousness pointed a finger. "You, Mr. O'Brien, are a troublemaker. Now take your pretty lady and get out of here. Battlefield, indeed. We haven't yet finished the *last war.*"

About the Author

Barry Friedman is a retired orthopaedic surgeon. He grew up in New Rochelle, NY, received his undergraduate degree at Lafayette College and his medical degree at New York University College of Medicine. Following an internship in Cleveland, he served during World War II as medical officer aboard USS Russell, a destroyer in the South Pacific. After the war, he continued his orthopaedic training at University of Iowa Hospitals, then returned to Cleveland where he practiced and conducted a training program for orthopaedic residents. He has received awards for teaching and research. His published writings include, in addition to a number of scientific papers, newspaper articles and short stories in national magazines. His previous novel, *Dead End*, a police procedural, was published in 1995. When he and his wife are not traveling or visiting with their three children and their families, they are at their home in southern California.